PRAISE FOR *MARCH OF CRIMES*

Jess Lourey named to Book Riot's "10 Funny Mystery Authors Like Janet Evanovich" list

"I laughed my way through this small-town mystery."

—Book Riot

"Earthy language, quirky suspects, and much related tomfoolery."

—*Kirkus Reviews*

PRAISE FOR *FEBRUARY FEVER*

Lefty Finalist for Most Humorous Mystery

"The best outing yet for Mira!"

—*Kirkus Reviews*

"Lourey skillfully mixes humor and suspense . . . and the mile-a-minute pace never falters. Another excellent addition to Lourey's very entertaining Mira James mystery series."

—*Booklist* (starred review)

"[An] incredible series . . . [*February Fever*] is a charming story with great dialogue [and] there are more months coming, so readers definitely have something to look forward to."

—*Suspense Magazine*

"I can't wait to see what Mira does next."

—*Crimespree Magazine*

PRAISE FOR *NOVEMBER HUNT*

"It's not easy to make people laugh while they're on the edge of their seats, but Lourey pulls it off, while her vivid descriptions of a brutal Minnesota winter will make readers shiver in the seventh book in her very clever Mira James mystery series."

—*Booklist* (starred review)

"Clever, quirky, and completely original!"

—Hank Phillippi Ryan, Anthony, Agatha, and Macavity Award–winning author

"A masterful mix of mayhem and mirth."

—Reed Farrel Coleman, *New York Times* bestselling author

"Lourey has successfully created an independent, relatable heroine in Mira James. Mira's wit and fearlessness enable her to overcome the many challenges she faces as she tries to unravel the murder."

—*Crimespree Magazine*

"Lourey's seventh cozy featuring PI wannabe Mira James successfully combines humor, an intriguing mystery, and quirky small-town characters."

—*Publishers Weekly*

"Lourey has a knack for wholesome sexual innuendo, and she gets plenty of mileage out of Minnesota. This light novel keeps the reader engaged, like one of those sweet, chewy Nut Goodies that Mira is addicted to."

—*The Boston Globe*

"Lourey has a talent for creating hilarious characters in bizarre, laugh-out-loud situations, while at the same time capturing the honest and endearing subtleties of human life."

—*The Strand*

PRAISE FOR *AUGUST MOON*

"Hilarious, fast paced, and madcap."

—*Booklist* (starred review)

"Another amusing tale set in the town full of over-the-top zanies who've endeared themselves to the engaging Mira."

—*Kirkus Reviews*

"[A] hilarious, wonderfully funny cozy."

—*Crimespree Magazine*

"Lourey has a gift for creating terrific characters. Her sly and witty take on small-town USA is a sweet summer treat. Pull up a lawn chair, pour yourself a glass of lemonade, and enjoy."

—Denise Swanson, bestselling author

"A fun, fast-paced mystery with a heroine readers will enjoy."

—*The Mystery Reader*

"With just the right amount of insouciance, tongue-in-cheek sexiness, and plain common sense, Jess Lourey offers up a funny, well-written, engaging story . . . Readers will thoroughly enjoy the well-paced ride."
—Carl Brookins, author of *The Case of the Greedy Lawyers*

PRAISE FOR *MAY DAY*

"Jess Lourey writes about a small-town assistant librarian, but this is no genteel traditional mystery. Mira James likes guys in a big way, likes booze, and isn't afraid of motorcycles. She flees a dead-end job and a dead-end boyfriend in Minneapolis and ends up in Battle Lake, a little town with plenty of dirty secrets. The first-person narrative in *May Day* is fresh, the characters quirky. Minnesota has many fine crime writers, and Jess Lourey has just entered their ranks!"
—Ellen Hart, award-winning author of the Jane Lawless and Sophie Greenway series

"This trade paperback packed a punch . . . I loved it from the get-go!"
—*Tulsa World*

"What a romp this is! I found myself laughing out loud."
—*Crimespree Magazine*

"Mira digs up a closetful of dirty secrets, including sex parties, cross-dressing, and blackmail, on her way to exposing the killer. Lourey's debut has a likable heroine and surfeit of sass."
—*Kirkus Reviews*

PRAISE FOR *THE TAKEN ONES*

Short-listed for the 2024 Edgar Award for Best Paperback Original

"Setting the standard for top-notch thrillers, *The Taken Ones* is smart, compelling, and filled with utterly real characters. Lourey brings her formidable storytelling talent to the game and, on top of that, wows us with a deft stylistic touch. This is a one-sitting read!"

—Jeffery Deaver, author of *The Bone Collector* and *The Watchmaker's Hand*

"*The Taken Ones* has Jess Lourey's trademark of suspense all the way. A damaged and brave heroine, an equally damaged evildoer, and missing girls from long ago all combine to keep the reader rushing through to the explosive ending."

—Charlaine Harris, *New York Times* bestselling author

"Lourey is at the top of her game with *The Taken Ones*. A master of building tension while maintaining a riveting pace, Lourey is a hell of a writer on all fronts, but her greatest talent may be her characters. Evangeline Reed, an agent with the Minnesota Bureau of Criminal Apprehension, is a woman with a devastating past and the haunting ability to know the darkest crimes happening around her. She is also exactly the kind of character I would happily follow through a dozen books or more. In awe of her bravery, I also identified with her pain and wanted desperately to protect her. Along with an incredible cast of support characters, *The Taken Ones* will break your heart wide open and stay with you long after you've turned the final page. This is a 2023 must read."

—Danielle Girard, *USA Today* and Amazon #1 bestselling author of *Up Close*

PRAISE FOR *THE QUARRY GIRLS*

Winner of the 2023 Anthony Award for Best Paperback Original

Winner of the 2023 Minnesota Book Award for Genre Fiction

"Few authors can blend the genuine fear generated by a sordid tale of true crime with evocative, three-dimensional characters and mesmerizing prose like Jess Lourey. Her fictional stories feel rooted in a world we all know but also fear. *The Quarry Girls* is a story of secrets gone to seed, and Lourey gives readers her best novel yet—which is quite the accomplishment. Calling it: *The Quarry Girls* will be one of the best books of the year."

—Alex Segura, acclaimed author of *Secret Identity*, *Star Wars Poe Dameron: Free Fall*, and *Miami Midnight*

"Jess Lourey once more taps deep into her Midwest roots and childhood fears with *The Quarry Girls*, an absorbing, true crime–informed thriller narrated in the compelling voice of young drummer Heather Cash as she and her bandmates navigate the treacherous and confusing ground between girlhood and womanhood one simmering and deadly summer. Lourey conveys the edgy, hungry restlessness of teen girls with a touch of Megan Abbott while steadily intensifying the claustrophobic atmosphere of a small 1977 Minnesota town where darkness snakes below the surface."

—Loreth Anne White, *Washington Post* and Amazon Charts bestselling author of *The Patient's Secret*

"Jess Lourey is a master of the coming-of-age thriller, and *The Quarry Girls* may be her best yet—as dark, twisty, and full of secrets as the tunnels that lurk beneath Pantown's deceptively idyllic streets."
—Chris Holm, Anthony Award–winning author of *The Killing Kind*

PRAISE FOR *BLOODLINE*

Winner of the 2022 Anthony Award for Best Paperback Original

Winner of the 2022 ITW Thriller Award for Best Paperback Original

Short-listed for the 2021 Goodreads Choice Awards

"Fans of *Rosemary's Baby* will relish this."
—*Publishers Weekly*

"Based on a true story, this is a sinister, suspenseful thriller full of creeping horror."
—*Kirkus Reviews*

"Lourey ratchets up the fear in a novel that verges on horror."
—*Library Journal*

"In *Bloodline*, Jess Lourey blends elements of mystery, suspense, and horror to stunning effect."
—*BOLO Books*

"Inspired by a true story, it's a creepy page-turner that has me eager to read more of Ms. Lourey's works, especially if they're all as incisive as this thought-provoking novel."

—Criminal Element

"*Bloodline* by Jess Lourey is a psychological thriller that grabbed me from the beginning and didn't let go."

—*Mystery & Suspense Magazine*

"*Bloodline* blends page-turning storytelling with clever homages to such horror classics as *Rosemary's Baby*, *The Stepford Wives*, and *Harvest Home*."

—*Toronto Star*

"*Bloodline* is a terrific, creepy thriller, and Jess Lourey clearly knows how to get under your skin."

—Bookreporter

"[A] tightly coiled domestic thriller that slowly but persuasively builds the suspense."

—*South Florida Sun Sentinel*

"I should know better than to pick up a new Jess Lourey book thinking I'll just peek at the first few pages and then get back to the book I was reading. Six hours later, it's three in the morning and I'm racing through the last few chapters, unable to sleep until I know how it all ends. Set in an idyllic small town rooted in family history and horrific secrets, *Bloodline* is *Pleasantville* meets *Rosemary's Baby*. A deeply unsettling, darkly unnerving, and utterly compelling novel, this book chilled me to the core, and I loved every bit of it."

—Jennifer Hillier, author of *Little Secrets* and the award-winning *Jar of Hearts*

"Jess Lourey writes small-town Minnesota like Stephen King writes small-town Maine. *Bloodline* is a tremendous book with a heart and a hacksaw . . . and I loved every second of it."
—Rachel Howzell Hall, author of the critically acclaimed novels *And Now She's Gone* and *They All Fall Down*

PRAISE FOR *UNSPEAKABLE THINGS*

Winner of the 2021 Anthony Award for Best Paperback Original

Short-listed for the 2021 Edgar Awards and 2020 Goodreads Choice Awards

"The suspense never wavers in this page-turner."
—*Publishers Weekly*

"The atmospheric suspense novel is haunting because it's narrated from the point of view of a thirteen-year-old, an age that should be more innocent but often isn't. Even more chilling, it's based on real-life incidents. Lourey may be known for comic capers (*March of Crimes*), but this tense novel combines the best of a coming-of-age story with suspense and an unforgettable young narrator."
—*Library Journal* (starred review)

"Part suspense, part coming-of-age, Jess Lourey's *Unspeakable Things* is a story of creeping dread, about childhood when you know the monster under your bed is real. A novel that clings to you long after the last page."
—Lori Rader-Day, Edgar Award–nominated author of *Under a Dark Sky*

"A noose of a novel that tightens by inches. The squirming tension comes from every direction—including the ones that are supposed to be safe. I felt complicit as I read, as if at any moment I stopped I would be abandoning Cassie, alone, in the dark, straining to listen and fearing to hear."

—Marcus Sakey, bestselling author of *Brilliance*

"*Unspeakable Things* is an absolutely riveting novel about the poisonous secrets buried deep in towns and families. Jess Lourey has created a story that will chill you to the bone and a main character who will break your heart wide open."

—Lou Berney, Edgar Award–winning author of *November Road*

"Inspired by a true story, *Unspeakable Things* crackles with authenticity, humanity, and humor. The novel reminded me of *To Kill a Mockingbird* and *The Marsh King's Daughter*. Highly recommended."

—Mark Sullivan, bestselling author of *Beneath a Scarlet Sky*

"Jess Lourey does a masterful job building tension and dread, but her greatest asset in *Unspeakable Things* is Cassie—an arresting narrator you identify with, root for, and desperately want to protect. This is a book that will stick with you long after you've torn through it."

—Rob Hart, author of *The Warehouse*

"With *Unspeakable Things*, Jess Lourey has managed the near-impossible, crafting a mystery as harrowing as it is tender, as gut-wrenching as it is lyrical. There is real darkness here, a creeping, inescapable dread that more than once had me looking over my own shoulder. But at its heart beats the irrepressible—and irresistible—spirit of its . . . heroine, a young woman so bright and vital and brave she kept even the fiercest monsters at bay. This is a book that will stay with me for a long time."

—Elizabeth Little, *Los Angeles Times* bestselling author of *Dear Daughter* and *Pretty as a Picture*

PRAISE FOR *SALEM'S CIPHER*

"A fast-paced, sometimes brutal thriller reminiscent of Dan Brown's *The Da Vinci Code*."

—*Booklist* (starred review)

"A hair-raising thrill ride."

—*Library Journal* (starred review)

"The fascinating historical information combined with a storyline ripped from the headlines will hook conspiracy theorists and action addicts alike."

—*Kirkus Reviews*

"Fans of *The Da Vinci Code* are going to love this book . . . One of my favorite reads of 2016."

—*Crimespree Magazine*

"This suspenseful tale has something for absolutely everyone to enjoy."

—*Suspense Magazine*

PRAISE FOR *MERCY'S CHASE*

"An immersive voice, an intriguing story, a wonderful character—highly recommended!"

—Lee Child, #1 *New York Times* bestselling author

"Both a sweeping adventure and race-against-time thriller, *Mercy's Chase* is fascinating, fierce, and brimming with heart—just like its heroine, Salem Wiley."

—Meg Gardiner, author of *Into the Black Nowhere*

"Action-packed, great writing taut with suspense, an appealing main character to root for—who could ask for anything more?"

—Buried Under Books

PRAISE FOR *REWRITE YOUR LIFE: DISCOVER YOUR TRUTH THROUGH THE HEALING POWER OF FICTION*

"Interweaving practical advice with stories and insights garnered in her own writing journey, Jessica Lourey offers a step-by-step guide for writers struggling to create fiction from their life experiences. But this book isn't just about writing. It's also about the power of stories to transform those who write them. I know of no other guide that delivers on its promise with such honesty, simplicity, and beauty."

—William Kent Krueger, *New York Times* bestselling author of the Cork O'Connor series and *Ordinary Grace*

MARCH
OF
CRIMES

OTHER TITLES BY JESS LOUREY

MURDER BY MONTH MYSTERIES

May Day

June Bug

Knee High by the Fourth of July

August Moon

September Mourn

October Fest

November Hunt

December Dread

January Thaw

February Fever

March of Crimes

April Fools

STEINBECK AND REED THRILLERS

The Taken Ones

The Reaping

THRILLERS

The Quarry Girls

Litani

Bloodline

Unspeakable Things

SALEM'S CIPHER THRILLERS

Salem's Cipher

Mercy's Chase

CHILDREN'S BOOKS

Leave My Book Alone! Starring Claudette, a Dragon with Control Issues

YOUNG ADULT

A Whisper of Poison

NONFICTION

Rewrite Your Life: Discover Your Truth Through the Healing Power of Fiction

MARCH OF CRIMES

JESS LOUREY

Text copyright © 2015, 2019, 2025 by Jess Lourey
All rights reserved.

Published by Thomas & Mercer, Seattle

www.apub.com

Amazon, the Amazon logo, and Thomas & Mercer are trademarks of Amazon.com, Inc., or its affiliates.

ISBN-13: 9781662519437 (paperback)
ISBN-13: 9781662519420 (digital)

Cover design and illustration by Sarah Horgan

Printed in the United States of America

MARCH
OF
CRIMES

Chapter 1

Ron Sims cleared his throat. "Convince people that Otter Tail County is safe."

Shouldn't have been too hard, what he was asking. Otter Tail County was plopped in the heart of gorgeous northern Minnesota. From the air, it appeared more lakes than land, a fistful of sapphires scattered across an emerald field. On the ground, at least in March, it smelled like melting snow and rich black dirt. Most residents didn't lock their doors, and they'd be sure to stop and ask if you were OK if they happened upon you stalled on the side of the road. Five bucks at a local café bought you coffee, juice, bacon, toast, and eggs done any way. Kids sold lemonade on corners come summer, about the same time of the year as the turtle races started back up. Norman Rockwell surely had the area in mind when he painted his folksy vision of America.

Convince people that Otter Tail County is safe.

Not only should Ron's demand have been a slam dunk, but as editor, owner, and publisher of the *Battle Lake Recall*, his request was reasonable. It's not like he was, say, *my gynecologist* requesting that I spin a shiny PR web across a whole county. I'd written articles for his newspaper since I'd relocated to Battle Lake, Minnesota, one year ago next month. I was known mostly for my passive-aggressive Battle Lake Bites recipe column, but there was room to expand. Writing one positive Otter Tail County article a week was well within my ability and job description.

As a decided plus, Ron was offering to pay me extra to punch out the PR column, and I needed the money. Badly. I'd taken a pay ding at the library to help it stay afloat after the county budget was slashed, and it looked like another cut was coming soon. The powers that be had threatened to fold us into Fergus Falls' larger library if we didn't trim costs even further. Taking more out of my salary would bury me under poverty wages. I currently made side money doing investigative work for a local lawyer, but that cheddar wasn't enough to cover a modest plate of nachos. The only bonus was that the girl Friday work for the attorney shambled me closer to obtaining my private eye license, a goal that required approximately a gazillion hours of supervised work.

Altogether, I made enough to stay afloat if I didn't treat myself to luxuries like, say, fresh fruit or dental floss.

This March, though, I wanted to do more than scrape by. I wanted to save a nice egg so I could treat Johnny Leeson to a romantic vacation. He'd been my #1 for months now, a Greek god sculpted of steel and drizzled with honey, his smile guaranteed to weaken my knees and tingle my tidbits. We'd been through a lot, he and I, most of it consisting of crises I had manufactured.

Crises that were punctuated by, um, *unexpected* outside events.

Last month had been the worst.

Last month, my heart had been shredded. My beautiful, whole-hearted, goofy friend Jed had been murdered on a train ride to Oregon, right in front of my eyes. I'd slept only in fits since, images of Jed playing across the back of my eyelids. Some of them were terrible, gray with guilt, his hands slipping through mine as he fell screaming into the abyss. Others were bright moments of his life, so real that some mornings I woke thinking he was still alive, a smile on my face.

And then I'd remember.

Johnny had been by my side ever since, nearly living at my place, and as much as my fear-brain was screaming at me to run, to end the relationship before it exploded on its own, my love-brain told me to stay put and cultivate gratitude. (It can get seriously noisy in my head, yeah?)

For once, though, I was listening to my love-brain. It had convinced me that because Johnny was leaving tomorrow for a week in Wisconsin, I should plan a getaway for when he returned. Something romantic, just the two of us, to show him how much I cared about him and that I appreciated all the thoughtful gestures he made for me.

All I had to do was come up with a destination and the money to cover it.

Cue Ron and his offer.

If you're keeping score, his request was reasonable, appropriate, and well timed.

But here's the thing.

I'd been involved in at least one murder case a month since I'd moved to Otter Tail County.

I didn't think a single one of the deceased would argue that the county was safe.

Of course, they *might* argue that the problem was me and not this neck of God's country. Before I relocated to Battle Lake nearly a year ago, the whole area was sweet and sleepy, with a nearly nonexistent homicide rate. The only problems they'd faced were of the small-town variety, like people driving their lawn mowers to the bar so they wouldn't get a DWI on the way home, or, if the rumors were true, your occasional Peeping Tom.

The alarming murder spike had coincided exactly with my appearance.

To be fair, before I'd arrived, I'd never stumbled across a single corpse, if we didn't count driving past the odd woodland creature taking a pancake nap on the highway. Sure, my dad was officially deceased, but I'd had nothing to do with that. Besides, his funeral had been closed casket. A career alcoholic, he'd killed another driver and himself in a head-on collision the spring of my junior year of high school. The situation wasn't cleanly murder or suicide, just a sad, horrible mess that made my mom and me as popular as goose poop in my hometown of Paynesville.

I ditched that wide spot on the map the second I graduated high school and shimmied up the road, landing in Minneapolis. Enrollment at the University of Minnesota led to a BA in English. I also waited tables, made terrible dating choices, and applied for my own career in alcoholism. When that didn't pan out like I'd hoped, I signed up for graduate school, possibly one of the first good choices of my adult life. I was a few classes in when I caught my musician boyfriend, hereafter known as Bad Brad, giving flesh horn lessons to another woman.

I packed up and hit the road once more.

Battle Lake was the only light that beckoned. My friend Sunny, a Battle Lake native, was traveling to Alaska to be with Rodney, her unibrowed lover. She needed someone to house-sit her double-wide on the outskirts of the tiny town, so I took over her life, including fostering her dog, a German shepherd mix named Luna. The house-sitting was only supposed to last through the summer, but in the unlikeliest of outcomes, I'd found I loved living in Sunny's slice of heaven. Her prefab house was the perfect size for me, Luna, and Tiger Pop, my calico kitty. Several picturesque outbuildings added charm to the land, and in the summer, I cultivated a nice-size garden right outside my door. On the opposite side, the silvery surface of Whiskey Lake winked at me when it was warm and offered a glassy ice-skating spot in the winter.

Besides the natural beauty of my home, as the town's head librarian (at least until we found someone qualified to take over) and a columnist for the newspaper, I was putting my English degree to good use. As a super bonus, I, a woman whose only consistent type had been "fixer-upper," had fallen hard-core for the aforementioned Johnny, a guy who was most certainly too good for messed-up me.

Otter Tail County had turned out to be weirdly perfect.

Except for those thirteen corpses, of course.

The first had been my murdered lover's. I literally stumbled over his body in the library last May. Next came a nasty surprise found sealed inside a safe in June. You guessed it—another dead body. This was followed by a scalped man I discovered in a cabin in July, a religious cult I uncovered—along with a dead body—in August, and . . . you get the picture, right? A murder a month, for nearly a year. That was why making this corner of the earth appear safe and welcoming was tougher than it looked.

Maybe the problem wasn't Otter Tail County or me.

Maybe the problem was me *in* Otter Tail County. And now Ron Sims was handing me an opportunity to rectify the situation by writing an ongoing puff piece to end all puff pieces: weekly features on the beauty, culture, and safety that was Otter Tail County. He'd asked me to start this very week, with a survey of the most popular community education classes the region offered: a bridge club, water aerobics, mountain climbing for cowards, a cooking class, and finally, yoga. Was this column falling into my lap a gift from Karma, offering me a chance to even the score? After all, other than its general corpsiness, Otter Tail County had been good to me.

Really good.

"Exactly what will you pay me to write these articles?"

Ron set down his coffee cup. The mug was old-school white porcelain, perfectly in keeping with the '50s-diner vibe of the Turtle Stew. And it wasn't a million-dollar, modern-trying-to-*look*-retro '50s diner, by the way. The building had genuinely not been updated since the middle of the century. It still housed a pie case by the cash register. The counter was lined with upholstered stools, two of which Ron and I currently occupied. We could have chosen a red Naugahyde booth on the diner's perimeter or a particleboard table in the center if they weren't all crammed with the buzzing morning rush. No matter where you sat in the Stew, though, you were guaranteed cozy food that tasted like home and took four hours to digest.

Ron grunted. "What am I paying you to write the Bites column?"

I wrinkled my nose. "Twenty bucks a pop, cash."

He shook his head. "Jesus."

"I know." I swirled a generous pour of half-and-half into my coffee. I liked it creamy, not sweet. "You told me I was lucky to get any money for it."

He had the decency to appear sheepish as he shrugged. "None of us thought you'd last long. I didn't want to fuss with paperwork."

I nodded agreeably. I hadn't thought I'd be around this long, either. "If you want me to take on another column, one with extensive research involved, you need to make me official. Put me on payroll, two-fifty a week, plus a travel budget."

He tipped back another chug of his coffee, his expression landing somewhere between "thoughtful" and "testicle cramp." The clank and scurry of the Turtle Stew's breakfast crowd held us in a bacon-and-toast-scented pocket of stillness. Despite an overpowering urge to fill the silence between us with nonsense words, a bad habit when I was anxious, I held my tongue. Ron might appear to be a disheveled middle-aged man with a penchant for energetically and publicly making out with his wife, drinking off-brand cola, and scratching himself in places that you should wash your hand after touching (he didn't), but I wasn't fooled. He'd proved his intelligence too many times to disregard.

He was also kind, though I'd promised him I wouldn't let anyone else in on that secret.

"I dunno about two-fifty," Ron finally said. He signaled for a coffee refill. "That's thirteen thousand a year. That's more than my wife makes."

As office manager, ads specialist, and layout supervisor, his wife was the only other on-the-books employee of the *Recall*. I had no doubt she made less than $13,000 a year. I also knew Ron made significantly more.

I tasted my coffee. Still too bitter. I tipped more cream into my cup. "You should pay her more, not me less. I have a degree."

He snorted. "An English degree. Not worth five cents on the dollar."

Ouch. *But at length the truth will out.* "I know all the movers and shakers in town."

"That's because you find dead bodies." He grimaced. "You're less of an ambassador, more of an undertaker."

I shrugged to cover a twitch. "I know the *Recall*'s procedures. You wouldn't have to train me."

"The job's easy. A monkey could do it."

Boy, was he slinging the truth arrows. This man could *negotiate*. Well, so could I. "I'm not going below $250 a week. If it's that easy, hire someone off the street to write the pro–Otter Tail column. Heck, you could make it a package deal and throw in my Battle Lake Bites feature." I hooked my thumb at the quiet lady two stools down. "Maybe she's interested?"

The woman had been sitting there since before I'd arrived. That commitment to a seat wasn't unusual in a small town. The older residents treated the cafés like social clubs, setting up camp for a morning or an afternoon to hear the latest news, sharing lemon bars and decaffeinated coffee with whoever passed through. Usually, I recognized all the old-timers. Not this woman. Her white hair hung in her face, somewhat disheveled under her hat, and she'd been cradling the same cup in her gloved hands since I'd noticed her. I was growing worried and figured drawing her into the discussion would serve my negotiations but also allow me to check on her. She might not be well.

Ron glanced over my shoulder and pointed, chuckling. "Her?"

I pushed his pointer finger down and lowered my voice. "Don't be rude." My cheeks warmed. I hated to make other people uncomfortable.

Ron didn't take a hint. He pounded a fist on the counter and called toward the owner of the Turtle Stew, who was behind the counter brewing a fresh pot of coffee, "Doris! Mira thinks that Ida's girl over there would like to write for the *Recall*. What do you think?"

Doris, a tired bowling pin of a woman, tossed a glance where Ron was pointing. I knew Doris only superficially. She was always at the Stew, her appearance somewhere between Eeyore and Droopy, bags big enough to pack resting under her eyes. If it was slow, she'd talk your ear off. Same if it was busy. In neither case would she ever smile.

But when her eyes landed on the elderly woman who was the subject of our conversation, Doris's face lit up. "I've had some bad staff here, the likes would steal, or not show up for their shift, or even spit in people's food. I could tell you stories, and will in a minute, but my point is, I know what a rotten employee looks like. That one on the stool? She'd be the worst you've ever hired."

Ron laughed agreeably.

My blush crawled all the way to my scalp. I don't know if I felt worse for the woman—Ida's *girl*? She was eighty if she was a day, but that didn't mean she was hard of hearing—or for me. It sucked not to be in on the joke. I kept my voice low. "What's so funny?"

After thirteen corpses, you'd think I'd have known better than to ask. My bad.

Chapter 2

Doris dumped the grounds, grabbed the full coffeepot, and took off toward the main floor of the restaurant, clearing plates as she went. "She's a doll," she said as she walked behind me.

I scowled, flashing side-eye at the woman on the stool. "I thought you said she'd be a terrible employee."

Doris shook her head, cackling. "She's an *actual* doll. Sewn together? A toy, not a person. Ida Gilbertson over at the Senior Sunset is putting them up all over town. It's a pet project. She'd be happy to learn she'd fooled you."

I jumped off my stool so fast I knocked it over, causing a clatter that shocked the restaurant. My heartbeat shot through the roof. "What the *what*?"

If I'd eaten already, I'd have barfed it up right then and there. The one thing creepier than a doll was a *life-size* doll. (Except maybe a life-size doll holding a ventriloquist's dummy with live birds on its shoulders. But I digress.) *I'd been sitting next to a mannequin I'd thought was a person for nearly twenty minutes.* That knowledge crawled like bugs across my skin. What if I'd accidentally touched it?

Ron nodded. "Yup. Ida's found her calling. She's crafting these big ol' dolls and donating them to businesses around town. She orders the heads and wigs from I-don't-know-where, designs the clothes herself, and stuffs them so they look real." He waggled his eyebrows.

"Guess your powers of observation aren't as keen as you thought, Ms. Detective."

I couldn't drag my eyes from the doll's hunched back. I studied her powder-blue overcoat, matching gloves, black slacks, stooped posture, and white hair. She was incredibly lifelike, except for the lack of breathing. "I can't sit next to that."

Ron pointed at the stool I'd vacated. "I recommend you give it a go, because I'm not switching. I just got this spot comfortable." He pretended to size up the doll. "Don't worry. I'll watch your back."

I didn't move.

He returned to his coffee, already tired of the game. "Fine. If you sit, I'll pay for your hotdish."

Dang. He knew me too well. It might be breakfast time, but the only meals I ever ordered at the Stew were Tater Tot hotdish or green bean casserole. Doris cooked them both perfectly. Rather than going fancy, she kept it simple, like God intended. For the totdish, that meant cream of mushroom soup mixed with burger (cow, turkey, or a special-order veggie crumble), salted and peppered, and topped with a golden field of tots. The green bean casserole had the same layout, except with beans in place of the meat and French fried onions instead of tots.

I slid gingerly onto my seat, keeping an eye on the doll.

I knew Ida Gilbertson. She was a gardener after my own heart, on the peculiar side but with her mobility and mental agility still intact despite eight-plus decades on the planet. She roomed next to her sister, Freda, at the Senior Sunset, Battle Lake's largest nursing home and assisted-living facility. Why in the world would such a placid woman create so much horror?

"You better believe you'll pay for my hotdish," I grumbled. "It's the least you can do for not telling me I was sitting next to Chucky this whole time."

The kitchen bell dinged, and my gaze shot toward the kitchen. Pavlov's dogs had nothing on me, not when there was hotdish at stake.

Doris returned to her spot behind the counter, slid the coffeepot onto the warmer, whisked two steaming plates from the window, and turned toward us. I clapped with joy. (You can judge, but at least I didn't let the drool slide down my chin.) My smile grew as she neared, my eyes Christmas-morning wide. I could smell the creamy, salty deliciousness, and I'd long since freed my knife and fork from their napkin.

Finally, after what seemed like decades, she set the heavy plate in front of me.

"Yay! I've been craving this all morning. I can't—" My grin fizzled. The silverware went limp in my hand. I tipped my nose toward the toast-colored slivers polluting the gelatinous peak of steaming tots. "What are those?"

"Almonds." Doris stood straighter. "I switched up my recipe. You can't fall into a rut in this world. Life'll just come up and sweep you away, and you're gone. Boom! Dead. You have to make the most of each moment. Take my cousin Len. He was all set to retire last week, and then he broke his leg. Sure, it was an artificial leg, but you still have to get those fixed. Had to drive all the way to Detroit Lakes. Actually, he had to have someone drive him . . ."

I wasn't listening. I was mourning my breakfast—so close yet infinitely far away. It wasn't that she'd mucked it up with fanciness, though I wasn't a fan of that. Rather, I'd recently discovered I was allergic to almonds. I'd bought a jar of the crunchy nut butter and slammed a third of it before noticing my palms were itching like fire ants were crawling beneath the skin. I stopped eating it, but it was too late. My face puffed up like an air mattress. The doctor at the Fergus Falls Urgent Care clinic diagnosed it as a late-onset food allergy and sent me on my way full of antihistamines and with a double-set EpiPen.

"I can't eat this," I said, interrupting Doris. "I'm allergic to almonds."

She retrieved a spoon from under the counter and made for my plate. "That's fine. I'll scrape 'em off."

My hopes momentarily soared—I could almost taste the warm, salty hotdish train sliding toward my stomach—until a thought struck me. "Wait, did you mix the nuts in, or did you only sprinkle them on as garnish?"

We locked eyes. As someone who'd long ago mastered the art of the lie, I recognized her expression. She was searching for her WHAT THE CUSTOMER DOESN'T KNOW PROBABLY WON'T HURT THEM file, because she had a new entry to add.

"Just garnish," she said, breaking eye contact.

Normally, I'd call out another liar on a fib that weak. It was a professional courtesy, if nothing else. I was considering letting it slide, though, because I wanted that hotdish bad. A small dose of almonds wouldn't kill me, right? Besides, was it really a lie if it made my life more delicious? I was on the verge of telling her to forget what I'd said about the allergy, that I actually loved almonds with a side of EpiPen, when I noticed her eyes widening at the exact moment the restaurant's front door donged, signaling a new customer.

A customer Doris clearly wanted to avoid. I swiveled to check it out.

And immediately regretted my decision.

Chapter 3

Battle Lake's mayor, Kennie Rogers—she of the country-music name and the death-metal soul, famous far and wide for her thick makeup, outrageous clothing, questionable politics, fake southern accent, and far-fetched business ventures—was striding into the Stew. She appeared to be sporting an ensemble from the Ride Me Barbie collection, starting with a tiny plastic cowboy hat nestled in her crunchy platinum beehive and plastic Barbie boot earrings dangling from her lobes. The accessories would have been ridiculous if they didn't so beautifully accent her sheepskin coat over a Western snap-front red shirt—currently more *front* than *snap*, what with her ample bosom pushing toward the light—and jeans so tight that her camel toe was closer to a camel *foot*. Bright-pink stiletto cowboy boots finished off the outfit.

Whoo-boy. My roller-coaster morning was taking another screeching dip.

It wasn't her outfit, which I had to admire for its sheer commitment to a single message. Nope. It was that she sought me out like it was her job, always wanting to involve me in her moneymaking schemes, either as a customer or a partner.

Before you say, "That doesn't sound so bad," here's a sampling of the businesses: a reused marital aid company called Come Again; coffin tables (place your coffee cups on it now and your body in it later!); a home bikini-waxing service; and her most recent, which she'd pitched to me last week, a raspberry-flavored hair tonic that, rumor had it, was actually a veterinary-class sedative. I didn't want to stick around to find out what was up next.

I tossed the totdish one last loving, regret-filled glance and slipped off my stool. Choose my battles and all that. "Ron, I have to skedaddle. Here's my final offer: you pay me two-fifty a week to write the column, and I'll eat the travel costs. I promise you the first article, the community ed class review, within a week."

I waved at Doris, who was still regarding Kennie like a child watched an incoming spoonful of cough syrup. I pitched my voice low, so as not to draw Kennie's attention. "Thanks for the coffee, Doris. If you can whip up an almond-free totdish, I'm all in. Next time, OK?"

Kennie hadn't yet noticed us in the back of the restaurant. She was working the crowd near the front door, and I'd never been more grateful for the Turtle Stew's side entrance. I could sneak out unseen! I turned toward the exit, a satisfied smile pinching my cheeks. Dang if I wasn't going to salvage this doll-and-almond train wreck of a morning.

"Mira James!"

Kennie's southern-tinged yell drew the attention of the handful of patrons who hadn't yet noticed her Western-themed resplendence. I shrank into myself, tossing all my eggs into the *she can't see me if I don't look at her* basket.

"Stay where you are, honey!" she continued. "I have a proposition for you."

My stomach dropped below Battle Lake's water table. I spun on my heels, committed to sprinting if need be. Unfortunately, I turned so fast that I collided with the nightmarish doll. Ida's freak show toppled toward the floor.

"I'm so sorry!" I hollered at the world, watching the crapfest play out in slow motion. My physical reflexes kicked in almost as soon as my apologetic ones, and I dived toward the doll, trying to catch it before it hit the ground. I slipped a hand under it a nanosecond before it touched tile. My plan was to keep it from smacking, in case there were any breakable parts. Instead, surprised by the doll's weight and density, I found myself falling along with the human puppet.

Something primal recoiled as I plummeted, a sickly-sweet smell causing my flight response to kick in, though I was off-balance and powerless to flee. The doll hit the ground with the weight and slap of a side of frozen beef. I tumbled on top of it immediately after. The doll's hat and wig went flying, and the coffee cup she'd been holding crashed to the floor. After a collective gasp, the restaurant went deathly silent, everyone watching me scramble to balance myself and fix this mess.

Something shrieked at me to run, something dark and terrible and slimy, but the terror was so great, so enormous, that it couldn't get ahead of my mouth, which was still trying to negotiate the social faux pas of tumbling the life-size doll. "Don't worry! I'll put her back just like I found her!"

I gathered the wig and hat, planning to slam them onto the doll and hoist her back onto the stool before the other patrons had a chance to process what was happening. That's when the terror caught up to me, crashing me finally, fully into the moment.

My slack-jawed horror was reflected in the face of every person in that restaurant.

They stared at the doll, their mouths agape. I followed their horrified gazes.

The only sound I could make was a greenish *oof.*

When the doll tumbled to the ground, its porcelain mask had slipped enough to reveal what looked like gray human flesh beneath.

I saw a hand reach forward to remove the mask the rest of the way. When the porcelain's coldness shocked my system, I realized that the hand was mine, and it was working without my permission.

A gentle tug, and the mask was free.

Underneath was a human corpse, female, her icy death stare aimed at the drop ceiling, her mouth a tight, angry rictus, as if she'd died rage-yodeling.

The mask dropped from my hand, crashing to the ground and shattering into white-and-red shards.

That's when the screaming started.

Chapter 4

Gary Wohnt regarded me with the steel-eyed gaze of a man regretting every life choice he'd ever made, every turn and decision that had led him to this moment.

I almost felt sorry for the guy.

Almost.

Gary was Battle Lake's police chief. When I'd moved to town last year, he'd weighed seventy-five pounds more and presented with a significant hair-pomade-and-Carmex habit. He'd also been dating Kennie and serving as gofer and sometimes bouncer at her geriatric sex club, though neither of those positions were in any danger of appearing on his résumé.

Since then, he'd experienced a literal come-to-Jesus, dumping the weight, the wet look, and, by all accounts, Kennie. The only thing that hadn't changed was how he consistently rode my nuts. Sure, he had a job to do, and his law enforcing butted up against my corpse catching with a regularity that I don't imagine he enjoyed any more than I did.

He could have been nicer about it, is all I'm saying.

Treated me like a partner rather than a criminal.

Take this zombie doll situation I'd tumbled into at the Turtle Stew. Somebody was going to find that hidden cadaver sooner or later. It was my bad luck that it had been me, sooner. Chief Wohnt should have handled me like a shaken witness in this situation, rather than studying me with those black eyes, flexing that muscle in his jaw like he had a popcorn kernel wedged in his teeth that he couldn't dig out.

He finally spoke. "You found the body."

He might as well have said "You're breathing," for all the surprise he invested into the words.

"Nope." My defensiveness burned up my good sense like it was made of rice paper. "The doll was there all along, in plain sight of every person in this restaurant. I didn't 'find' anything."

His jaw twitching doubled. Two popcorn kernels. "Yet it was *you* who discovered the corpse hiding inside the doll?"

Someone had pulled a sheet over said corpse and cleared the Turtle Stew of everyone but me, Doris, Ron, Kennie, and Gary's two deputies. One of the deputies was questioning the other three witnesses while the second taped off the region around the body. I tried not to look.

I hadn't recognized the woman before she'd been covered, but that didn't mean much—her face had been heavily made-up under the mask, exaggerated blue eye shadow and garish lipstick rendering her rheumy eyes and eternal scream clownish.

I shuddered all over again but held my wobbly ground, pointing toward the body. "I discovered that corpse like Columbus discovered America."

The deputy currently cordoning off the crime scene made a noise like a teeny set of tires screeching to a halt, a Barbie car slamming on the brakes just before hitting a tiny chicken crossing the road.

Gary made no sound.

Instead, thunderclouds rolled down his forehead and shaded his deepwater eyes and I caught the slightest whiff of steam. Were his black eyes turning a green tornado color? Time stood still as he leaned toward me, looking for all the world like he was going to bite off my nose and spit it onto the floor. I held myself still on the stool farthest from the corpse, the spot I'd selected the second Gary had ordered me to sit. He wouldn't hurt me in front of all these people, would he?

"Mira James," he growled into my ear, "I am sick and tired of meeting you over dead bodies. Do you understand?"

I nodded. I wasn't a fan myself.

"If it were up to me, I'd have taken you off the streets months ago. We'd have fewer murder investigations, and I'd have less pains in my ass." He growled in frustration. "But it turns out I need a legal reason to lock you up. My number-one job from this moment forward is to find. That. Reason."

I jumped off the stool, fear giving way to fury. "That is the stupidest thing I've ever heard!" I gestured toward the body on the floor. "You should be worried about who killed this woman, not what I'm up to."

His face relaxed not at all. "Who killed this woman and what you are up to seem to be connected," he snarled. "So why don't you stop wasting both our time, because I'm confident there's something you want to tell me."

I puffed up all 125 pounds of myself, any last shred of self-preservation fleeing in the face of anger. I hadn't *wanted* to sit near a huge doll. I would have given all my money *not* to find a corpse underneath the hat and wig. And I sure as hell was not going to sit here and be harassed for my bad luck.

"Yep." I planted my fists on my hips. "There sure is something I want to tell you."

He drew back slightly, his mouth tight, the barest hint of surprise in his eyes.

I set my shoulders. "Here it is." I drew in a deep breath. "I want to tell you that you're a mean bag of dog turds."

The deputy made the itty-bitty tire-screeching sound again.

"You tell him, girl!" Kennie called from the other end of the counter.

Ron and Doris said nothing, their faces somber.

I ignored Kennie and leaned forward, forcing Gary to step back. "I also want to tell you that I'm late for work."

I began striding backward toward the rear door, not sure if he'd let me go.

He watched me moonwalk away, his gaze predatory. He said nothing. I was quaking inside, but no way was I gonna let him see it. I spun at the last minute, ripped open the back door, and stormed away, returning to ease it closed before it slammed shut.

There was righteous and then there was rude.

After I made sure it closed quietly, I gulped in the brisk March air in great big servings. We were officially in the first week of spring, and for once in Minnesota, it actually felt like the thawing season. Still, this early in the day, the temperature was barely above freezing. I hurried away from the restaurant, passing a handful of people walking the hunched-penguin stroll of Minnesotans in spring, eyes on the ground, ever watchful for ice or, worse, melting ice. The trees tall enough to be visible over Battle Lake's downtown businesses curled like winter skeletons, perfectly reflecting my mood.

I shuffled up the street toward the library, where I'd parked my car in anticipation of starting my shift after meeting with Ron. My hands were shoved deep in my pockets. I hoped that everyone back at the Stew thought I'd left because I was angry. I didn't want them to see the tears bubbling up.

Screw tears. I began to full-on sob.

I kept it smooth on the surface because people hurt you if you showed weakness. The truth, though, was that I was terrified. And broken. And sad. I didn't want to find more bodies. I didn't want to be a murder magnet. Most importantly, I missed Jed, and the woman's body at the Stew had brought back the visceral pain of his recent funeral.

I'd thought I'd disassociated better.

Jed was one of the first to welcome me to Battle Lake and had been one of my closest friends ever since. He'd been a goofy, Shaggy-esque hippie who relocated spiders rather than killing them, who was always broke because he felt bad charging people for the handyman work he completed around town, who'd been one of the last innocents, a pure puppy ball of love and kindness. Sure, he smoked too much pot, was disorganized, and had an off-again, on-again relationship with personal hygiene, but his heart and home were always open.

Jed wasn't supposed to travel with me and Mrs. Berns when we took the train to Portland last month. He'd tagged along because he thought it would be fun to train-trip with me.

He'd died saving my life.

A sob escaped my mouth and splintered in the March air. I didn't bother to try and hide it because, really, who was safe around me? I wiped away hot tears. They were immediately replaced by more.

I'd never felt responsible for my dad's passing, but maybe I should have, because it sure seemed like everyone who came close to me was pulled into an invisible death vortex. It was simply a matter of time until they all suffered a horrible fate. Up until now, I'd been able to convince myself that as tragic as all the other Battle Lake deaths had been, none of them had been connected to me, none of them particularly close. Even Jeff, the first corpse I'd found, had been in my life for only a matter of days. I could keep his death, and all the ones that followed it, at some distance.

Jed's murder had changed all that.

I blubbered some more, swiping at the snot rolling out of my nose. That poor woman back at the Turtle Stew. What had happened to her? What family was she leaving behind? What had her last moments been like? The tears were coming so fast that I could hardly see. Good thing most people were already at work and the foot traffic was light. The library was a straight shot from the Stew.

I swiped at my face again.

Through my clearer vision, I saw someone standing in front of the apothecary a half block ahead. He looked familiar. I rubbed both eyes. He wore an old army jacket. From behind, I couldn't see his face, only his curly hair.

My heart leaped.

I knew why he looked familiar.

It was Jed, back from the grave.

Chapter 5

I bolted forward, chasing Jed into the apothecary. A thrill-fear, light and sharp, separated skin from muscle. My brain was spinning webs from hope. I'd witnessed him thrown out of a moving train, but I'd never seen him land. The train had been speeding over a deep valley shrouded in mist and darkness. His body hadn't been discovered.

What if Jed had survived the fall, my sweet, goofy Jed, and he'd found his way back to Battle Lake? Stranger things had most certainly happened.

The paste in my mouth made it difficult to swallow. I raced into the apothecary's welcoming warmth. The door closed behind me. The man in the army fatigue jacket—Jed, I was sure of it—stood in the main aisle, a row of candy on one side, the till on the other.

He turned so I could see his profile.

The suffocating paste in my mouth dropped into my stomach with a hollow echo. He wasn't a man at all. He was a boy, an unfamiliar child of maybe eight years.

Of course it wasn't Jed. Jed was gone, forever.

I'd never see my beautiful friend again.

What I would see was a parade of corpses, one a month, give or take, like that poor woman someone had stuffed inside a doll disguise and planted on a stool. The sticky clot in my stomach began to harden, but I ignored the pain. I needed to cement it far below the surface. Who had murdered that woman and why, I did not know. I would not let my brain go there. Getting involved in other people's business had cost me Jed.

I dug my fingernails into my palms to return to the moment. I needed to focus, to pull my brain out of the macabre track it had boarded.

"Can I help you?" A worker appeared from behind the shelves, her smile not slipping a whit as it landed on what was surely the slimy swollenness of my cry face. She wasn't one of the usual teenagers who worked here, but I often shopped later in the afternoon, when school was out. Come to think of it, what was the kid in the fatigues doing in the drugstore in the middle of a school morning? The worker must have read my thought bubble, because we both turned toward him at the same time, at the exact moment he was sliding a candy bar into his sleeve about ten feet away.

The cashier's bristles rose in concert with her mouth opening. I beat her to it.

"I'm buying his candy."

He swiveled, aware he'd become the topic of conversation. His hand flew guiltily up his sleeve, where he drew out the candy bar with a magician's finesse, as if he'd been holding it in plain sight all along, bargain hunting rather than stealing.

"I said I got it," I said, pitching my voice toward him. "Grab me that box of Nut Goodies next to it."

His expression made clear he thought I was playing him and he didn't know the game. Equally transparently, he was guessing that we'd seen him shoplift. Playing the wise card of following instructions until you see your opening, he reached into the bright green, red, and white box I'd directed his attention toward and drew out a single Nut Goodie.

(Time for an important customer service announcement: If you're not familiar, Nut Goodies begin with a maple center spun of sugared unicorn smiles. Perfect peanuts top that blessed center, and then a deliciously creamy, milky chocolate coats the whole works. As a Minnesota original and one of only a handful of candy bars with the courage not to be penis-shaped, the Nut Goodie held a special place in my heart—as well as in my coping-mechanism drawer.)

"Not the bar," I clarified. "The *box*. It's been a long day already."

He didn't want to do what I asked, that's what the set of his shoulders told me. I could tell he was smart, though, and almost as good at reading people as I was. Probably he'd grown up in a volatile household, too. Not knowing what words would set off the adults around you, or what actions would drive them to raging anger or worse, made a person exceptionally good at sussing out the meaning of the subtlest of gestures, from a lip twitch to a hip cock.

Ask me how I know.

The kid grabbed the unwieldy Nut Goodie box with one hand, strode toward the counter like he was auditioning for a Bee Gees video, slapped the box down, and yanked two other candy bars out of his pocket, neither of them the bar we'd seen him steal. He used all three to salute the cashier and me before strutting out of the apothecary. I caught a whiff of cigarettes and unwashed hair as he passed, though he appeared surface clean. I reevaluated his age. He was closer to eleven, maybe twelve, though small for his age, the top of his head barely reaching the bottom of my ears, and I was a modest five-six.

Maybe it was because he resembled Jed, or the way he'd chosen to own this situation he had no control over, but I found myself liking the kid. I even found a small smile creeping up my lips. The boy had style.

"Foster care," the cashier muttered, yanking me out of my thoughts.

She was about my height but had at least ten years on me. "What?"

"Little D, they call him. I don't know what his actual name is. He's new to the school system. Guess he was homeschooled somewhere, or maybe he was in a foster home in a different town? Anyhow, he's staying with the Fords, that big Colonial-looking house on Country Road 78 south of town? He's one of their temporary children." She cocked her eyebrow. "I seen him smoking with older kids and skipping school. No good, that one."

"That must be hard," I murmured, watching through the front window as he disappeared from view. "To be in foster care."

She made a scoffing sound. "Better than living on the streets. You sure you want this whole box of Nut Goodies?"

Yeah, I was sure. Unless she had a gross, in which case I'd take that, too. I reached into my pocket for cash. I was done talking with her. I didn't like that she didn't like someone I liked.

The front door donged and her sour mouth tipped down further. "Speaking of no good . . ."

I glanced over my shoulder. A guy in his early sixties strode in. He was thin-lipped and sharp-nosed, and his bald head was covered in swollen, tough-looking lesions. I guessed his hands were equally afflicted, but they were shoved too deep into his pockets to know for sure. I grabbed my change and the Nut Goodies, turning down the bag she offered. I wasn't willing to hide my addiction.

The older guy walked toward the rear counter, where the pharmacy services were. The cashier strode over to meet him. "Here for a prescription, Eustace?"

I didn't hear him respond. I found myself not wanting to leave quite yet, though. In fact, I very urgently wanted to know what his prescription was for. It was the same part of me that liked to look in people's medicine cabinets when I visited, or to open closed doors. The more secrets you knew, the less you got hurt in this life. I tiptoed around an endcap and toward the rear of the apothecary.

Eustace was hidden from where I stood, but his voice matched his appearance—short and sharp. "The price the same?"

"Always," she said. "Cash?"

He grunted. I heard the crinkle of paper.

"Vemurafenib. That sound right, Eustace?"

He mumbled another affirmative.

Disappointed, I made for the front door. I'd hoped he was picking up something I'd heard of, like cootie spray or Viagra, not Femur-whatever, which was probably something to help with that painful-looking rash. Ah, well. Such was life.

Speaking of life, mine was marginally better than it had been five minutes earlier, now that I had enough Nut Goodies to kill a diabetic. Denial, some might have called that, or compartmentalizing. Me, I called it survival.

I debated schlepping the Goodies over to the Fortune Café, the coffee shop owned by my pals Sid and Nancy, and enjoying one or seven of them over a cup of coffee. I'd been robbed of my breakfast, after all, and I didn't need to be at the library until noon since my best friend, Mrs. Berns, had taken the opening shift. The first hour or two on weekdays were usually slow, at least until the day care parents showed up. She and I'd agreed that would be the best time of day for her to learn to run the place on her own.

Mrs. Berns had been an octogenarian residing at the Senior Sunset when I first landed in Battle Lake. Plot twist: she was not even close to ready for a nursing home. She'd since turned ninety, rented an apartment, and scored about a million more dates than women half her age, me included. She'd also weaseled her way into a position at the library, plus somehow managed to become an assistant private investigator for my nonexistent PI agency. I grumbled about her omnipresence in my life, but I loved having her around. She was outspoken and hilarious, strong as steel.

She'd also recently taken to dyeing her hair blue, but ironically.

Today, I imagined she'd have it freshly curled, her lipstick a perfect coral ring drawn way outside the lines. Same with her eye shadow, which she applied using her lids as more of a suggestion than a goal. I guessed she'd be sporting her lilac palette today.

Hey, you know what made this guessing about Mrs. Berns's appearance particularly easy?

I was looking at her right now, through the front window of the apothecary. She was across the street, dropping a letter into the blue mailbox.

Which meant no one was watching the library.

Chapter 6

I charged outside, making a noise somewhere between a strangled burp and a cluck. (Some days, *I* acted more the nonagenarian.)

"Mrs. Berns!" I hollered across the street. The words floated out in white plumes, the ion smell of late winter crowding my nose.

She let the face of the mailbox close and waved at me with her free hand. "Morning!"

After the traffic—two pickup trucks and a rusty sedan—rumbled past, I scooted across the icy Main Street, careful to keep my feet close to the ground. I almost bit it once, faring better when I reached the salted sidewalk. Mrs. Berns watched serenely.

I was out of breath when I finally reached her. "What are you doing here?"

She made a show of staring at the huge metal mailbox, then at me. "You know what these are for, right? They swallow your letters and poop them out in a new location."

I made that prying-a-rock-from-a-swamp noise again. "Not *here* at the *mailbox*. *Here* away from the library! You were supposed to open an hour ago."

"Of course I did that." She nodded as if the matter were laid to rest and then began to walk up the street, away from the library. Had dementia finally tracked her down?

I scooted to catch up with her. "Great. But you know that after you opened the library, you were supposed to *stay* there . . . and help people?"

She stopped at the street corner and glanced at her watch. "You're close, but you don't have it exactly right. You said, 'Once the library is open, *someone* needs to be there at all times.'"

My forehead plonked into my palm. I had actually spoken those exact words. I'd *assumed* the someone would be her, but I guessed I hadn't spelled that out. "Who's watching the library, Mrs. Berns?"

"A lantern."

I gargled with my tongue. "A light is watching the library?"

"Not a light." She rolled her eyes like I was the dumb one. "A *lantern*. And you're not going to like her one bit."

My brain raced through the sticky pinball track of possibilities and landed on the soundalike that made the most sense. "An *intern*?"

Mrs. Berns waved at the air in front of her. *Tuh-may-to, tuh-mah-to,* the gesture said. But then a thought stopped her, and she grabbed my wrist. "I heard you found another body. One of those creepy dolls Ida is making, but this one with a secret center." She cackled and dropped my hand. "Anyhow, I was on my way to see you. That's why it's good we got the lantern when we did or I would've had to close down the library to come help you. We're on the job on this one, right? What clues do you have so far?"

"No clues," I groaned, gently turning her around to face the direction she must have come. We didn't have an intern, and I needed to see who was running my library. The way my day was going, it was probably a pack of raccoons in a trench coat. "Also, we are not 'on the job' on this one. I don't know who the dead woman is, how she died, or why she was put in a doll, and it's none of our business. We have a library to run."

"You mean I don't get to eyeball the body?" She rummaged in her purse. "Because I ordered a fingerprinting kit online, and I'd hate to see it go to waste. Do you know you can get anything online these days? I'm saving up for a remote control airplane as we speak."

She tugged out a neatly packaged box with the words Super Sleuth KidKit on the front. It featured a graphic of a young girl in a houndstooth deerstalker cap, staring at me through a magnifying lens. The kit was unopened.

"You hang on to that." I kept my free hand on her elbow so she couldn't slip away and also to keep us steady on the slick street. "I'm sure we'll need it, but not today. Gary Wohnt is on the scene, and no way would he let you in, even if . . . scratch that, *especially* if you said you wanted to help him 'solve the crime.'"

"Hi, Eustace!" Mrs. Berns called out as the older man exited the apothecary across the street from us. He must have heard her, but he didn't so much as glance our way.

I kept us motoring toward the library, balancing the box of candy on my hip. "You know him?"

"Sure. He's a wacko pinko nutjob."

She said it in such a friendly tone that it took me an extra moment to process the words. "He's a Communist?"

"If that means he lives in the woods, growing his own food and refusing to pay taxes as a protest to government involvement in overseas wars, then yep, he's a Communist."

"Huh." Eustace suddenly grew more interesting. I wished I'd paid more attention to the name of the medicine he'd picked up. Femurjobbie?

"I'm surprised to see him in town, actually," Mrs. Berns said thoughtfully, mincing up the street. "He used to come by the Sunset to visit his dad. That's how I know him. Sometimes I'll see him around, bartering firewood or canned vegetables for something he needs at the hardware store, and I'll say, 'Hey, Eustace Dickens, how's the simple life,' and he'll say, 'Just fine, Mrs. Berns.' See? He's a good guy."

That wasn't a lot to go on, but it didn't cost me anything to believe Mrs. Berns and file Eustace away accordingly. "Thank you for that riveting story. Now tell me more about the intern. Let's start with the basics. Is he/she human?"

"She, and yes. Human."

I relaxed not at all.

"Kennie dropped her off," Mrs. Berns continued. "Have you seen the mayor yet today? Looks like a rodeo clown barfed on her, and it was the kind of barf that shrinks your clothes so tight that you'll need the jaws of life to cut you out of them. Anyhow, Rodeo Kennie brought a lady with her, said some words about the woman contributing to the library, and that because of the lady's generosity, she would get to be our lantern."

I shook my head. "That makes no sense. We don't even have an internship program, let alone one you can buy into."

"My thoughts exactly. Well, not exactly. Mine were more along the line of 'Get out of my library, lady, except first cover my shift.'" Mrs. Berns punched an angry fist in the air, then transformed it into a proffered handshake to demonstrate her interaction with the intern before continuing. "Kennie has a new business scheme, by the way. You're gonna like this one."

The image of Kennie noticing me in the Stew flashed big on my mind screen. "I don't want to hear a lick about any new Kennie business venture."

"Interesting choice of words." Mrs. Berns hooted. "You'll find out why soon, but I think you're going to be perfect for the job. I'll let Kennie tell you all about it. In the meanwhile, speaking of licking, what's the news on the Johnny Leeson front?"

The library loomed ahead and to our right, and thank all that was good, it was still standing. Maybe the intern wasn't so bad after all. "Things are fine, I think. Tomorrow morning he leaves for a trip to Wisconsin. He's looking into grad school again."

Johnny was as smart as he was hot. He'd earned a horticultural bachelor's (on top of being a lead singer for a local band) and had always meant to attend grad school for an advanced degree in the field.

His father's cancer and then death had sidetracked that plan, but only temporarily. I completely supported his dreams. We'd just have to figure out how to make them work.

Mrs. Berns screeched to a stop. "If he moves to Wisconsin, where would you live?"

To be honest, I didn't want to consider that too closely. That was why I'd elected to keep the *we'll figure out how to make it work* Band-Aid slapped across the top. Out of sight, out of mind. "We'll cross that bridge when we get there. For now, I want to plan a getaway for when he gets back. Where do you think we should go?"

She shrugged. "I hear Battle Lake is nice this time of year."

I laughed. I couldn't help it. "I was hoping for something a little more exotic."

"Try Urbank," she said, naming the dot of a town up the road. "I hear they have authentic nachos on the bar menu."

"Thanks for the hot tip." I was still laughing. There was no one better at distracting me from the bad stuff than Mrs. Berns.

"Stay clear of the cabins on Clitherall Lake, though," she said, her voice suddenly serious. "Apparently, the Peeping Tom has been spotted there."

I'd heard the rumors. Some dude had been flashing his pork and beans into women's windows around town. I didn't know what made guys think that was something we'd want to see, but the only thing less welcome than a penis out of context was two penises out of context. "Anyone you know actually seen him?"

"I wish!" Mrs. Berns waved her hands in the air, karate-style. "I'd neuterize him."

"Neutralize," I corrected.

She raised her eyebrows.

"Oh," I said. "You were being literal. You'd take his nuts."

She wrinkled her nose. "If he has any. Men who spy on women are a bunch of wieners, not a ball between them. At least five different women, all ages, all around town, have claimed to see this one. He runs before they can get a good description, except they all agree he's not a big fella. I say bear traps outside of windows should take care of the problem."

"I hope he gets caught soon."

We crossed the street. The library parking lot was empty—odd but not unheard of at this hour. The sidewalk that led to the front door had not been salted yet, which made for treacherous walking. I needed to call the city and get the groundskeeper out here ASAP. If this was the worst of the library's status, though, I was getting off easy.

I held the door for Mrs. Berns. She stepped inside and pointed at the front counter, removing her winter jacket as she did so. I followed. I had my own parka half-unzipped before I saw what she was indicating.

A woman was sprawled on the floor, a fluffy white doll near her head.

The air squeezed out of me, and my box of Nut Goodies dropped to the floor.

"Meet your new lantern," Mrs. Berns said, her voice oddly calm.

Chapter 7

I charged forward and dropped next to the woman, scrabbling to check her pulse. My quick movements startled both her and the white doll, which turned out not to be a doll at all, but rather a miniature poodle with eyes like buttons.

The woman leaped partway up and clambered away from me. I mirrored her shocked movements, automatically taking stock of her appearance, even as I tried to make sense of what she'd been doing spread-eagled on the floor. She was in her late fifties if I had to guess, her $400 dye job and subtly tailored clothes suggesting money. Buckets of it.

"What is wrong with you!" she yelped.

"What's wrong with *you*!" I responded. My heartbeat thumped at my wrists. "You were lying on the floor."

She patted her chest, reaching for the dog to calm it.

Mrs. Berns strode toward us. "Told you that you wouldn't like her." She held her hand toward me. "Take your coat?"

I finished removing my parka and handed it to her, my hands shaking. Mrs. Berns headed to the back room, presumably to hang up our jackets. That left me with the intern and her dog, all three of us still on the floor, but hopefully her poodle the only one sporting the eye boogers. I smoothed my hair and tried again. "What were you doing on the ground?"

"Meditating." The woman rose gracefully to her feet, cradling the poodle in one arm. She used the other to arrange her clothes.

I stood, too. "On the floor?"

"On the *earth*."

Dammit, Mrs. Berns was right. I didn't like her even a teensy bit. "Let's start over." I held out my hand. "My name is Mira James. I'm the head librarian. You are?"

"Christie." She indicated the poodle. "And this is Vegan, my vegetarian service dog."

"You've got to be kidding me." I scanned the perimeter for hidden cameras as I walked over to gather up my precious Nut Goodies. "I am speaking literally. Somebody is pulling my leg here."

Christie huffed. Dog still tucked in her arm, she glided behind the counter, pulling out a purse that, based on the conspicuous brand name it was lettered with, cost more than my car. "See for yourself."

"Why the hell not?" I strolled over to read the piece of thick paper she'd fished out of her purse, setting my box of candy on the counter. Sure enough, Mrs. Christie Maroon held a letter on a medical office's letterhead. Vegan was medically required to reduce her anxiety. I studied the white fluff in her arms. Poor guy didn't look nearly up to the task. He was drooling himself and quivering, likely surfing the waves of WTF coursing off me.

"Fantastic. Your name is Christie, your dog's name is Vegan, and you are licensed to carry him wherever you deem necessary. What are you doing in my library?"

I had had exactly enough. Unfortunately, the Universe hadn't, because Mayor Kennie Rogers swept into the library as the last sentence left my mouth. Bad Brad, of all people, followed at her heels.

Yes, Bad Brad, the ex-boyfriend who had driven me out of Minneapolis and into the arms of Battle Lake with his extracurricular exploration of other ladies' privates. In a further chucklefest from the Universe, BB had chosen to follow me to Battle Lake a few months back, mistaking my lack of communication as an indicator that Otter Tail County was a great time.

He'd been a bass player back in Minneapolis and formed a band, Iron Steel—"twice the metal"—as soon as he hit town. He'd been respectful of my relationship with Johnny and even rousted up a couple dates of his own with some nice area women. He seemed to be fitting in just fine, though his current sneaky grin assured me that I didn't want to know what he was doing with Kennie.

"Christie is saving your sweet patootie, that's what she's doing here." Kennie smiled grandly, picking up my sentence where I'd let it drop. "And you could use some good luck, considering that I just left the Turtle Stew, and believe you me, Chief Wohnt is gunning for your neck." She waved her hands in the air. "But enough of that unpleasantness. Christie here is an ambassador of the Seeking Life Under Many Names organization. You've heard of them?"

I had not.

"They send rich people to the country to learn to be a redneck," Mrs. Berns said matter-of-factly, returning to the room. "It's like a mission trip, but they spread idiocy instead of Christianity."

I coughed to cover my spit take.

Christie arched her eyebrows. "We most certainly do not. SLUMN is a domestic study abroad organization that promotes cultural sensitivity."

Mrs. Berns shrugged and made for the book-return bin. "If you say so."

"I heard about the organization on NPR," Kennie said, drawing the conversation back to herself. "I called them and put Battle Lake, and specifically your library, on SLUMN's donor list. They chose us at the beginning of the month. Whee!" She clapped her hands and, impossibly, widened her heavily caked eyes. "In return for hosting two of their prominent members for four weeks, they'll make a generous donation to the village of Battle Lake. Enough to run the library for a year, and then some."

She beamed lasers toward me. Her meaning was clear: *Play nice if you want to keep the library afloat.* I had a more pressing question. "You listen to NPR?"

"Pfft," she said, waving away my question. "I am a cultured woman."

In the way that yogurt was a cultured food, I supposed. Her radio must have gotten accidentally jammed on the station. Still, life was all about letting some things go. "All right, tell me the score. Who is the other SLUMN"—I heard it as soon as I said it and stopped myself, just barely, from rolling my eyes, ears, and anything else that could rotate—"member who will be studying 'domestically abroad' here in Battle Lake, and what do I need to do on behalf of the library?"

Christie placed the quivering Vegan on the counter, where he peed a little out of sustained terror. Somebody needed to set that poor animal free. "The other member is my husband, Donald. He and I are staying at the Battle Lake Motel for the month. Each week, we work at a different business in town. He's at the Senior Sunset this week, and I'm here. You'll be pleased to learn I have a background in marketing."

I'd be pleased to learn no such thing.

"Any questions?" she asked.

Mrs. Berns held an armful of books that needed restocking. "I've got one. How do you manage to be both boring and arrogant? Usually folks pick one or the other."

I shot my hand into the air, more sensitive to the library budget than Mrs. Berns was. "I have two questions, actually. What hours do you want to work, and what do you want to do while you're here?"

"That's more like it!" The joy was written plainly across Kennie's face. She loved to be the town's puppet master. "You are absolutely gonna love having Christie around. She's a queen among women, well traveled and smart."

Christie and Kennie exchanged obsequious glances before Kennie blessed Bad Brad with her attention. I was horrified to see him light up like a skyscraper at dusk.

"The paperwork, please," Kennie asked him.

The briefcase Bad Brad had been carrying looked out of place with his otherwise Jim-Morrison-on-a-bender appearance. He set it on the counter next to Vegan and jerked out a sheaf of papers. Before I could see what the papers were, I was distracted by Kennie unsnapping her Western-style blouse.

"Whoa, missy," I said, shielding my eyes. "Think of the children."

"Pshaw." I heard another snap. "I'm not going to flash anybody. This is one of my businesses, though not the one I need your help with. It's the prototype shirt for my Modern Cowgirl line. Check it out and be impressed."

I peeked through my fingers. I wouldn't last long in the wild—all a predator would have to do to lure me out of my den was pique my curiosity. I was elated to discover that Kennie wore a tight pink tank top under her now-open snap-front shirt. Her breasts pushed against the thin fabric like two Macy's Thanksgiving Day parade floats, but still. They were covered.

"Not those, honey, though they are spectacular, aren't they? The shirt's magic is here." She pointed at the interior button hem. A thin bit of silver the size and shape of a pencil was sewn into the cloth. "This one is a flask." She tugged out the cylinder, popped off the top, and tipped it into her mouth. "It only holds a single shot. I had to sacrifice quantity for fashion."

Mrs. Berns, who'd given up the facade of working to lean against the front desk, nodded as if that were the sanest thing Kennie had ever said. "Better than no shot at all."

Kennie winked at her, replaced the now-empty cylinder, and pulled out a second object, this one flatter than the first. "This side contains a lady tool."

"I've met some lady tools," Mrs. Berns said, cackling. "They wouldn't fit in there."

Brad shook his head. "Naw, a lady *tool*. Like a Leatherman, but for a woman? Kennie and I invented it."

Kennie scowled, clearly not ready to share credit. "*I* invented it, Bradley constructed it. All the clothes in my Modern Cowgirl line contain a flask plus a secret weapon that every lady can use. That's what sets them apart from your average stylish Western wear." She unsheathed the silver object.

"Looks like a metal nail file to me," I said, leaning in.

"It is," Kennie said. "It's also a screwdriver. And a pen."

Mrs. Berns's face lit up. "Could be used to pick locks, too."

Could it be? Had Kennie Rogers finally had a good business idea?

Chapter 8

I didn't want to admit it, but I'd actually like to own one of those lady tools.

"The best part of all of this," Kennie said, pulling out the pen so she could initial the top of the forms Brad produced before tucking the tool back into her shirt and snapping it closed, "is that it is fashionable! But enough about my genius. Let's return to the task at hand, the library. We're going to double its usage."

Kennie pointed at the papers she'd just initialed. "They're city-approved welcome packets. You're going to canvass Battle Lake and hand them out to anyone who isn't an active library user. The packets were Christie's idea! She calls this a focused thrust."

Surprisingly, Mrs. Berns let that low-hanging fruit pass unpicked, going for more books from the return bin, pausing only to nudge Bad Brad's briefcase into the pee puddle with her elbow. "Great idea. I think Christie'd be perfect at handing out welcome packets. She'd really get to meet the locals going door-to-door."

Christie regarded Mrs. Berns with flinty eyes. She didn't like being told what to do, that much was evident.

"I suppose I would," she said through clamped teeth.

Mrs. Berns nodded happily. "Great! With that settled, you can all clear out so we can get to work. The library is an important institution, and we have a public to serve."

Who was she fooling? The only person lazier than Mrs. Berns was, well, no one. Taking books out of the bin was already more work than I'd seen her accomplish in a single shift. I had questions for Kennie, too. I wanted a hard commitment on the library's budget, in writing, before I started ass-kissing Christie. I might have also had an itty-bitty inquiry about the identity of the body at the Stew. Not because I was going to get involved, mind you—simply to sate my curiosity.

Kennie read my mind. Sort of. "While I'm here, I'd like to discuss my new business venture that I already told Mrs. Berns about. Bradley and I have a grand idea, and we want you to be a part of it."

Her words caused Bad Brad to swell. I hoped it was with pride. Guess the budget and dead-body talk could wait.

"Maybe later?" Just because she'd had one good idea didn't mean the next one would hold up. "Because Mrs. Berns is right. We have a ton of work to do around here. In fact, we have a group of preschoolers to prepare for. They're arriving any minute for reading hour, and this time of year, we have to put down a tarp to catch all the runny noses."

"Time to run!" Kennie trilled, just as I'd expected. Sticky kids were not her jam. Bad Brad wasn't far behind. Christie lingered a moment, donning her parka, possibly trying to figure out how to reclaim some personal power from Mrs. Berns. Wisely, she chose to instead grab the sheaf of papers and follow Bad Brad and Kennie out the door.

Mrs. Berns appeared alongside me. "Phew," she said. "Glad to see them go. Did you see how hairy that Christie woman was? Gave me the heebie-jeebies."

I tucked my chin toward my neck. "I didn't notice that she was particularly hairy."

I actually had noticed, but I was sensitive about hairiness. In one of those fun life twists, I'd been born with thin hair on my head and an ape pelt on my arms. In high school, I'd shaved a swirling line through it, like a flesh peppermint stick, and then brushed the unshaved hair over the mowed spots. It'd turned out OK, I thought.

"You did too notice," Mrs. Berns said. "It was embarrassing how much you were staring at it."

I blushed, even though I was pretty sure I hadn't stared. Christie had sported a healthy covering on her arms and along her jawline, too. I imagined Battle Lake did not provide the aesthetic services she'd grown accustomed to. "She wasn't that hairy."

Mrs. Berns snorted. "She brought in some quinoa and cardboard nuggets for breakfast this morning. I watched her eat it. While she was chewing, she dropped some crumbs on her chin, and a hermit crab darted out of a hair patch on her cheek to grab 'em."

I cleared my throat. There really must have been hidden cameras somewhere. Maybe they'd been surgically implanted in my scalp. That would've explained a lot of happenings in the past year. In any case, I wasn't going to argue with Mrs. Berns. If she needed to vent by focusing on Christie's appearance, let her. I would remain neutral. I didn't particularly like the woman, but her appearance was no one's business but her own, and if she could save the library, we needed her.

Plus, I needed Mrs. Berns here and happy so I could duck out for a bit and talk to Ida Gilbertson at the Senior Sunset. Not because I was interested in solving the mystery of the Turtle Stew corpse, obviously. I had a few questions about the doll, and maybe I could introduce myself to Christie's husband when I was there, that was all. You know, as a polite gesture, one that could cement SLUMN's contribution to the library.

"Hey, I'm going to run to the Fortune Café for some coffee," I lied. "Want any?"

"No thanks," Mrs. Berns said. "I would like to go to swim aerobics with you tonight, though."

"What?"

She tugged the list of community classes that Ron had asked me to visit out of her pocket. "I found it in your jacket. Swim aerobics tonight, indoor mountain climbing tomorrow morning, then bridge club, cooking class, and yoga."

That explained why she'd wanted to hang up my jacket. Probably she was looking for anything relating to the scene at the Turtle Stew and had had to settle for my research list. "I'm not doing those classes for fun. Ron wants me to write an article."

"Duh," she said. "And I plan to attend every one of them with you. A lot of bad things can be said about you, Mira James—and I know because I'm the one who says them—but the truth is, it's never boring when you're around. We'll have a lot of fun at those classes."

I doubted it. I had only a week to hit them all, and reading their descriptions had brought up images of uncomfortable chairs and dull people. None of it sounded fun, particularly to a non-joiner like me, but it would be less painful if Mrs. Berns were there. Maybe. "You can come with if you agree not to call Christie hairy to her—"

"Werewolf mug," she coughed into her hand.

"—face, or make any scenes. We'll be attending as observers only." She nodded.

Satisfied, I went for my jacket. "You sure you don't want anything from the Fortune?"

"Positive," Mrs. Berns said. "But you can say hi to Ida for me." There was comfort in having a friend who knew me so well.

Chapter 9

Dirty cotton clouds scudded in front of the wan sun, shading the treacherous streets with fake dips and valleys that made walking all that much more difficult. I'd gambled that I'd be safer on foot than behind a wheel for this short distance, and so I'd left my car at the library. That had seemed a safe bet until I went ass over teakettle right outside the Senior Sunset.

My fall was so spectacular that the front desk worker ran out to check on me. After we ascertained that I was OK besides the bruised bumper and black-and-blue ego, I helped her layer more salt on the front walk. Then I made my way to Curtis Poling's room to say hi on my way to hunting down Ida.

Curtis Poling was Battle Lake's communal memory, and some days I wondered if he was our conscience as well. He'd helped me to solve more than one mystery since I'd moved here. Older than Mrs. Berns, he was nearly as popular as she was with the opposite sex. I racked it up to his beautiful, thick, snowy hair, perfect teeth that he removed each night, and a mind as sharp as a diamond point.

I found him at the window of his private room, finishing the Friday *New York Times* crossword puzzle with a pen.

"Hey, Curtis!"

He didn't look up. "What's a three-letter word meaning 'talk smack about'?"

"Does *D-I-S* work?"

He scribbled it in. "Yup." He scowled. "You kids today are wrecking the language, by the way."

I smiled. "I'm twenty-nine years old, Curtis. Hardly a kid."

He returned the grin, but it faded quickly. "I heard about the body."

I crossed my arms. "Any idea who it was?"

"Not that I've heard, but I'll tell you if that changes." He studied me. "How are you doing?"

The one question most likely to bring me to tears. I fought valiantly against them, taking a stab at a lame joke. "Couldn't be better. A body a month keeps the doctor away, don't you know."

He tipped his head. With the sun breaking out of the clouds behind him, it was difficult to read his expression. "Bad luck is nobody's fault."

I nodded. I had to get out of here before he hugged me and I melted into a puddle of Nut Goodie–flavored jelly. "Ida around?"

"She is. Room 405, if she's not in Abraham's room." He tapped the crossword puzzle absently. "The police have already talked to her. Not sure what sort of shape they left her in."

"Who's Abraham?"

Curtis leveraged a cane to stand. I'd never seen him use one before. He also appeared to be moving slower than usual. I didn't like what that signaled. "You know Abraham," he said, "though not by name. He's the gentleman who's been in a coma for a year or so, sent there by a heart machine that failed him."

I'd heard talk of a man in a coma being transferred to the Sunset months ago, but for obvious reasons he was not someone I'd visited. "Why would Ida talk to a comatose guy? Did they know each other before he was admitted?"

Curtis grimaced. "No, they did not. Abraham has become popular recently, however, ever since Ida's sister, Freda, organized an Abraham-sitting club. It originated out of the goodness of her heart after a visiting doctor mentioned Abraham might awaken sooner if he was touched and talked to. The man is only in his late fifties, I believe, and the whole situation is a real shame. So Freda started sitting with him, and then Ida joined, and soon the other ladies began taking shifts."

"That's nice of them."

"Well, it's not just the ladies now." He shook his head. "Not since Freda won at bingo last Friday and swore it was due to rubbing Abraham's lucky hand. That's the right one, I understand. Now everyone wants to sit with him. The nurses tell me some are even piling trinkets into his 'lucky hand' in the hopes of increasing their own good fortune."

I envisioned a stack of Mardi Gras beads, incense sticks, and pennies teetering in the poor man's palm. "What? They're erecting altars on a comatose man?"

He shrugged. "There's worse ways to spend time."

I didn't know whether to be offended on Abraham's behalf or stop by and slip a Nut Goodie and my business card into his hand. I could've used the extra luck, no lie. "I better head out. I'm supposed to be working, but I wanted to check in with Ida and make sure she's doing OK."

"Always nice to see you." Curtis let himself onto his bed, more of a fall than a sit. He definitely was feeling his age. "Go easy."

"I won't bother her if she'd rather be alone," I said, mildly offended that he'd think otherwise.

"I meant go easy on yourself."

I left without a goodbye, promising myself that I'd stop by for a longer visit later in the week, after life settled down a bit. Finishing a crossword puzzle with Curtis and dipping into the peanut M&M's stash he hid in the back of his closet was one of my favorite ways to spend a cold evening.

Curtis's prediction that Ida would be in Abraham's room played true. I found her sitting next to him, eyes squeezed shut, gripping Abraham's wrist with one hand and a rosary with the other. She was a stocky woman, as old as Mrs. Berns but not as nimble. Her hair was short and white, her face lined, her age lying heavily on her with her sparkling eyes closed.

I let the door close silently behind me and took stock of the room. It was the same size as Curtis's but seemed much newer. Abraham rested in the bed, still except for the steady, soothing rhythm of his chest rising and falling. He was covered by a blanket and wore a T-shirt. It was comforting, somehow, that they didn't have him in scrubs.

His only visible flesh—hands and arms, head—was pale and slack, his arms skinny as sticks. I wondered what the odds of him coming out of this coma were and found myself wishing that Ida's plan to keep him stimulated and somehow wake him up would work. The only furniture was his bed in the center of the room and a chair and table on the perimeter, both draped with fresh flowers.

The smell of lilies was cloying.

"Ida?" I whispered it, but she jerked as if I'd slapped her. Her face did not relax into its characteristic smile. She ducked her chin and clutched her rosary tighter. "Curtis told me the police were here. How are you doing?"

"The dolls were supposed to make people happy." Her voice was a husk of its normal self. Ida and Freda had historically been the social center of the Senior Sunset, cruise directors on this boat into the afterlife, and they relished their role. I knew Ida as bubbly and easygoing, Freda as a little sharper, but both were equally fun loving. It hurt to see Ida so deflated.

I tried to remember the last time I'd seen her. It'd been weeks, certainly before she'd started making dolls. I'd have remembered that.

I put my hand on her shoulder. "It's not your fault, what happened."

I mostly believed that, but part of me wondered whether one should expect this sort of thing when they created life-size dolls. That crap was demon bait. There was no good reason to mention that to Ida, though.

A sparkle in Abraham's hand, the one nearest Ida, caught my eye. I stepped closer and peered down at the assortment of baubles balanced in his palm. The residents really were leaving him small offerings in hopes of increasing their luck.

"That's what the police said, too." Ida snuffled. "They don't know who the poor woman is. They think sometime last night someone dressed her in the doll clothes I sewed for the Turtle Stew doll. One of the officers discovered my original stuffing in the dumpster behind the café. He had me identify it."

I leaned over and hugged her. She felt soft and bony at the same time. "That must have been hard."

I felt her nod. "Police Chief Wohnt asked me so many questions. I couldn't answer any of them!"

Hoo boy, did I know what that ride felt like. "Do you have someone to be with today, Ida? I don't want to leave you alone."

"I'm not alone. I am here with Abraham." She pulled away and patted his arm, her smile beatific. "Two of the ladies gave me their shifts today so I could pray with him. Isn't that kind?"

Kind of weird, but who was I to judge? I worshipped at the feet of Queen Nut Goodie. "I'll be at the library all day today. Call over if you need anything, OK?"

"I will." She reached into the old-lady Kleenex pocket—her sleeve— and drew out a tissue. She was blowing her nose as I left. For a moment I thought I saw her eyes flash at me as the door wheezed shut, the most peculiar canny expression in them, but I dismissed the thought.

Chapter 10

I suspected Ida returned to her rosary after I was out of sight. For a moment, I envied her faith. How nice to be able to find internal strength at the low times rather than seeking sugar, liquor, or men, like I usually did. I smiled, imagining a combination of the three, specifically some sort of Nut Goodie shot that I could enjoy with Johnny. I was so focused on the delicious possibilities—add whipped cream (to Johnny, of course)?—that I smacked into an orderly as I rounded a corner.

"So sorry!"

He grabbed my shoulders to balance me, gripping them a little too long. "My fault," he said. "I'm new here." He smiled the slippery grin of the lech. I stepped back and out of his meat hooks.

His name tag read DONALD. *Of course.* Christie's husband. He looked like a perfect match for her, too. The tall, middle-aged man somehow managed to make the navy-blue volunteer scrubs look expensive. It might have been the thick gold rings he wore, or the constricted, puffy lips and aquiline nose that suggested he was one generation shy of collapsing the genetic line through inbreeding.

I held out my hand. "My name's Dolores." I didn't have a good reason for the lie, which made it a waste of a perfectly good superpower.

He tapped his name tag, the slimy grin still on his face. "Donald."

"You're new here?"

He took my question for a come-on. "Who wants to know?" He waggled his eyebrows. I knew in that moment that he was the kind of guy who assumed every waitress wanted to bone him.

"Dolores," I repeated, playing dumb to match his gross. "Didn't I already tell you my name?"

A shadow crossed his eyes. He knew I was playing with him. "I have to get back to work."

I watched him walk away. It took to the count of three until he turned around, either to make sure I'd left or to watch me from behind. He glared when he caught me doing the same. I won the stare down. Putz. Now I just had to hope he didn't visit Christie while she was volunteering at the library.

I zipped my jacket as I stepped outside. The cold felt cleansing after Donald's sticky eyes. I'd met many a Donald in my life; most women had. He's the guy who feels owed your attention, and who calls you names when he doesn't get it. I'd do my best to avoid him until he and Christie had completed their service to Battle Lake, and then I'd forget I ever met him.

I breathed deep. So much hope and potential were contained in the rich, loamy smells of thawing earth. I knew it was a false sun shining down, not nearly warm enough to melt all the ice, but I decided I'd start my seedlings that night anyway. I'd refashioned one of Sunny's dilapidated outbuildings into a makeshift greenhouse, stapling heavy-duty plastic over the gaping holes in the roof and south wall. My thermometer let me know that my hard work kept the shed's temperature a good ten degrees above freezing at night and as warm as eighty-two degrees during the day.

I'd dug up a barrelful of black dirt last summer. It rested in the greenhouse's corner. Last week, Johnny had brought me a hundred peat pots and planting trays, extras from the nursery he worked at over the summers. As a final bounty, my seed packets had arrived yesterday, perfect rectangles of promise. Tomatoes, bell peppers, burpless cucumbers, watermelons, radish, beets, lettuce, spinach, thyme, oregano, basil, parsley, cilantro, sage, zucchini, and eggplant. I'd also ordered five pounds of seed potatoes and a bag of onion sets, but those wouldn't come until the ground was thawed.

The world could throw dead bodies at me, but I would seek out life. I would make things grow. I would nurture health, and green, and tender seedlings. I'd pour love and attention on them.

Imagining tender sprouts lightened my step. Not a lot—it was still icy—but some. I tromped along, visions of sinking my fingers in good black dirt making me smile. I would grow huge and healthy vegetables this year, kohlrabi and watermelons so big that they'd look right at home on the set of *Land of the Lost*, one of my favorite shows growing up.

It was good I kept my feet close to the glacial ground as I dreamed big dreams. It gave me a better foundation when Little D jumped out from behind a building.

"I need to talk to you," he whispered, his young face tight and pale. "You're the only one I trust."

Chapter 11

If his revelation was true, it revealed profoundly bad judgment. Plus, I didn't like that he'd scared me. My heartbeat was still fluttering. "Shouldn't you be in school?"

"Shouldn't you be at work?"

Hm. "Let's walk and talk."

He fell into step beside me. He was much nimbler than I was on the sidewalk. Up close, it was clear that other than his hair, Little D looked nothing like Jed. Yet there was something fundamental about him that brought to mind my dear friend. Some small energy, or maybe a smell or the way he carried himself. A too-familiar ache settled into my chest.

"I know who you are," he said.

Such an interesting statement, that. It becomes even more fascinating if you let the person fill in the blanks after. My pulse had quieted, and I'd regained my confidence. I would take charge of this conversation.

So I said nothing.

He didn't either for the longest time, but he finally cracked. "You're a detective. Right?"

I shrugged, an honest answer rather than a tactic. Last November, I'd decided to pursue my private investigator license. I'd enrolled in a class that taught all the basics and signed up for a database that provided an amazing amount of information for a flat monthly fee. The hitch was my discovery that Minnesota required *six thousand hours* of supervised investigative work before issuing a PI license. I was pecking away at that number through my odd-job work for a local attorney, but it was slow going.

So. I wasn't a detective, but I'd been paid to do detective work.

We stood at a crosswalk, waiting for traffic to stop. "I could help you," he said. "Spy on people, I mean."

I gave him side-eye. "What makes you think I want to spy on people?"

"Doesn't everyone?"

Damn, I liked the kid. No way was I letting him know it, though. "Spying on people is illegal."

He puffed himself, taking up more space as he walked. "I followed you to the nursing home, and you didn't even notice. I work there sometimes, you know. I sneak in liquor or cigarettes, or other stuff they're not supposed to have. I could do the same for you."

I spread my hands, indicating the open street we were walking across, and almost slipped for the second time that day. "Look around. I'm free. I don't need someone to smuggle me anything."

"Not that," he said. "I could help you gather dirt on people, and you could pay me."

We were now safely across the street. "I'll pass." I was already babysitting Mrs. Berns on the job. I didn't need another mouth to close.

A Battle Lake police car appeared up the street, pulling into the cop shop. Probably one of the deputies from this morning's horror show at the Stew. Little D noticed the same thing. His face drained of color.

"Gotta run!" He took off into an alley, agile as a mountain goat. "Think about my offer."

I shook my head. What was this world coming to, with people stuffing corpses into doll suits and kids skipping school to run contraband? *Blah.* I wanted nothing to do with any of that. I'd sure like to know if Gary knew whose body had ended up at the Stew, though. I turned around within steps of the library—Mrs. Berns was fine on her own for a little bit longer (denial could be a powerful pair of sunglasses)—and penguin-scuttled toward the police station.

I hoped with all my might that I wouldn't find Gary Wohnt inside. It was much more likely one of his deputies would be personning the place, somebody more forthcoming with information. My luck deserved a turn, right?

Wrong.

My stomach deflated as I entered to find Gary filing papers.

The Battle Lake police station foyer was an open space with a '70s feel, housing three desks, beige locked file cabinets along the back, and stiff wooden chairs if you had the lousy luck of waiting for something or someone. Off to the left was a hall that led to a fistful of jail cells, old-fashioned ones with bars and everything. A bathroom and storage room were off to the right. Gary swiveled around upon my entrance and regarded me with venomous eyes.

At least I think he did. He hadn't taken off his mirrored sunglasses yet.

"I'm here as a journalist."

His lip twitched. "Does Ron know?"

"Know" was such a slippery word. How could we be sure what anyone truly *knows*? "He has me on a special assignment with a focus on Otter Tail County."

That was 100 percent true. It had zero application to this situation, but that affected its truthiness not at all. I soldiered on. "I want to know if you've identified the body in the Stew or have a cause of death." Also 100 percent true. The best lies always were.

He locked the file cabinet with a key that snapped back to his waist when he was done. I idly wondered where I could get one of those leashes for Mrs. Berns. She was forever losing the library keys.

Gary removed his sunglasses and set them on the cabinet before striding over to his desk. He slid behind it and clicked on his computer. My heart leaped. He was looking up stuff for me! This was a first. I tamped down my triumphant smile. My relationship with Gary had achieved a new level. No reason to gloat.

It took all of four minutes for me to realize he was actually ignoring me.

Ninja-level ignoring.

I scowled and stepped toward his desk, smacking my hands on it and leaning forward. I was close enough to smell his cologne, something light and pleasantly masculine. Definitely not his signature Old Spice. "As a member of the press, I am entitled to any information you have as long as it is not protected."

"Not true." *Click. Click clack click.*

Really? I'd seen that work on a TV show once. I stood up straight. "Then, as a witness, out of the kindness of your heart, at least let me know how that woman died."

Clack click clack.

An acidic flame began to flicker in my stomach. Gary was being rude. And I'd had a helluva day. If he wasn't going to spill all the details, I could understand that, but he at least owed me her cause of death. He knew I hadn't had anything to do with it. Didn't he? "Look, I deserve to know." I crossed my arms and set my chin. "If you're not going to tell me, I will have to find it out through other channels. That means—"

He was up and out of his seat before I could finish my empty threat. His speed took my breath away. He grabbed my upper arms with a force just west of pain and leaned in close, his physical presence overwhelming. "The body is at the ME's in Fergus Falls. We do not have a positive ID or a COD. Don't get involved. If you do, I will arrest you."

My breath still hadn't returned. When Gary had lost all that weight, it revealed a chiseled form underneath, all sinew and muscle. I could feel his strength as a solid, hot force. Gary and I had butted heads more times than I could count, but he'd also shown me compassion in the past. This new energy, borderline erotic, was discombobulating. I opened my mouth and squeaked.

His face was inches from mine. I could smell the coffee on his breath, his new cologne. He glanced at my mouth, made a frustrated noise, and returned to his chair and computer. He was done with me.

I backed out of the police station.

I would need to take the rest of the day off.

Chapter 12

Self-medication was an art with three components.

The first was reliability. The second was convenience. The third, and most important, was duration. I was a master of all three requirements.

First, reliability.

I stood in my greenhouse, so pleasantly warm that I'd stripped down to a black tank top and my faded Levi's, the ones that hugged my curves (butt and gut) and felt as soft as a blanket. I hadn't bothered with a bra or underwear, and I'd left my shoes and socks inside the door so I could walk barefoot, admiring my blue toenails. My hands were shoved deep inside the black dirt I'd collected last summer, kneading out clumps and releasing the pregnant scent of living earth. The soothing that came with squeezing dirt was as reliable as anything I'd ever experienced.

Next came convenience, the most undervalued of the three spokes of self-medication.

On a shelf at head level, I'd laid out three Nut Goodies cut into bite-size pieces, angled so that I could scoop them up with my tongue. Next to my candy buffet, I'd placed a glass of red wine with a straw in it. My garden boom box played my favorite Nina Simone CD, filling the shed with lush, velvety jazz that would loop on itself until I chose another CD.

Food, drink, and music, all within reach of the dirt. Voilà, accessibility.

Finally, duration.

At two o'clock in the afternoon, the greenhouse was lit like a sunroom, but if I took my time, which I fully intended to do, I could be here past sunset. Because I'd be working into the dark, I'd placed candles and a box of matches on shelves around the room. I'd light them as the sun began to set and garden by candlelight.

If I were a cat, I'd be purring.

But then a scratch at the window startled me, draining the peace I'd worked so hard to cultivate. I withdrew my hands from the barrel of dirt, my pulse a sick thud at my wrists. Was the Peeping Tom visiting me in bright daylight? I stepped closer to the window. It was dirty, revealing only the shadows of the trees lining the back of the shed, hiding it from the road.

There was only one thing to do: open the door and see who was out there. It wasn't courage; it was efficiency. I could stay inside the shed, scared and wondering for the rest of the day, or I could stuff all the terror into a two-minute period. Except in the cases of clowns and evangelists, I always recommend the latter.

I slipped my feet into my shoes and stepped outside. The difference in temperature between the greenhouse and the outdoors was shocking. The pleasant dusting of wet heat froze on my arms, and my nipples immediately reported for duty.

"Hello?"

Dirty white snow, my outbuildings, my car, my house. That's all there was to see. I made my way to the rear of the shed. The snow was lighter and icier here on the wooded side. The only tracks in evidence were deer prints from before the last thaw. I forced my shoulders to relax down out of my ears. No Peeping Tom. No crazed, doll-stuffing murderer. I must have heard a branch scratching the window. Silly nerves.

I scoured the forest one last time for good measure and returned to the front of the shed.

I left my shoes outside the door and stepped into the greenhouse, the warmth embracing me again like a lover. My smile and calm returned almost immediately. If dealing with a corpse a month taught you anything, it was to celebrate peace where you find it. Once my skin temperature matched the sultry air, I leaned over and looped a Nut Goodie chunk into my mouth, washing it down with a slurp of red wine.

I plunged my hands into the barrel of dirt all over again, kneading it, feeling the warm soil caress my skin. Before the scratch on the window, I'd worked through the top two-thirds of dirt, crushing clumps between my fingers, breaking them up and stirring them so it'd be easy to scoop into the tiny seed pots. As I bent over the barrel as far as I could go now, I realized I'd need an implement to reach the bottom third.

I surveyed the shed. I stored all my garden tools here, but a rake or a hoe would be too awkward and long. I needed something with a short handle that I could spear through the dirt. My eyes landed on my grandma's rusty garden shears. Gardening ran in my family. My grandma passed her love of it to my mom, who passed it to me. The shears no longer functioned for their original purpose, but I'd hung on to them after my grandma died as a reminder of the good stuff.

I reached for them, soil sifting off me and onto the floor. Gripping the handles in both hands, I cleaved the soil, pushing down, down, down until the tip of the shears came in contact with the barrel's floor. With a movement like churning butter, I began to stir, finding an almost meditative rhythm, verging on sexual for the pleasure and focus it brought me. The combination of a sugar high and wine and the stirring trance worked its magic, and my shoulders loosened completely for the first time in months.

I would plant my seeds. I would care for them.

I would do my job for the library and the newspaper. I would love Johnny.

I would *not* discover any more corpses.

I think my next pledge would have been to appreciate my friends, or check in on my mom, or maybe even to eat fewer Nut Goodies. I'll never know, though, because the hands that suddenly grabbed my hips bludgeoned the good thoughts right out of my head.

Chapter 13

"Aigghhh!" I yanked my hands out of the barrel and spun, peeing my pants a little. That would have been the least of my worries if the hands on my hips hadn't been Johnny's. As it was, the pants peeing hurtled to the top of the list.

The last I'd seen him was two nights ago, when we'd rented a movie and popped some corn, cuddling on the couch. I'm pretty sure both of us had assumed our next interaction would be urine-free.

"I'm sorry, Mira! I thought you heard me." He stood back, hands up, probably afraid of the wild-eyed harridan wielding a pair of rusty shears. Maybe he even, for the first time in our relationship, wondered if I actually was a murderer. I wouldn't have blamed him.

I set the shears on a nearby bench and put my hand over my heart, trying to steady the pounding. "How long were you standing behind me?" Now that I knew he wasn't a killer, I needed to know how much of my hip-grinding soil churning he'd witnessed.

He dropped his hands, and a slow, sexy smile crawled up his face. "One minute, two tops. I knocked, and then when I came in, I said your name. I thought by the way you"—he pointed at my lower half—"were moving that you knew it was me."

A nuclear blush bomb detonated on each of my cheeks. "Can we both agree that that was what was happening?"

I expected him to laugh. He stared at my mouth instead, gazing with that intent hunger that worked like kindling at my neck, heart, and sweet spot. My heart ramped back up for a very different reason. Damn, the man was good-looking. His dirty-blond hair was thick and curling, longish in a way that had stopped being popular in the '70s but that he managed to make J.Crew handsome. His deep-blue eyes were storming, promising heat and release. I could almost taste the cinnamon of his soft, lush lips.

The way he was looking at me, I could tell I soon would.

The pulse at my throat fluttered like butterfly wings. Johnny unzipped the neck of his parka and pulled it over his head. He raised his hands, revealing a sliver of his sculpted stomach, perfect lines pointing toward his lean waist. Underneath the jacket, he wore a soft white T-shirt that hung beautifully from his broad shoulders, giving just the promise of the muscled chest underneath.

I may have groaned a little.

I reached toward him. "My hands are dirty."

He removed his shirt by way of response. "Things are about to get a lot dirtier."

I was OK with that.

Johnny lit the candles after the sun set. I lay nestled in his arms, our clothes a makeshift blanket beneath us. My seeds hadn't gotten planted, but I sure had. My finger played lazily alongside the ridge of his hip bone, down his strong thighs, and back up. His mouth was tangled in my hair.

"Is that what you stopped by for?" I asked him playfully.

He chuckled into my scalp and kissed it. "Actually no, but I'm not complaining. I came over to see if you wanted to go out for dinner. I tried calling, but no answer."

I indicated the shed. "I've been out here since I got home. I probably should get a cell phone one of these days, but I like being able to slip away from the world."

"I know you do." He put his hand under my chin and tipped it up to land a deep, warm kiss on my mouth. The shed was still warm enough, but barely. "You sure you have to check out that swim class tonight?"

I sighed. I wasn't sure, but I'd promised Ron that I'd write the article and Mrs. Berns that she could come with me. My swimsuit and towel were already packed in my car. "When are you heading out for Wisconsin?"

"Early tomorrow. Before sunup. I'm going to miss you."

I loved how good he was at expressing his emotions. Not for the first time, I wished I could meet him there. "We'll have the trip when you get back. Five whole days together. You'll probably get sick of me."

"Not a chance." The playfulness had left. He stared into my eyes, his hand still under my chin. "Mira, I love you. I want to be with you."

I sat up, reaching for my clothes. Of course he knew I loved him, too. "Want to know where I'm taking you for our getaway?"

He stayed put on the ground, appearing uncomfortably vulnerable in his nakedness. "I . . . sure."

His disappointment made me sad. I knew he wanted me to tell him I loved him, too, but I could only be me. "Me too! It'll be a surprise to both of us." I smiled, but he wouldn't mirror it. I babbled to cover my discomfort. "I promise it'll be amazing, though. You might even need a passport."

I stood, shaking soil off the clothes I'd been lying on. I was going to be a fine sight in the pool. They'd probably have to change the water after I got out. I bent over to tug on my Levi's.

"You're beautiful." He was still so serious.

The tears pushing at my eyes surprised me. I leaned down and gave him a peck on his lips. "You are, too."

I zipped my pants and slipped on my tank top and was out the door.

Chapter 14

"You smell like a brothel left out in the sun," Mrs. Berns informed me matter-of-factly on the drive. "Forget showering before you get in the pool. You should do one of those prison hose-downs. Otherwise everyone is going to wonder who's packing the tuna sandwich."

I steered the car into Fergus Falls, responding the only way I could. "Thank you."

"You're welcome. It was Johnny, right?"

Her question caught me off-guard, so much so that my reply came out sharp. "Who else would I sleep with?"

Mrs. Berns punched my arm. "Don't get smart with me! I'm not the one who plays hot and cold with that boy. I don't know why you make it so hard. He loves you, you love him."

"We're exclusive!" I clutched the steering wheel as if to communicate my indignation. "And he knows that I love him."

"Whatever. This isn't high school. And the YMCA is up here."

"I know where it is." More or less.

The lot was surprisingly full. We parked, checked in at the front, and made our way to the locker room. I was heading to the showers, still stinging from Mrs. Berns's spot-on criticism, when I saw her pull out a string bikini.

"What do you think?" she asked.

I gaped at the yellow wisps of cloth. "I think that floss will get stuck in your teeth."

Her grin widened. "I can't wait for the kids to see me in this. About time this culture was introduced to a real woman's body." She hooted and slapped her knee. "It's going to make everyone squirm!"

I shook my head in admiration. Mrs. Berns had reached the Promised Land, the tipping point in life where wearing an ill-fitting swimsuit becomes more uncomfortable for the witnesses than for the wearer. Me, I was still sheepling, dreaming of a day where my boobs stuck out farther than my belly.

She dropped the bikini on the bench so she could remove her elastic-waisted pants. "Hey, can we stop at the smelt fry in Underwood on our way home? We're gonna work up an appetite swimming."

"Sounds like a plan to me." I snatched my own swimsuit and made my way to the shower.

In case you didn't know, smelt were a tiny fish fried up whole, which was how the meal acquired its two popular nicknames: "fries with eyes" and "calzones with bones." For $7.99, the local Elks club would sell you a plateful with a side of fries, a buttered white dinner roll, and pickle slices for garnish. I was salivating just thinking about it. I'd never eaten smelt before moving to Battle Lake. Now I couldn't get enough of the Friday night fish fry.

The shower water took longer to run clean than I would have liked. When I returned to the locker room, having changed in private, I found Mrs. Berns putting her best boob forward, wearing nothing but her string of a bottom. She grinned at me. "Figured you'd want to see old-lady jugs so you knew what you had to look forward to." She did a little helicopter dance with them.

"You're a real pal." I held up my towel so I could see only her face. Her boobs looked just fine, all swoops and folds and curves. I wasn't comfortable with anyone's nudity, though. "You ready to go swim?"

"Yup!" She tied on her top, which was sized more like a pasty than a bra.

Fergus Falls public pool, here we come.

We followed the signs and the tart reek of chlorine until we reached the enormous room housing the Olympic-size pool. The front desk person had informed us that the northwest end of the water would be cordoned off for the aerobics class. Neither Mrs. Berns nor I knew which direction was northwest, but we agreed that it was likely the shallow end, the one packed with kids wearing water wings in one corner and mostly middle-aged women in the other. The entire opposite end was arranged in lanes clotted with swimmers, their arms a front-crawl blur. The noise was a cacophonous echo of squeals and splashes.

Mrs. Berns earned a lot of stares as she strutted toward the shallow end. I shouldn't have been surprised at how many of them were admiring. If you were an alien landing in the US, you'd think that skinny, young, and big of boob was the only acceptable body type. Mrs. Berns was none of those, yet she was healthy, and she was confident, and she was herself. Hanging around her made you want to be yourself, too, and it turned out lots of people wanted more of that in their life.

When she reached the far side of the pool, Mrs. Berns crouched down to address the only person in the shallow end wearing a swim cap and a plastic whistle around her neck. "Is this swim aerobics?"

"It is." The woman smiled and indicated her class of a dozen women, all of them wet as seals and staring open-mouthed at Mrs. Berns's bikini. "You must be the *Battle Lake Recall* reporter and guest. We were just talking about the excitement you all had up your way today."

I bristled. Surely she couldn't know about the doll corpse in the Turtle Stew. News traveled fast in small towns, but Fergus Falls was twenty miles from Battle Lake. Had something else happened that we hadn't heard about?

"Pam over there works in the hospital." The instructor tipped her head at a particularly sour-faced woman in the group. "She said the coroner identified the body inside the doll that was found at that café."

Chapter 15

Goose pimples dotted my arms despite the room's steamy heat. "Who was it?"

The women in the pool exchanged glances, possessive of their secret now that there were outsiders on the scene.

"Mira here found the body," Mrs. Berns interjected. "She has a right to know."

Pam's hand flew to her mouth. "You're Mira James? The librarian who finds all the corpses?" She drew closer to her wet compatriots.

My stomach flopped. This was not a reputation I wanted to precede me.

"I'll give you all one more chance to tell us," Mrs. Berns said, hands on hips. "Or I'll jump into your human stewpot and pee like it's my job."

Pam, the sour-faced and apparently loose-lipped hospital employee, scowled. "You don't need to be mean. It's just not professional to share private information. HIPAA, and all that."

The swim instructor rolled her eyes. "You already told every one of us here. I don't know why you're giving them such a hard time. You said the woman's name is Rita Theisen, and that you thought she was a part-time nurse at the Senior Sunset."

I sucked in my breath. Ida, and the canny look I thought I'd imagined, had just taken on a new significance. But there was no way Ida was involved in a murder, right? My intestines slid greasily. "Mrs. Berns, we have to go."

"I'm one step ahead of you."

I waved at the instructor. "Sorry! I'll be sure to write good things about your class."

We kept silent until we reached the locker room, and then until we were inside my car for good measure. "This doesn't look good for Ida," I said once I'd started the car.

"Or Eeyore."

"Eeyore?"

"You know. Doris. The woman who owns the Turtle Stew?"

How had we shared a nickname for her and never known? "What does Doris have to do with this?"

Mrs. Berns clicked her buckle into place. She'd insisted on wearing her bikini top under her unzipped parka, no bra, no shirt. The yellow scrap of fabric glowed. "She's Rita's sister. They own the Stew together. Rita is a silent partner. I'd heard they were going through some real tough financial times. Her sister murdered in the Stew? If she loses business because of it, it might cost her the restaurant."

"But Doris was there when the doll fell off the stool! She never said anything about it being her sister."

Mrs. Berns shrugged. "You said the corpse wore a lot of makeup under the mask. Rita never wore makeup when she was alive. Plus, she was wearing clothes Ida had sewn for a doll. You and I've both seen enough dead bodies to know that the same person alive looks a lot different dead, especially if you don't know who you're peering at and you don't get a close look." Mrs. Berns shook her head and glanced out her window at the early-spring moonscape. "Poor Doris. Her sister was dead in their restaurant and she didn't even know."

I drove in silence, sadness giving way to frustration, which led to a seething anger unlike anything I'd experienced before. I believed both Ida and Doris to be good people. One of them was about to be short-listed for murder, and the other was surely heartbroken at the loss of

Rita. Maybe both, if Ida had known Rita at the Sunset. We wouldn't be in this position if I hadn't moved to Battle Lake. I knew that as well as I knew my own name.

I joked and I deflected, but come *on*.

If every room you walked into smelled, it was only so long until you realized it was you bringing the stink. I was attracting murder to Battle Lake. Over and over again. My dad's death had been only a warm-up. Since then, karma or fate or my energy had distilled into a deadly concentration. I was the silent killer, a walking version of high blood pressure, slaying anyone who wandered too close.

A vision of Johnny—sweet, sexy, tender Johnny—gripped my heart and twisted it. I couldn't bear to lose him, to be somehow responsible for anything bad happening. I was gripped with a sudden brutal clarity. I knew what I must do. "Mrs. Berns, I need to drop you off at home."

"Duh."

"Quick-like, though. Instead of going out for smelt."

She turned away from the window to study my face. Her voice was sharp. "You look like you're going to do something stupid."

I quieted the fearful burble in my heart. If I overthought this, I'd lose my courage. I loved Johnny too much to chicken out. "It'll be the smartest thing I ever did. I should have done it a while ago."

I screeched in front of her apartment and pushed her out before making my way to Johnny's. The pain was too deep to feel anything. Numb, I let myself in with my key and raced to his bedroom, where he was reading in bed.

"Johnny!"

He dropped his book and jumped up, the blankets falling off his warm, beautiful body. His face was the picture of concern.

How I wished I'd been dealt a different hand, one that would've let me crawl back into bed with him right now, like a normal person, and sleep cradled in his arms until he had to leave before sunrise, kissing me gently on his way out so he didn't wake me and I could sleep in.

But that wasn't in my cards.

I needed to end things with the love of my life. It was the only way to protect him.

"I realized I don't love you." My voice sounded desperate, even to my own ears. Was I crying? Bleeding? Falling to pieces? "I want to break up. Now. Forever."

He wore only boxers slung low on his hips, and ran his hands through his hair. His face broke at the edges. He reached for me, then pulled back. I wanted to beg him to hold me, convince us both that I didn't mean it, that we could figure out together how to keep him safe, but that wasn't how it would work for us.

Chapter 16

"Get off me!"

The huge, meat-heavy doll was crushing me.

No, I was drowning in a suffocating *sea* of dolls, their plastic skin chafing mine, their leathery, gloved hands crawling toward my throat, their wiry hair stuffing my mouth and cramming my throat. I pushed, and the heaviest doll yelped but did not budge. I screamed, and she whined. There was a crash, glass breaking. I realized my eyes were closed.

I ripped them open.

I was splayed in my bed. Luna, Sunny's sweetheart of a German shepherd, was curled next to me, her hackles up, avoiding eye contact. I'd been pushing at her, but she hadn't left my side. Tiger Pop watched warily from a shelf. The crash had been the empty wine bottle I'd fallen asleep next to colliding with the floor.

When Luna saw I was awake, she began to furiously lick my face, whining. I clutched her fur, holding her. "I'm sorry, baby. I'm so sorry. I was having a nightmare."

The previous evening returned in bloodred patches.

I'd dumped Johnny because it was the only way to save his life.

I wasn't having a nightmare; I was living one.

Panic clawed the edges of my consciousness with its untrimmed, yellowed fingernails. I leaped out of bed to stay ahead of it. I swept up the broken glass, dished out food for Luna and Tiger Pop, rinsed their water bowls, and refilled them with fresh water. Luna kept close to my heels, ignoring her food. I watched her through the Plexiglas shower door as I washed my hair, told her everything would be OK, but both of us knew it wouldn't be.

Johnny and I were through.

I'd broken his heart and mine rather than risk having him go the way of my dad, Jeff, Jed, Rita Theisen, and the ten other bodies that'd shown up since I'd moved to Battle Lake.

Suddenly, I found it difficult to draw a breath. I gasped shallowly, reaching out to the shower bar. What had I done? How could I have broken up with Johnny, then downed a bottle of wine so I could pass out? Was I insane? He was everything I wanted in a partner: kind, smart, sexy, loved to garden, knew my past and still wanted to be with me. The panic crawled up my throat to choke me from the inside. I turned off the water.

I couldn't live like this. I had to fix it.

I needed to apologize to Johnny, tell him that my fear for his life had driven me to be such a fool, beg him to take me back. He would, right? The second-to-last thing he'd said to me was that he'd love me forever. He believed in second chances, and third, and fiftieth, right?

"I will make this right." Voicing this out loud kept the panic at bay.

For the first time since I'd woken up, Luna's tail wagged, tentatively.

"You heard it, Luna!" Her tail thumped against the floor. "I will fix this."

Old me ran from commitment, from the hard work of a relationship, from Minneapolis, from Paynesville. New me would stay and fight. New me was a grown-up who accepted responsibility for what was hers and let others do the same. I would get dressed and go see Johnny right now. I had almost convinced myself I could turn back time when a realization stopped me in my tracks, turning my stomach cold: Johnny was halfway to Wisconsin by now.

That was all right, I told myself, a giggling fit bubbling at the edges of my awareness. Probably better, in fact. The time apart would make us both realize how much we loved each other and let the memory of last night's asshattery fade. I'd make the plans for our getaway and sweep him off his feet as soon as he returned. I'd make it all up to him, but away from Battle Lake, safe.

That was it. I had a plan.

It had the familiar feel of a brittle surface fix, the throbbing of reality pushing against it, threatening to rip apart my weak rationalizations. Like a modern-day, small-town, Midwestern Scarlett O'Hara, however, I would not let reality ruin my hope. Johnny and I would cool off. He would return. I would apologize. Everything would be OK.

OK?

I nodded at myself.

Luna whined.

I scratched her behind the ears. I needed to get out of the house before I drove all three of us bananas. I toweled off, tied my wet hair into a bun, tugged on my clothes, grabbed my keys, and made for the door. The air was crisp, the sharp morning sun hurting my eyes. I crunched across the frozen lawn to reach my car. Ribbons of frost drifted off the windshield as I scraped it, my nostrils filling with the smells of cold and white. My wet bun hardened in the brisk air. I let my car warm up for a few minutes before I took off, trying not to look at the gardening shed as I waited. It reminded me of how efficiently I'd ruined everything.

Because the temperature was colder than it had been in a week, the roads were less slippery than I'd grown accustomed to. Committed ice is a much more predictable surface than melting ice. Probably there was some life lesson there, but I wasn't in the mood to philosophize. Today would be about action. Ooh, I liked that. Action. Movement. I knew what hotel Johnny was staying at. I would have flowers sent there to let him know I wanted to talk, and that we were still on for our trip when he got back.

Once I sent some positive energy that direction, I'd check in on Ida and then Doris before opening up the library. I'd visit the mountain-climbing club over lunch. I'd also write my Battle Lake Bites column for the *Recall* and submit it ahead of schedule. Tonight, Mrs. Berns and I would attend the Battle Lake Card Club so I'd have more research for the series Ron wanted.

My shoulders relaxed as I took the first deep breath of the day. Everything would be perfect and orderly and tucked in.

My step was lighter as I entered the Senior Sunset, where I was told Ida was likely in Abraham's room. I wondered if she'd taken more shifts from the other ladies today. When I knocked quietly on his door, though, no one answered. I peeked inside. The room was empty.

Except for Abraham, of course.

I felt momentarily bad for lumping him in with the furniture. I slipped inside to make amends. I couldn't risk any worse luck, and I'd sure as shooting welcome some good fortune. I covered my nose to filter the cloy of lilies. I wasn't sure how to pitch my voice, so I settled on a hair above a whisper.

"Hi, Abraham. I heard that it's good for your brain waves to be talked to and touched. I don't know you well enough to do the second one, but if it's OK with you, I can do a little bit of the first. Not for very long, mind you. I have to find Ida, and then stop by the Turtle Stew and see Doris." I cleared my throat. "Not sure if you've heard, but Ida makes life-size dolls, and some sicko hid Doris's sister's body inside one of the dolls and set it up in the Turtle Stew, the restaurant Doris and her sister co-owned. Tragic, huh?"

You'd think it would feel weird to talk to a comatose stranger, and I'm not gonna lie, it started out that way. Suddenly, though, against all logic, I found myself wanting to share *everything* with him. "Do you know where the Stew is? It's right downtown. Not sure where you were from before you were transferred here. You must be single, though. Curtis said you don't have any family. You're probably lucky."

I dropped myself into the chair nearest Abraham's bed. "Family is nothing but trouble. At least mine has been. Take my dad, a career alcoholic. He didn't heal himself, so I grew up feeling like I needed to take care of two people—him and me. That drew other men to me, dickish moths who sensed something wasn't quite right and were attracted to my light. And I just shone brighter. Not in a good way. Not in a 'phoenix rising from the ashes' way, or a 'shine bright like a diamond' way, or even a 'this little light of mine' way. Nope. It was in a beacony, 'I'm really good at fixing people so limp on over, mole-eyed losers' sort of way. And that turned out about as well as you'd expect, every time."

I patted his hand, ready to apologize for my intensity, and a shiny bauble fell out of it and clunked to the floor. "Sorry for upsetting your altar! Looks like someone left you a pretty brooch." I dropped to my hands and knees to locate the piece I'd seen drop. I found it in a shadowy corner under his bed and returned it to his palm, a rhinestone pendant the size of a quarter and inset with a gold *M*. I picked up my monologue where I'd left off.

"Here's what really surprises me about how I used to date, Abraham: how long I kept doing it. Kept shining that fixing light, all the while surprised when it attracted what it was designed to attract. Moving to Battle Lake extinguished that toxic beacon. And you know what? Once that dimmed, I could see clearly what a good guy looks like." I crossed my arms and sighed, my voice dropping. "It looks like Johnny Leeson, except that I dumped him. Last night. Because I was afraid he would get murdered if he stuck around me. You maybe haven't heard about me, but—"

A movement outside Abraham's window snagged my eye.

I leaped to my feet and rushed to the glass in time to catch a flash of fatigues and curls.

It was Little D, spying on me.

Chapter 17

My blood pressure surged.

"Sorry, Abraham! Gotta run. Thanks for the support, though."

I scurried toward the door and let myself out the back of the Senior Sunset. By the time I reached the rear courtyard abutting Abraham's window, Little D was nowhere to be seen. Had he followed me all the way to the Sunset, or was it just coincidental that he'd peeked into Abraham's window when I was in there? I did not like the thought of anyone following me, not one bit.

I zipped up my winter jacket, tucking my hands into my armpits for warmth. It was chilly outside, particularly with the building blocking the thin sunshine and my hair still damp. I turned to go back inside, but the door had locked behind me. Of course. That kid was going to pay. I was in the process of jogging around the front when a sniffling caught my attention. It was coming from the bushes lining the side of the Sunset.

Aha! Little D, get ready to suffer for making me follow you outdoors. I pounced, stopping just short of full-on grabbing the person behind the scrabbly bushes.

It was Ida Gilbertson of all people, cradling a bag of lemon drops. From the pooch of her cheeks, it appeared as though she'd already mainlined a bunch.

I glanced around the shadows, still convinced Little D must be hiding nearby. "Ida, what are you doing outside? It's freezing."

She pointed at the bag. "I'm not allowed to have sugar. It interferes with my medication." Except, with her mouth so full of lemon drops, it came out more like this: *foo foo foofoofoofoogar, feeferfeefer feffication.*

I held out my hand, my lips pursed. "Then you probably shouldn't have them."

She let me help her up before handing me the bag of lemon drops, which I shoved into my parka, raising my eyebrows at her cheeks. She sighed and spit them out into the dirty snow like yellow machine gun bullets. "The sugar makes me feel better."

I impulsively wrapped her in a hug. "I know what you mean."

We stood like that, embracing in the bushes, both shivering in the spring cold, until I let up. "You heard who the body was?"

She nodded and we started crunching our way toward the front door. "I didn't know Rita very well. She was only part-time, a rehabilitation nurse. I don't know that I ever saw her over in the assisted living wing." Ida stopped and stared at her feet. "It's sad she's dead, of course, but that's not why I was sneaking the candy."

I let the silence play out.

"It's Helen," she said. "Helen Ripley? She's two doors down from me. She's spreading rumors."

"What kind?"

"Pure awful nonsense. She's telling people that I know who killed Ruth, and that I shouldn't be allowed to schedule Abraham time because I am as good as a criminal. What if I don't get to see him anymore?"

Damn. High school never ended, did it? "Have you tried talking to Helen?"

"Talk to her? I want to do way worse." Ida balled her hands into fists. "I want to inflict bad credit on her. I want to steal one of each pair of her socks. I want to move her recliner so it takes all day to get it just right again."

That was some fierce old-lady cursing for sure. I led Ida gently around to the front of the building, holding open the Sunset's main door for her. "She probably deserves all of that, but I think you should just talk to her, first. It's best to try and figure stuff out rather than go straight to worst-case scenario."

Look at me, dispensing advice I'd never followed in my life. As an immediate karma check, the back of my neck prickled. I smelled the perfume—yeasty gardenias—before I laid eyes on the face.

"Just the ladies I wanted to see!"

Kennie Rogers stood in the Sunset's gray lobby. Neither Ida nor I broke stride. "Now slow down, you hear." Kennie landed a claw on each of our shoulders. We had no choice but to stop and face her. In what I assumed was a new Modern Cowgirl ensemble, she wore winter boots outfitted with silver spurs, snow pants tailored to look like assless chaps, and a fringed suede jacket, all topped off with a ski cap with a cowboy-hat brim (envision a deflating ten-gallon perched on her head).

"Cheesus." I whistled.

"I know, right?" She lifted a heel and spun one of her spurs. "These here come off and can be used to cut either material if you're quilting or throats if you're defending yourself."

Modern Cowgirl, indeed.

Kennie turned to Ida. "Honey, I stopped by because I want you to make a doll that looks just like me."

Ida grew pale. "I'm not making any more of those."

asKennie wheedled, "I want to feature it in my bedroom."

I almost asked her what for before I caught myself. That's one of those questions you simply do not ask, right up there with "Why are there underwear in the bathroom garbage?"

"Ida's been a little traumatized these past two days, Kennie," I said. "I don't think she wants to make any more dolls right now."

"Well, think about it." Kennie handed Ida a paper grocery bag stuffed to bursting with feathers and glittery cloth. "I'll provide the wardrobe and pay you a hundred dollars."

I could see Ida calculating how many lemon drops that would buy. I wanted no part of this. "I have to run."

Kennie grabbed my elbow. "Not so fast. We haven't talked about that job proposition yet."

I twisted my arm free and backed away, donning my best fake smile. "Later."

Her eyes narrowed. "Perfect. I'll stop by the library."

That woman could not recognize a blow off, and she'd already cost me enough time. Rather than confirm, I skedaddled to the Turtle Stew, where I was surprised to discover that Doris wasn't at her restaurant for the first time in recorded history.

"Preparing for her sister's funeral tomorrow," the middle-aged waitress told me, not looking up from the table she was washing.

Her name tag informed me I was speaking with Jan. I tested a theory out of curiosity. "Did you know Rita well, Jan?"

She shrugged and looked at me with eyes and hair the color of the water she rinsed her rag in. "She didn't come around much."

That's what I'd thought. A lot of people seemed to know who Rita *was*, but didn't actually *know* her. It struck me as odd that she co-owned one of the most beloved restaurants in town but I'd never met her. "Do you know what time the funeral is?"

I'd make a point of attending. It would give me a chance to flesh out who Rita had been. Plus, as someone who'd attended many funerals, I knew they were held for the living, not the departed, and showing up went a long way.

I glanced at my watch. Without Doris here, that meant I had fifteen extra minutes in my morning, and I was only two blocks from the cop shop. I still wanted to know how Rita had been killed. For all I knew, she might have dressed herself like a doll and taken her own life somehow, though my gut told me that wasn't the case. Anyhow, I wanted to put it to rest once and for all, and I might be able to get someone inside the police station to spill if Gary wasn't around. It was worth a try at least. I could stroll past the station and simply keep walking if I spotted Gary inside.

I made my way outside, skimming the ice all the way to the cop shop. Only one navy-blue police car was parked out front, but I didn't know who usually drove it—they all looked the same. I risked a peek through the front window. The bald deputy with the handlebar mustache was personning the front desk with no Gary in sight. Perfect. I dug a notepad and pen from my inner jacket pocket and sauntered in like I owned the place.

"Hello, Deputy?"

He started from behind the computer. Clearly he'd been looking at something he wasn't supposed to be. Boobies, if I had to guess, which worked in my favor. If he was packing guilt, half my job would be done for me.

"Yes?"

"Mira James with the *Battle Lake Recall*. Ron Sims sent me over to get an update on the body found in the Turtle Stew. We"—note the royal *we*, technically still not lying—"know that Rita Theisen is the name of the deceased, and we have reason to believe she—"

"Was murdered between midnight and two a.m. two nights ago?"

I was going to say, "We have reason to believe she worked at the Senior Sunset," but OK.

Chapter 18

The deputy leaned back and kicked his boots up onto the desk, nearly losing his balance as he braided his hands behind his head in the most stereotypical illustration of nonchalance that I'd ever witnessed. I didn't know what was stopping him from blowing on his nails and shining them on the front of his shirt, and by the way, what was that gesture ever meant to signify besides buffoonery?

"Rita Theisen was murdered?" I asked.

He yanked his boots off the table and dropped them to the ground with a clank. "Wait, you said you already knew that!"

I pretended to scribble on my pad.

"What are you writing?" he asked, his expression pained.

"The information. Don't worry. Police Chief Wohnt and I spoke just yesterday about how, as a member of the press, I'm entitled to any information you have as long as it is not personal." Gary had told me explicitly that I was wrong on that front, but we *had* talked about it.

The deputy slapped the front of the desk as he stood, his mustache quivering. I put him in his late fifties and didn't know much about him except the rumors that he split his work time between Battle Lake and Fergus Falls. I wondered if he was worried his slip would cost him this job. "Well then, be clear that I didn't say she was murdered, just that we know it was the drug that killed her. It could have been suicide, technically. She had that bump on her head, of course, but they think that happened when her body fell off the stool, after she was already dead."

Shee boy. He was a piece of work. "She overdosed?"

"Naw. Well, not like you'd think. It wasn't a narcotic she ingested. It was cancer medication, and she didn't have cancer. Either someone forced her to take it, tricked her into taking it, or she had one very odd habit." He took off his hat and ran his fingers through his hair. I noticed he wore no wedding ring, which was the last piece of the puzzle I needed to peg his type. He wanted to impress me with the information he had. He was the guy who wished he never had to take the uniform off so people knew they were supposed to respect him, the kind who started conversations with "Between you, me, and the wall . . ."

But typing him wasn't why I'd stopped writing. It was the information he'd given me, possibly the weirdest cause of death I'd ever heard. Who would give a woman a non-narcotic? Or, if she'd taken it herself, why?

"You're not writing anymore."

I stuffed the notebook into my pocket. His loose lips were not good for the police department, but they'd been peaches and cream for me. "I think I have everything I need here. Thank you."

"Do you want my name?" He smiled. "So you can quote me."

My answer would have been "sure," if not for Gary walking in, his face the color, shape, and attitude of a boulder hurtling down a cliff toward me.

Chapter 19

I spun back around to the deputy. "When does winter parking end?"

He looked confused. "April first."

"Well, that's all that I need! Thanks so much for the information. Chief Wohnt, your staff is super helpful. You should be proud."

I scooted around Gary and into the icy March air, speed-shuffling toward the library. I gave it three minutes, tops, until Gary forced the deputy to tell him what I'd really been asking about, and I wanted as much street as possible between Gary and me when that happened. It wasn't my fault the deputy was a talker. I certainly hadn't broken any law. Still, I'd feel safer inside the library's brick. Gary would be less likely to ream me out with other people around.

Five minutes and I was almost there. I heard voices coming from the parking lot before I could see who was speaking. The anger was palpable.

"I saw the text you sent her!" a woman yelled. "You propositioned her! For all I know, you slept with her, probably in one of those old folks' beds between shifts."

I rounded the corner at a jog, hoping I wasn't going to have to call for help to break up a fight. I found Christie and Donald just outside the door twenty feet away, Christie's face purple, Donald's expression bored. They hadn't spotted me yet. Christie raised her hands to let loose another round of harsh words, this one juicier than the last.

I was clearing my throat to announce my presence and hopefully end the argument when a hand darted out of the thick juniper bushes and yanked me in. It was Mrs. Berns, hidden behind the greenery in full winter gear. What, did they offer a bush-crouching class over at the Senior Sunset? Come to think of it, that wouldn't be a bad class for private eye licensure.

"What are you doing?" I whispered.

"Snooping, obviously," she whispered back, rolling her eyes at the idiocy of my question.

"Why?"

"Because I got rid of cable." She pinched my arm. "What do you think? They're people we know, and they're fighting about sex! What could be more fun?"

"It's time to open the library, Mrs. Berns."

I tried to stand, but she yanked me back down. We'd kept our voices low, but the rustling branches and crunching snow must have drawn Christie's and Donald's attention.

"Who's in those bushes?" Donald called.

Mrs. Berns stood and brushed shrubbery off her slacks before striding confidently toward him. "Mrs. Berns. I work with your wife here at the library. It sounds like you're dipping your wick in other people's candles?"

He had the grace to look abashed, pursing his sphincter-shaped lips. "She's wrong. I didn't cheat with anyone."

I had no choice but to step onto the sidewalk as well. Christie glared at me. Donald didn't even bother to glance at my face, his eyes on my chest, though the only sight less titillating than a pair of A-cups had to be a pair of A-cups in a winter jacket. Dumbass.

Mrs. Berns flicked his arm. "If you're going to be gross, you should be less stupid. Propositioning other women when you're already married? If you're gonna throuple, you have to let the other two know. Otherwise it's a vicious circle, though I don't know why it's called that. Vicious triangle makes more sense, what with all those sharp edges."

"OK," I said, leading Mrs. Berns toward the front door. "We have to open this place up."

"Do I know you?" Donald asked, his eyes now on my face, incurious. He wore an ankle-length quilted jacket that might have flown on a Colorado mountaintop but looked ridiculous in Battle Lake. Something about him made me want to punch him right in his throat. I bet he got that a lot.

"Nope," I said, not caring whether he was trying to embarrass me by pretending that I was forgettable or actually didn't remember that we'd run into each other in the Sunset yesterday. I'd already grown to loathe the arrogance conveyed in his puffy yet rectal mouth, and this was only the second time I'd seen him. I swished past without another glance. Mrs. Berns followed, while Donald and Christie stayed just outside the door, presumably working on their tans.

"If that man was dogshit, I'd buy a new pair of shoes rather than wipe him off," Mrs. Berns said. "Do you understand what I'm saying? I'm saying he's gross."

"I got that."

She reached for my coat, but last time she'd done that, she'd riffled through my pockets. I held my hands out for her jacket instead.

"You find out any more about Rita's death?" she asked as she unzipped it and handed it to me.

"She OD'd on cancer medication, and she didn't have cancer," I said, walking toward the back room. "The police don't know if it was suicide or murder, though I got the impression the latter makes more sense."

She followed me to the break room. "And you talked to Ida?"

"Yep. She's hanging in there. Except some woman named Helen is bullying her at the Sunset."

Mrs. Berns sucked in a breath. "Helen Ripley?"

"Yeah. You know her?"

"Bossy old hen," Mrs. Berns said, wrinkling her nose. "I'll take care of her. How about Doris? Check in on her?"

"She wasn't working. I'm going to her sister's funeral tomorrow. I can pay my regards then."

"I'll join you." Her pause was long. Too long. "How's Johnny?"

By her tone of voice, it was clear she knew I'd stopped by his place after I'd dropped her off. Her tone wasn't playful, like it usually was when she asked about him. "Fine."

She smacked the back of my head, only enough to embarrass me. "Don't mistake me for one of the dolts you can lie to. You look like you messed up something big. If it wasn't Ida, Doris, or the investigation, then it was Johnny. What'd you do this time?"

I rubbed the back of my head, but that wasn't the part of me that hurt. "We got in a fight."

She stuck out her chin. "That doesn't sound like Johnny."

"Fine." I twisted my hands. "I broke up with him."

Mrs. Berns dropped her purse. I expected her to make fun of me. Instead she looked stricken, which shook me more than anything she'd ever done.

"What?" she asked.

"Don't worry about it." I picked up her purse and handed it to her. "I can fix it. I wasn't myself last night, is all. I was scared that Johnny would get murdered if we stayed together. I realize that's foolish. Isn't it?"

She still wasn't talking.

"You're worrying me," I said.

She finally spoke, her voice sad and old. "You can't keep playing with that boy like that. One of these times he isn't going to come back."

I blinked rapidly to fan the tears. "Yeah, well, it's not this time," I said with a confidence I did not feel. "I'm going to send him some flowers so he knows that I messed up. I'll make it up to him when he gets back." I artificially lightened my voice. "We still on for the class tonight?"

She nodded. I didn't like her gloom. I really could fix this. She didn't need to worry.

I made one last attempt at changing her mood. "We'll have fun!"

She snorted. "Fun? Bridge club in Battle Lake? It's going to be a sea of vitamin B breath, dry skin, and micropenises. But I'll do it because I love you."

"Thank you." Her doubts about Johnny weighted my stomach like a stone.

When I saw Kennie walking in, that cursed new job offer on her lips and Bad Brad at her heels, I was almost grateful for the distraction.

Almost.

Chapter 20

As a public employee on the job, I was trapped and Mayor Kennie knew it. Still, I backed up until I was against the far wall behind the counter.

"Stop looking for an escape," she said, removing her winter cowboy hat and unsnapping her fringed suede coat. "This isn't going to hurt."

I winced. "That's what you said about the home bikini-waxing service."

"You didn't even let me go down there!"

"I might be dumb, but I'm not stupid."

"That's true," Mrs. Berns said, nodding agreeably. "Kennie, I've been meaning to ask you—why are you hanging out with Bad Brad so much?" She pointed at the shaggy doofus. "You two doing the 'how's-your-father?'"

Bad Brad stared guiltily at his shoes. Kennie drew herself taller.

"You know, the lust and thrust?" Mrs. Berns prodded.

Still they kept silent.

"Rocking the Casbah?" she offered helpfully.

"Good lord," I said, interrupting her. "Leave them alone."

It was more for me than them. The idea of Kennie and Bad Brad being intimate wasn't the grossest thing I'd ever envisioned, but that wasn't saying much, since I'd accidentally crashed a masked geriatric orgy last May. I shuddered. But the more I thought about Kennie and Brad together, at least with their clothes on, the more it worked for me. They were sorta perfect for each other, actually, both of them a cunning kind of ditzy, both horndogs, both currently Battle Lake residents. Successful unions have been built on less.

"Thank you," Kennie said, patting her crispy hair. "My personal business is just that. Though interestingly, Mrs. Berns's line of inquiry is right in line with the financial proposition I have for you both."

Ohh, that couldn't be good. Kennie stood between me and the front door, but I bet I could break the glass on the nearest window. *Exit, air, help.*

Mrs. Berns, on the other hand, clapped her hands with glee. "Count us in!"

"We don't know what the job is!" I objected.

She tapped her nose with her pointer finger. "I do, and I've got a good sniffer for this sort of thing. I can tell you're going to like this one." She lined up the fingers of one hand and used them like a sound barrier to keep her comments from reaching Kennie and Bad Brad, though her loud voice negated the gesture. "Finally, right? Kennie Rogers has lobbed some real stinkers our way."

Kennie cleared her throat, but Bad Brad jumped into the space, too excited to stay quiet.

"It's the best idea ever! A Minnesota phone sex line." His eyes bubbled with enthusiasm.

I had a different reaction. Time froze. I was paralyzed, my thoughts the only movement inside me. Bad Brad thought a phone sex line was the best idea ever. Dear God. Exes were like a reminder of how far you'd come, right? And you should celebrate your personal evolution rather than hate yourself when Future You meets up with sad or tragic evidence of Past You. Yep, that was it: I'd celebrate that I was no longer dating Bad Brad, rather than regret that I'd ever slept with him.

Time rushed back.

"But a modern one!" he continued. "We use cell phones. But they're also *sell* phones, used to sell Minnesota phone sex!"

Right. God help me, I had to ask. "What exactly is *Minnesota* phone sex?"

Kennie jumped in, shooting Bad Brad a *you better not interrupt me again* glance, sharp as a knife. "Minnesota phone sex is like regular phone sex, but with the accent. Plus, you know, less dirty talk, more innuendo."

Cheese and rice, she was for real. Kennie Rogers intended to open a phone sex business, and she was offering me a job as one of her operators. What was worse, it didn't seem like the foulest idea she'd ever dreamed up. True, her large animal–sitting business, Home for Your Horse, had set the bar low, particularly when her clients realized she was boarding the animals in her teensy Battle Lake backyard, but still. Even a stopped watch was right twice a day.

Christie chose that moment to enter the library. She walked past Kennie and Brad, holding herself stiffly as she made straight for the central computer behind the front desk. Donald was nowhere in sight.

"Like I stated," Mrs. Berns said, ignoring her, "I'm in. I was born for it, don't ya know."

"Nice accent," I said. "I'm afraid I'll have to pass, though." Potentially profitable idea or no, I couldn't see how talking sex with strangers using my best Minnesota accent would win me any favors with Johnny.

Mrs. Berns could. "If you take the job, you'll have extra money," she said. "You can use it to take your boy someplace extra nice when he gets back from Wisconsin."

Kennie clapped her hands. "Perfect! I'll consider Mrs. Berns a yes and you a strong maybe, Mira James. We start tonight at my house. I have a convoy of truckers distributing ads in the finest restrooms across the country. Our clients will be expecting our prettiest ladies to be on the phones beginning at ten sharp!"

Mrs. Berns tapped her chin. "I'll have to wear my sexy-time lingerie."

I choked on my own spit. "The people calling won't be able to see you."

"I know, but I'm a Method sex talker. I have to *feel* it."

Oh no.

"I understand completely," Kennie said. "That's why I'll be providing bottomless wine for all my workers."

That did sweeten the pot. But wait, what was I thinking? I couldn't participate in phone sex. "Is operating a business out of your house even legal?"

"I should say so. I ran it by Gary Wohnt, and he said he didn't want to hear another word. If that's not complete permission, then I don't know what is." She smiled and then switched to a sad face. "On an unrelated note, on my way out from visiting with Gary, I couldn't help hearing that Eustace Dickens is being investigated for the murder of Rita Theisen."

A smashing sound made us all jump.

"Sorry!" Christie's face was ashen. "I dropped the stapler."

"Relax," Mrs. Berns said. "I drop that thing all the time and still can't figure out how to break it."

I didn't think that was why Christie looked so panicked.

Chapter 21

Kennie ignored the stricken expression that Christie was struggling to hide. "One of Gary's deputies explained that Eustace and Rita had been dating. When they think there's been foul play, the partner becomes the primary suspect."

This news was not nearly as interesting as Christie's countenance as Kennie spoke. My wealthy intern had a vested interest in this conversation, for all that she was trying to appear otherwise. Was it Eustace's name or Rita's that had triggered her? I flashed back to the argument she'd been having outside the library with her husband. Was it connected? My curiosity sniffed the air like a hound. I owed Ron a recipe for the Battle Lake Bites column. It wouldn't hurt to do some extraneous research at the same time, starting with Donald and Christie, our little town's newest benefactors.

Kennie wrapped up her gossip, not adding anything new, and left the library with a flourish, Bad Brad following her like a manservant. Christie prepared to do more canvassing with library welcome packets, and I set Mrs. Berns up at the front counter to help patrons before making my way to one of the computers.

Out of deference to my work ethic, I began by researching material for my food column. Battle Lake Bites had started out as an outlet, my way to take childish swings at the town I found myself in, as if the choice to live here weren't all on me. As I began to take responsibility for where I was—in life as well as geographically—I began to recognize the beauty of Battle Lake. That's when the column morphed into a sociological study of the eccentricity that was Minnesota food, a cuisine remarkable only for how little chewing it required: hotdish, lutefisk, klub, "salads," cream soups.

Usually, to locate recipes for the column, I'd google "bizarre Minnesota food" and put my own twist on whatever appeared. The stranger it got, the more positive letters the newspaper received. I didn't feel like going outlandish today, though. I craved normalcy. Part of me wanted to run a Tater Tot hotdish recipe, but I felt like Doris might read it and think I was judging hers.

(She'd be right, by the way. Almonds had no place in totdish.)

But I wouldn't kick a woman when she was down. Instead, I decided on the spot to start a themed focus for the column. I would home in on a different ethnicity each day. Otter Tail County's makeup was predominantly Norwegian, German, and Swedish, and I definitely wanted to feature an Ojibwe and Lakota week to celebrate the county's original residents. I'd ease readers into the theme slowly by starting with German, the food I had the most experience with because my grandma was of German descent.

I fondly remembered sauerkraut-drenched family get-togethers when I was young, before my dad's drinking made it impossible to attend social events. These were gatherings accented by cuts of meat that most people would consider awful, though I later found out it was actually spelled "offal": tongues and hearts and feet and cheeks. It couldn't be too hard to make up a few recipes with those ingredients, I thought.

I began typing.

> This week's Battle Lake Bites column will be the first in a series honoring our ancestors, from the Native Americans who first settled this land to Scandinavians who reproduced like rabbits. We'll begin with a German theme, dedicated to my grandmother

Bernadine Haehn, whose family first moved from Germany to Wisconsin in the late 1800s before settling in central Minnesota. My grandma Bernie was the queen of comfort food, and I think she would have gotten a kick out of these recipes, which together will make a complete, well-balanced meal of entrée, side dish, and beverage. Ingredients available at your local grocery store.

Schweinshaxe

Ingredients

1. Meaty pig knuckles, 1 per person
2. 1 clove minced garlic per knuckle
3. 1 teaspoon salt per knuckle
4. ½ teaspoon ground black pepper per knuckle
5. ½ teaspoon caraway seeds per knuckle
6. 2 tablespoons olive oil per knuckle
7. 1 tablespoon apple cider vinegar per knuckle
8. 1 whole onion, sliced, for every two knuckles
9. 1 can of beer

Whisk together the garlic, salt, pepper, caraway seeds, olive oil, and vinegar and place it in a large plastic Ziploc along with the knuckles. Release all the air and knead the sealed bag, making sure the marinade is evenly distributed. Let sit 8 hours, or overnight. Preheat oven to 350 degrees. Place sliced onions in a shallow baking dish along with the contents of the can of beer (approximately ½ inch of liquid). Distribute knuckles evenly in pan, making sure they're not making a fist. Bake uncovered for 3 hours, or until meat falls off bone and skin is brown and crusty.

German Potato Salad

Ingredients

1. 2 pounds red or Yukon Gold potatoes
2. 4 slices bacon, diced
3. 1 red onion, finely chopped
4. ¼ cup cider vinegar
5. 1½ tablespoons honey
6. 1½ teaspoons salt
7. ¼ teaspoon pepper
8. Chopped chives or parsley, for garnish

Peel and quarter potatoes and boil in salted water until fork-tender. Drain. Cut into ¼-inch slices while still hot. While potatoes cook, fry bacon, saving the drippings. Remove bacon, add onion to the pan, and cook until transparent, stirring frequently. Add vinegar and honey and bring to a boil. Pour over the warm potato slices and toss to coat. Taste for salt and pepper. Add the bacon and toss again. Sprinkle chopped chives or parsley on top as a garnish.

Krautini

Ingredients

1. Good vodka
2. Sauerkraut
3. Pitted queen olives

Chill your martini glasses. Pour 2 shots vodka and 1 table-spoon sauerkraut juice into a martini shaker with a handful of ice. Let sit while you stuff sauerkraut into 3 olives. Shake

the martini and pour through the sieve into a chilled glass.
Garnish with 3 olives and a smile.

As I typed, I wondered if my grandma's food had been as good as I remembered or if everyone had simply been drunk when eating. I'd maybe stumbled onto the explanation for German food. Ah, well, I liked it. I proofed my article and emailed it to Ron, excited to dig into the real research. Specifically, I wanted to know more about Christie and Donald Maroon, plus Rita Theisen and Eustace Dickens.

I had no intention of getting involved with the investigation. I just wanted to be informed.

For $49.95 a month, I had access to a database that culled and organized a wild amount of information on pretty much anybody—all legal documents, addresses, even reviews they wrote for online products. People who were paranoid about their information or personal data being on the internet didn't know the half of it. No one could hide in this cyber world.

The Maroons had a particularly deep online trail—more than five hundred hits came up on their name. I skimmed the first few. The information was redundant. They had married in 1973 and had no children. They'd come by their money through their medical research enterprise, which was poised to go public this coming April. Shares were predicted to sell at a record-breaking price due to the company's well-publicized breakthroughs in cancer research as well as a heart implant that was in the final stages of FDA review and showed tremendous promise as a cost-effective pacemaker replacement.

Was there a connection between the fact that Rita Theisen had died from cancer medication and the Maroons' company doing cancer research? It seemed tenuous. More pressing was Christie's accusation that Donald had slept with someone he worked with at the Senior Sunset. It couldn't have been Rita, could it? She was dating Eustace, after all. I filed both questions away.

The rest of the articles documented the Maroons' extensive philanthropy, from donations to volunteer work to mission trips. If you read about them without ever meeting them, you'd believe they were saints. The story they'd told Kennie about being a part of SLUMN's domestic study abroad program checked out, so I turned my search to Rita.

Rita Theisen was her married name, though she'd divorced two decades earlier, exactly two months after meeting and marrying Andrew Theisen. Since then, she'd earned a Licensed Practical Nurse degree from the community college in Moorhead, racked up an impressive stack of speeding tickets, and bounced from one job and apartment to another, all of them located in northern and western Minnesota. The one job she'd never held was waitress at the Turtle Stew, though sure enough, she was listed as co-owner with her only sibling, Doris Pitowski. I made a note to myself to add Polish to my list of themed recipe columns and dug deeper into Doris's affairs.

She and her sister had inherited the Stew from their mom and dad in 1986. The Stew came without debt and had remained solvent with, according to tax returns, a steady if not particularly impressive profit. That was until three years ago, when the Stew began operating with deep losses. What would account for that? The Battle Lake economy had been steady for years. The Stew was always packed at mealtimes. I tried a few more searches but could find no accounting for the downturn in profits. I'd need to ask around.

My last search was on Eustace Dickens. The computer took longer than usual to scour the internet. The arms on the "still searching!" clock ground around, and around, and around. When the results finally appeared, I sat back in my chair.

Eustace had only one hit, a newspaper article from the early '70s. In this day and age, how could that be? I clicked on it.

Decorated Vietnam Veteran Drops Out

Eustace Dickens, one of the few living U.S. recipients of the Vietnamese Military Merit Medal for courage and rare self-sacrifice, is no longer willing to claim his award. Dickens was awarded the honor for rescuing several Vietnamese children from a forced labor camp despite heavy enemy fire. Dickens took a bullet to his right leg in the rescue mission and was honorably discharged from the military. Upon his return to his hometown of Battle Lake, Minn., Dickens became an outspoken opponent of the war and one of the most recognized antiwar protesters in the state.

In a statement released to the press, Dickens has chosen to formally relinquish his medal, step away from the war protest movement, and "live separate from the follies of man and the crush of idiocy."

I could definitely relate to that impulse. Eustace must have been successful at staying below the radar, because there was no more information to be found.

I had much to ponder.

My eyes wandered to the library's front windows, which offered a view of icicle fingers pointing down from bare trees, and the sidewalk and Main Street beyond. My gaze unfocused as I tried to fit the pieces of research together. Rita Theisen had been a bit of a nomad, refusing to work for or with her sister despite staying close to Battle Lake, even moving here a couple years earlier. According to Kennie, she'd been dating Eustace at the time of her death, which had been either murder or suicide by unprescribed cancer medication.

Someone had dressed her body in clothes and a mask designed for a life-size doll, then precariously perched it on a stool in the café she co-owned with her sister. Meanwhile, two rich weirdos had come to Battle Lake on some mildly insulting cultural mission, throwing around money, cash acquired largely due to their company's successful cancer research. Christie was guarded; Donald was slimy.

That was everything I knew. What a clusteryuck.

Based on that, you know what would have been the best thing for me to do? Avoid getting involved. I had literally zero insights to offer. No good could come from me stepping into the middle of this. There wasn't a single thing that would compel me to get involved.

At least, not until three men walked past the library windows, each of them carrying a limp body hoisted on his shoulders.

Chapter 22

The sight hit me like a gut punch. I jumped up so fast that I knocked over my chair. Had murder become industrialized in Battle Lake? Were people now hoisting corpses around out in the open? It had been bound to happen, I supposed.

I found my tongue. "Call 911!"

"You don't have to yell," Mrs. Berns said from immediately behind me.

I jumped. "How long have you been standing there?"

"Long enough to notice what you're looking up. Also, long enough to see the city workers hauling the last of Ida's town dolls to the police station. They were rounded up this morning. Can't have any more corpses hiding in plain sight."

Of course. Those were Ida's freak show dolls the men were carrying, not limp, super-dead bodies. I swear, if I hadn't had a million reasons to hate dolls before, I sure did now. Gross. I laid my hand over my heart and willed it to stop racing.

Mrs. Berns pointed at my computer screen. "Snooping on Eustace, eh? Not much there. The man has been living in the woods since the seventies. Too tender a soul to be out in the world. I don't know why you didn't just ask me about him."

I cocked my head. That was a good point. "What else do you know?"

She held her hands, palm up. "That's it. The guy is good at keeping a low profile. I do know how you can find out more, though."

"How?"

She walked to the front desk and grabbed a welcome packet. "Drive out to his place and give him a library card."

It was a pleasant day for a drive, actually. The sun was high in the sky and full of promise, the roads clear. The radio *and* the heat in my old brown Toyota Corolla had elected to work at the same time, a rare occurrence worthy of celebration. I drove, cocooned in a cloud of toasty heat and '80s arena rock. I'd ordered a bouquet of daisies and tulips sent to Johnny's hotel room along with a note before I'd left the library. My food column was written, and if I stopped by the mountain-climbing group on my way back to the library, I'd be on track to complete the first pro–Otter Tail article on schedule.

I felt no urgency to investigate Rita's death. It was sad, for sure, but I was not involved. I'd introduce myself to Eustace to assuage my curiosity as well as welcome him to the library, and that would be that.

Everything was falling into place just fine.

According to Mrs. Berns, a Eustace sighting was as rare as spotting a leprechaun, and the fact that I'd spotted him at the apothecary yesterday meant a year of good luck. That level of remoteness also meant he probably didn't eat a lot of fresh food, at least this time of year, so I'd stopped by Larry's on my way out to pick up some fruit and veggies to bring along with the welcome packet. The apples, bananas, peppers, and celery emptied out the last of my cash, but if I kept my budget lean until I turned in my first new column, I'd survive.

Mrs. Berns's directions led me to a secluded patch of land at the terminus of a dead-end road three miles east of Battle Lake. No Trespassing signs dotted the edge of the thick hardwood forest, all elm claws and grasping oak branches, but I wouldn't be going into the woods. I'd stay on the road. Plus, I was a city employee. Pretty sure that made me immune to trespassing.

I threaded my car through the low-slung branches, their sharp talons scraping and screeching along the Toyota's roof. If we hadn't had a few good melts, I doubted I would have been able to drive in. As it was, I barely made it, crunching through crusty snowdrifts that reached halfway up my tires. This road was definitely minimum maintenance and saw few motorized vehicles. Come to think of it, how had Eustace gotten to town yesterday? According to my database, he had neither a driver's license nor a registered vehicle. That didn't mean he didn't drive an unregistered car—a lot of old farmers in the area did it—but it was definitely something to follow up on.

Or not.

I rounded a final bend in the crotchety road, and Eustace's farmhouse came into view.

"House" might have been a generous description. It was more of a shack, the size of the average American living room, constructed of sturdy-looking logs with a tar paper roof patched with mismatched shingles that looked as if they'd been scavenged from ditches after a windstorm. A pile of wood nearly as tall as the shack teetered next to it, and on the other side of that, an old, hand-crank well sprouted from the ground.

A single outbuilding the same size as the house stood on the western perimeter of the small clearing. It appeared sturdy, or at least straight, but it was also constructed of a patchwork of materials. A series of wooden poles in front of the outbuilding displayed a stretched-out animal hide. Next to that was a hand-hewn table, its rough, blood-stained surface interrupted by a wicked-looking knife. Nearby, an oddly familiar shape lay on the ground, neutered by snow. It was round and a few feet across. An outhouse was on the opposite side of the clearing, maybe thirty feet from the main shack. I guessed Eustace didn't have running water.

There were no vehicles in sight, not even rusted-out ones.

I shut off my car, grabbed the welcome pack and sack of groceries, and stepped outside, hoping that I'd be able to back out through the drifts when the time came. Smoke from the chimney suggested that Eustace was inside, or at least had been recently.

"Hello?" The air smelled pleasant, like woodsmoke and winter thaw. When no response came, I went to the door and knocked.

No answer.

I stepped off the front stoop and peered in a window. The interior of the shack consisted of a single room with a fireplace on the far end. A hook held a cooking pot over the crackling flame, and a grate at the bottom suggested Eustace sometimes cooked or grilled on it. A single bed hugged one wall and a desk the other. Two closed cabinets likely held clothes or food and tableware, or both. A well-stocked gun rack was nailed to the wall. In all, the interior was clean and simple. It reminded me of that one-room pioneer cabin that every Minnesota kid had to visit on a field trip. There was something almost comforting in it.

Less heartening was the sharp sound of a gun cocking directly behind me.

Chapter 23

I whipped around, hands in the air and heart in my throat. My quick movement startled Eustace, who was stepping out of the woods, his feet laced in snowshoes. I'd heard the sound of a branch breaking, not a gun.

"Sorry to alarm you," he said, his eyes wary. His voice was deeper than I'd remembered, and scratchy. I wondered if he'd spoken a word to anyone since picking up his medication. "I didn't know anyone was here."

He held up two dangling rabbits, death rendering them both impossibly long and relaxed. "Hunting."

I sagged against the door. "Sorry I was peeking in your windows." I meant it, and not just because I'd gotten caught. When Eustace had stalked into the apothecary, he'd seemed so tense and angry. In his natural habitat, wearing a worn winter parka and a plaid Stormy Kromer, he seemed more like a kindly woodsman. Even his skin lesions appeared less red.

"Not much to see." Was that humor behind his eyes? Sadness? I couldn't get a bead.

I lamely held out the welcome packet. "My name's Mira. I'm the Battle Lake librarian, and we need to raise our number of patrons to ensure the library stays afloat for everyone."

He didn't pull his eyes off my face. "I'm not much of a reader."

I shrugged. "Never too late to change that."

The nascent humor blossomed into a smile, revealing surprisingly white teeth. "Probably true." He held up the rabbits again. "I have work to do. You're welcome to leave your packet on my front porch, but I can't promise you it wouldn't end up as kindling."

He walked over to the shed, where the animal hide was strung, and removed the knife from the nearby table with a practiced move. A quick, slick thrust of the blade, and one of the rabbits' fur was sliced up the middle. He gave a smooth tug, and voilà—all the fur was gone except for the unlucky rabbit's feet.

Twenty yards separated us, and his back was to me. I wasn't sure how to play this. He hadn't done anything wrong, as far as I knew. I'd already told him I was a librarian, so I couldn't just start asking him about Rita. Could I? Based on the little I knew of him and his austere lifestyle, I gambled that he'd prefer directness.

I cleared my throat. "There's a funeral tomorrow."

His shoulders stiffened. Four clean whisks and the fur was cut from the feet.

"I also heard that you and Rita Theisen were friends."

He swiveled so I could see his outline, all sharp nose and thin lips under his flannel cap. He opened his mouth to speak and then snapped it shut.

I sighed. "I was the one who found her body at the Turtle Stew."

He pivoted more quickly than a human should be able to. He held the bloodied knife in one hand and the rabbit pelt in the other. I became acutely aware of how little I actually knew about the man, and that only one consistently forgetful person knew I was out here.

"What do you want?" he asked, all humor gone.

The groceries I still held felt patronizing, but they were all I had left. That and the truth. "I brought you groceries because you remind me a little bit of my dad. I came out here because I heard you were dating Rita and had been questioned in her death, and I wanted to find out if you know what happened to her because I feel guilty about it even though I didn't know her."

His eyes sharpened and then grew distant. He returned his focus to the rabbit carcass, his back again to me. I thought he was done talking, but then I heard his voice, barely. "I loved her, and I miss her. I do not know why or how she died."

I stood for another quiet moment. He wasn't going to talk any more. I set the sack of groceries on his front porch, got in my car, and drove away.

I was almost back on the main road before I realized what the familiar shape under the snow had been. It was a tractor tire, the old kind that you transform into a sandbox for little kids. We'd had one in my own backyard growing up.

My dad had played with me in it all the time.

Chapter 24

It was a bit out of the way, but I stopped by my house before visiting the climbing club north of town. I had housecleaning to catch up on, plus my animals deserved some love. They both clamored for attention when I walked into the double-wide, following on my heels as I refreshed their water. Luna and I played catch on the front lawn for twenty minutes while Tiger Pop watched us archly from the warmth of the window.

When Luna sprawled on the snow from exhaustion, I went back inside to hand-wash dishes and peek inside my fridge. It was empty except for condiments and the marauded remains of my box of Nut Goodies. My cupboards fared better in terms of quantity, but not quality. They were stuffed with the B-team impulse buys, those foods that looked like an adventurous treat in the store but transformed into an undelicious chore once you got them home: Cajun rice mix, a quinoa salad kit, four bottles of flavored balsamic vinegars. I should have asked Eustace if I could stay for lunch.

I tell you what, though: taking stock of my cupboards was making the idea of being a Minnesota phone sex operator look better and better. I returned to the fridge and grabbed a Nut Goodie, munching on it as I made my bed, started a load of clothes, and ran the vacuum across the floors. Once I had the place in decent condition, I petted Tiger Pop till she crackled with static, brushed

Luna, and told them to be nice to each other before I took off for mountain climbing.

The plan was to duck into the climbing gym recently added to a wing of the Lake Christina Hunt Club, interview the director, and return to the library so Mrs. Berns could have a break. I was a few miles south of town, halfway to the hunt club, when I passed a big white Colonial house. I'd driven past it a hundred times before but never thought much of it until now.

According to the apothecary cashier, though, this was the home of the Fords.

Little D's foster family.

I pulled into the driveway, grateful for the library welcome packets for the second time that day. The Fords' yard and home were the opposite of Eustace's—spacious, well maintained. The house had a two-car attached garage as well as a rust-free, older-model sedan parked in the driveway. I didn't know what the Fords did for a living, but apparently they made decent money.

I parked, hauled myself out, and crunched across the driveway to the shoveled walk. Ringing the doorbell set off a cacophony of noise on the other side, mostly a dog barking followed by at least two different children crying.

The woman who answered the door was harried, in her late thirties with hair askew, a toddler on each hip, her gaze suspicious. "Yes?"

I held up the packet, hoping my smile appeared genuine. "Mira James, head librarian at the Battle Lake Public Library? We're in the middle of a welcome campaign hoping to introduce more of the community to the library's benefits."

Her distrust fell away and, with it, at least five years. She set both toddlers down, patting their diapered butts. "Andrew," she called into the house, "come get Pearl and Evan!"

When she turned to me, a smile much nicer than mine was planted on her face. She brushed her hair behind her ears before reaching for the packet. "Thanks so much for coming out. I've been meaning to get the younger ones in for your children's reading hour. I've heard good things about it. It's just so hard to coordinate with nap times."

I glanced behind her. The living room was decorated with shabby but serviceable furniture, and children and toys littered the floor. A graying black Lab sprawled on the ground, wagging his tail as a preschool-age child climbed on him.

"You have quite a dynasty back there."

She smiled. "I run a day care."

"You're more patient than me."

I meant it. I loved story time at the library because I had the kids for only sixty minutes. If I had to feed, water, and supervise a whole crew of them, I'd last a week before wondering how much I could get for them on eBay. "You also provide foster care, don't you?"

Her eyes narrowed. "Where did you hear that?"

My question had been clumsy, so it didn't surprise me that she'd slapped her suspicions back on. I could do better. "I ran into a new kid in town. Little D? I think he's one of yours."

Her mistrust stepped aside to make room for taciturnity. "He is."

Maybe I *couldn't* do better. I was bungling this. "I didn't mean to offend you. He seems like a nice kid, maybe a little wild. I liked him."

She didn't soften. "I can't speak about my foster children, except to say that I do my best with each of them. I'm sure you understand."

Translation: *You're an idiot. Go away.*

"Of course. Sorry to bother you." I nodded toward the packet now hanging loosely at her side. "Hope to see you at the library!"

She closed the door without a goodbye. I'd offended her, but I didn't know if it'd been my clumsy questioning or something she was hiding about Little D. I didn't suppose it ultimately mattered. I wasn't even sure why I'd stopped by, except now I knew that Little D had a roof over his head and a dog to play with.

I was still mulling over Ms. Ford's hot-and-cold body language when I pulled into the Lake Christina Hunt Club's circular driveway ten minutes later.

Otter Tail County had almost half a dozen hunt clubs, a mix of a luxury resort and a zoo where you could shoot the animals. Like most hunt clubs in the area, Lake Christina's main building was designed to resemble an enormous log cabin. Also in keeping with most hunt clubs, summer was their busiest time of year. In an effort to make their business more consistent in the between seasons, as well as to become more of a family destination, this past fall, they'd begun building a huge wing onto the main lodge. Opposite the two dozen hotel rooms, it held two waterslides and a climbing wall.

When I stepped inside the lobby, I was greeted by walls of glassy-eyed animal heads. The front desk was empty, so I walked into the addition I'd come to visit. The construction was so new that the waterslides hadn't been turned on yet, and the carpet was still off-gassing.

I was glad I'd forgotten to invite Mrs. Berns. She believed that if new carpet could do it, she could, too. I'd learned that the hard way when we had the weathered carpet in the library break room replaced.

"Can I help you?"

A guy about my age, wearing black pants and a white button-down, emerged from a door to my left. He held a fistful of Oreos and looked weirdly angry for a guy eating cookies. I must have been off-gassing some negativity myself.

"I'm Mira James. I'm looking for Ed? The director?"

"You're not looking for him. You're looking *at* him."

I scowled. Nobody liked to be corrected, but if you combined it with a lame joke, it became unbearable. "Lucky me. Thanks for agreeing to the meeting."

He popped the cookies in his mouth and indicated that I should follow him. "This way to the climbing wall. We're all set for your demo."

"What?" That was what my face said, I hoped. My mind had left the building. I wasn't afraid of heights; I was *terrified* of them, to the point that if I was forced up high, I was overcome with the urge to jump, the quickest way my brain could see to end the fear.

He smiled, forgetting the Oreo Golden Rule: you cannot show your teeth for at least five minutes and two glasses of milk after eating one. "You can't write an article about Climbing for Cowards if you don't actually climb!"

"Um, yeah I can." I rolled my eyes. "It's called an imagination."

He chuckled. He was enjoying this way too much. "You'll be fine. All the harnesses are new." He let his eyes drop to my stomach, where I was carrying a Nut Goodie baby. "It's great exercise, too."

My scowl deepened to a forehead ravine. "You have cookies in your teeth."

He snapped his mouth shut and glared at me. "Let me show you how to step into the harness," he said through tight lips.

I craned my neck and stared at the ceiling, three stories overhead. A dozen different rappelling lines were soldered to it, each of them angling close to the divoted climbing wall, each bump a rainbow color against the brown base. "How about *you* scale the wall first?"

"No can do, friend." He pointed at his own round belly and bowed legs. "This body only goes one direction, and that's forward."

"You don't climb, but you manage the climbing center?" Also, did he mean he couldn't back up? If so, he shared that trait with my first car, a 1973 Mercury Cougar, more boat than automobile.

"It's the family rec center," he said, shrugging. "Climbing is only a part. But yeah, my cousin owns the hunt club. He gave me this job. Are you in or not?"

"Fine." I did need the exercise. Plus, how bad could it be? The equipment was all new. The padding on the floor was thick. Monkey bars used to be my favorite playground equipment. These were all things I told myself as he tightened the climbing gear in movements so personal that I wondered if I should have given him my phone number first.

Once he had all the straps tight, he gave me a ridiculously sack-like pair of climbing shoes and a helmet. I let my longish brown hair out of its bun and tugged the helmet on. I was pretty sure it would be useless if I actually plummeted from three stories, but it did boost my morale ever so slightly. I clicked the helmet into place and tied the laces of the seedpod shoes. All geared up, I had nothing to do but try.

"Start here," he said, pointing to yellow-rimmed handholds. "If you follow the same-colored grips, you'll stay on the easiest route. See the yellow gong up there?"

My eyes followed where he indicated. From this distance, it was the size of a teacup. "Yeah."

"After you dong it, you can come back down."

I wanted to dong him. Instead, I dug into the rock-climbing wall. My harness gave me a sense of safety, hugging me, holding me like an adult bouncy swing. I curled my toes into a ledge a foot off the ground, appreciating the malleability of the ridiculous shoes. I reached for a hand grip just within my grasp and used it to balance as I tucked my other foot into a yellow ledge higher than the first. The initial ten feet were scary, but once I got a feel for it, I started to enjoy it. In fact, I reveled in it, reaching for one yellow handhold after another, curling my toes around slippery knobs, sweating, straining.

"Look down!"

"Screw you!"

I might have been having fun, but I wasn't stupid. The higher I reached, the greater the distance between the lemon-colored grips. I refused to look around, but I could feel space opening up behind and around me, daring me to leap. I grew monkey arms and legs, balancing and swinging, surging ever higher, until . . .

Gong.

The sound rang out over the enormous space of the family center, echoing off the silent waterslides and the floor-to-ceiling windows.

My grin was huge, visible only to me. I had done it.

Then I made the mistake of turning around.

OhmygodIamsohighwhatwasIthinking.

My grip slipped. I almost caught myself, grabbing on to the same knob with both hands, but my terror sweat was immediate, my hands slippery.

My upper half gave way, followed by my lower, and I plunged.

Chapter 25

The harness caught me with near-whiplash force three feet shy of the floor.

I gasped, blinking rapidly. I was OK. I was alive. The ceiling was way up there, and I was down here, near the ground.

"Holy shit did you come down fast!" Ed tipped me so I was on my feet, but my knees gave way. He caught me and held me there while I swallowed down the nausea. "You're supposed to let me know before you release."

"I thought I was going to die," I said, when I could finally speak again.

He stepped back, his face strained. I imagined he was playing out how my article describing this experience was going to look. "You OK?"

I felt my stomach. It was still there. "I'm fine. I thought you said this was good exercise."

He chuckled and began to undo the straps. "Happy to see these straps work so well. We hadn't tested them out yet."

My jaw dropped. "You're lying."

He shrugged. "Hey, you're a natural at climbing. Going up, anyhow." He sneaked a glance at my face. "You'll want to practice coming down."

"I'm never doing that again." I stepped out of the harness, my joints still wobbly.

"You'll make sure to write that the straps work, right?"

I ran my hands over my sweaty face before removing the helmet and shoes. "I will write that the straps work. Anything else?"

He rustled in his back pocket and brought out a sleeve of cookies. "Want one?"

I did not. After promising ten more times that I'd write a good review of the place—and I would—I stepped into the refreshingly brisk spring air, grateful to crunch across the parking lot to my car. I might have been good at climbing, but when life tripped you like mine did regularly, you wanted to keep your feet on the ground.

I pointed the Toyota toward town. During its normal operation, Battle Lake Public Library was open six days a week, ten hours a day, and I ended up working most of those. I didn't feel even a little bit guilty about leaving Mrs. Berns alone to run it. We had no scheduled events for the day, and Christie should've been back soon to help her, if she wasn't already there. I hated to admit it, but Christie showing up to help might turn out to be a good thing, not even counting the money her organization was bringing in or the usefulness of the welcome packets she'd designed.

I was brainstorming more ways to get the most of her expertise when I pulled into the library parking lot.

The ambulance positioned near the back door smacked those thoughts out of my head.

When I saw them wheeling Mrs. Berns out on a gurney, I stopped breathing.

Chapter 26

I bounded out of my car so fast I don't think I even turned it off. "Mrs. Berns!"

She lifted her head weakly, her skin pale. "I'm going home, Mira."

My voice broke. "No!"

The EMT holding the end of the gurney closest to the ambulance set it down.

"Hurry!" I yelled. "Pick her back up! Get her help!"

The EMT didn't move, so I shoved him. A small crowd had gathered outside the library, hands over their mouths, tugging their sweaters closer to their bodies. Why wasn't anyone moving quickly?

I grabbed Mrs. Berns's hand. It felt cold and featherlight. "What happened?"

The EMT I'd pushed squinted at me, rubbing his arm. "She collapsed," he said. "We think dehydration."

I felt Mrs. Berns for broken bones or a fever or anything I could touch. "People don't die of dehydration."

Mrs. Berns swatted at me and made a scoffing noise. "Who said anything about dying?"

"You! You said you were going home."

"That's ridiculous. I meant Wadena, not heaven. That's where these nice gentlemen drove from. It was the closest hospital with an ambulance to spare. I know I've told you that's where I was born."

My mouth opened and closed. I was a big ol' landed fish.

"We'll check you out in the rig," the second EMT said, grunting as he released the pin holding his side of the gurney before sliding it into the back of the ambulance, "but I think you'll be fine. If your vital signs are good, we won't even need to bring you to Wadena. We'll let you go with some electrolytes and a recommendation that you take it easy and check with your personal physician today or tomorrow."

My legs went out from under me. I landed on the cold sidewalk, a jag of ice digging into my palm. Mrs. Berns was going to be all right. I waved away the EMT when he rushed over to help me. "I'm fine. Also, sorry about shoving you."

"She's such a drama queen!" Mrs. Berns hollered from the back of the ambulance. "Do you have any Popsicles in here?"

Someone broke from the crowd and helped me to my feet. My legs were a little quivery for the second time that day. I wobbled to the rear of the ambulance, where the non-pushed of the two EMTs was taking Mrs. Berns's blood pressure.

"How did you get dehydrated?"

"Lack of liquids is my best guess." Mrs. Berns tapped the blood pressure cuff and spoke to the EMT. "I'm trying to beat my high score. Does this thing go above 140?"

"I need you to be quiet," he said.

"Mrs. Berns." I put my hand on her foot to get her attention. "Why haven't you been getting enough liquids?"

She zipped her lips until the EMT finished. "Life, I suppose. Too much to do, not enough time for sitting around and drinking."

"Promise you'll take better care of yourself."

Her eyes narrowed. "If you promise that you'll take Kennie up on her job offer."

I gasped. "Please tell me this isn't all a ruse to get me to commit to Minnesota phone sex."

Both EMTs raised their eyebrows but managed to keep their expressions neutral. They'd heard way worse things, right?

"Don't be silly," Mrs. Berns said. "I would not fake passing out and call an ambulance with the sole goal of getting you to work a phone sex line." She squeezed the bicep of the man who'd taken her blood pressure and winked at him. "I might do it to get your phone number, though, son."

He looked like he was considering it.

I envisioned my dismal cupboards, my bare fridge, the energy it would require to argue. All the fight was gone from me. "Fine. I will take Kennie up on her business proposition, as long as I get to hang up when I want to and I can work on the article I owe Ron while I'm talking."

Mrs. Berns held out a hand. "Deal."

I shook it. It felt unusually cool and papery. I wondered if she was dealing with more than dehydration. I made a vow to bring her to the doctor myself.

After she checked out with the EMTs, she wanted to go home and rest so she'd be ready for bridge club. I tried to talk her out of going, but she wouldn't have it. We agreed to a compromise: She could come with if she let me know if she was feeling dizzy, in which case I'd bring her straight to the hospital. If she felt good, we'd stick it out and head to Kennie's for the inaugural phone sex training.

(Mrs. Berns revealed that the name of Kennie's business was Minnesota Hot Dishes, by the way. I didn't hate it.)

Mrs. Berns got a ride home from the EMTs, which was unorthodox, but so was everything else about her. After the ambulance drove away, I herded everyone back to the library, helped those who needed it, and generally ran the place, which was blessedly uneventful. I even had time to call Mrs. Berns's doctor. Her regular lady was out of town, but the receptionist promised to call back and let us know if she'd make a special office visit for Mrs. Berns the next day, a Sunday. I said that'd be great.

Christie returned that afternoon looking wind-slapped, which made sense, considering she'd gone door-to-door the whole day. She said she had a potential dozen new sign-ups and offered to spend the rest of the afternoon updating the library's website. *Yes, please.* I finished a shelving job I'd started, removing books that hadn't been checked out in more than a decade and shipping those off to our sister library in Mississippi. If Christie came through with the donation, I'd be able to stock the shelves with fresh books.

I had two hours to kill after I closed down the library. I stopped by the nursing home to check on Ida. Both she and Curtis were out. I peeked in Abraham's room. He had all new decorations—notes, candles, a plant, a pair of shoes under his bed, two sets of dentures stacked on his chest, and all-new trinkets resting in his palm: a rose quartz rosary, bits of ribbon, a black-and-white photograph of a WWII pilot, and a lottery ticket. I wondered where the rhinestone button had gone, and where all the previous gewgaws were being stored.

Abraham's hand very much reminded me of the Led Zeppelin altar I'd started when I got my first apartment in Minneapolis. It had begun as a few of their album covers that I came across in a garage sale and expanded to include posters, incense, a candle melted into the mouth of a wine bottle, and ticket stubs from the first Robert Plant solo tour. The altar hadn't made me particularly lucky, but then again, it hadn't hurt anyone, either. I supposed the same could be said for Abraham's.

Ever a fan of hedging bets, I scrounged through my pockets. They contained only a Nut Goodie wrapper and a shiny coppery penny. I placed the penny in Abraham's palm, held it for a moment as if we were lovers, and slipped out of the room.

Chapter 27

"Welcome to the Battle Lake Bridge Club! What's your pleasure?"

"Avoiding card clubs, but here I am, so what are ya gonna do?" Mrs. Berns said to Helen Ripley, Ida's nemesis, before stepping around her to check out the dessert bar on a nearby coffee table.

If I'd known Helen was the card club's president, I might not have agreed to this stop. I didn't like that she'd bullied sweet Ida, especially during such a tough time. Still, Mrs. Berns and I were here, in a church basement and surrounded by card tables full of poker and corn chips, and so I thought we might as well make the best of it.

Helen turned to me. "How about you? What is your favorite card game?" She smiled expectantly, taking a delicate sip of coffee.

"I like a good game of Wrinkly Dick," Mrs. Berns called out around a mouthful of brownie.

The coffee Helen had been drinking came out her nose. "Excuse me?"

She reached for a napkin off a nearby table and patted delicately at her face. She sported the perfectly styled white hair of a First Lady from a bygone generation, her purple pantsuit crisp and clean and made of that half-plastic material that the elderly wore more often than not. Except for a cane she leaned on moderately, she appeared to be in good physical shape.

"Wrinkly Dick." Mrs. Berns made her way back to my side, rummaging in her purse for a deck of cards. "It requires a normal deck, plus the joker. You deal the cards equally to all players and take turns drawing from the hand of the person to your right. Your goal is to pair off all your cards and not be the last one holding the Wrinkly Dick. You know, the joker."

Helen stared at Mrs. Berns. "You mean Old Maid, of course."

"Of course I *do not*. You'd be lucky to end up with an old maid. We get wiser and more resourceful as we age, not to mention that we're sorceresses in the bedroom. A wrinkly dick, on the other hand?" She shrugged. "No use to anyone."

Mrs. Berns shuffled her cards as she walked toward the nearest table. "Mira, care to join me?"

You bet your last dollar I did. From now until the end of time.

Wrinkly Dick was, not unexpectedly, a huge hit with the mostly female card club, most of whom were sixty years old and up. I also learned only the broadest concepts of bridge, a game with more rules than a Victorian first date.

Throughout the night, both Mrs. Berns and I talked up Ida, who we learned was a regular card club member but had forgone tonight because she was feeling ill. Most ladies tossed shade Helen's direction when we brought up Ida. We left the church basement confident that Ida would be getting a lot more social offers.

Outside, we wrapped our jackets tight against the chill night air. Mrs. Berns asked the question I'd been dreading: "You ready?"

"The *world* isn't ready for Minnesota phone sex. But a deal's a deal."

"Darn tootin'." Mrs. Berns was smiling as she shoved her mittened hand in mine.

We walked the half mile to Kennie's small rambler near the water tower. It was lit up like a party house when we arrived, though only she and Bad Brad were inside, four black burner phones lined up on the living room end table like the weapons in a twisted, cellular game of Russian roulette.

"I'm so happy you came!" Kennie said, clapping her hands. Her outfit tonight was the mullet of dress suits, with the business on top in the form of a fitted, double-breasted jacket and the party below by way of a skirt so short it transformed us all into amateur gynecologists.

"Save it for the callers," Mrs. Berns said, removing her parka and holding it out for Kennie. "You said there'd be wine?"

Kennie pointed a red-tipped talon toward the jug on the counter.

"They still make Ripple?" I asked. I wasn't complaining. "Quantity over quality" was my liquor motto—and possibly my new phone sex mantra as well.

"They do not," Kennie said. "I've been saving a case in my basement for a special occasion."

"What's that smell?" Mrs. Berns asked.

I sniffed the air. Uff da.

"My new perfume." Kennie waved air from her neck toward us. "It's called Lust for Life. Like it?"

Mrs. Berns strode to the jug of Ripple and unscrewed the cap. "If I wanted cats to stay away from something, that's what I would use."

Kennie's face lit up. "Thank you! And grab me a glass while you're at it."

I tugged a pocket notebook and pen out of my jacket before hanging it on the coatrack by the door. "I'll take a glass, too. And if you don't mind, I'll be working on an article tonight. Maybe you won't even need me."

"Oh no, we'll need you," Bad Brad said. He wore a loose T-shirt, track pants, and those frat boy slip-ons that brought to mind kegs and hot dog farts. Come to think of it, why was he wearing sandals? Those were definitely not March shoes. Was he staying at Kennie's? I eyed the two of them. Their body language was not giving anything away.

"Are you answering the phones, too?" I asked him.

He nodded and pointed at the black cell nearest him. "This one has a separate number, for anyone who wants Minnesota phone sex with a man. We don't want to discriminate."

I felt the tiniest bit better about the whole thing. "What's the script?"

Kennie chugged her glass of Ripple like it was water. "No script. You let the caller lead. Use your strongest Minnesota accent, and get Minnesota kinky."

"Minnesota kinky" was not a thing, I didn't think, unless you considered lovemaking with the lights on racy. I didn't know how that would translate down the phone line.

"Shouldn't we be in separate rooms?" I asked. Because the only thing that could possibly make Minnesota phone sex more uncomfortable was having people I knew hear me attempt it.

Mrs. Berns handed me a wineglass and spoke under her breath with the intent of a whisper but the volume of a normal conversation. "So you can, you know, take care of business if you get caught up in the moment?" She made a circular gesture in the vicinity of her waist.

I held my glass of wine toward Kennie. "Do you have anything stronger?"

Kennie beamed. "We'll see." She plopped on the couch next to Bad Brad and crossed her feet demurely at the ankles, causing her thighs to squeak like an indignant restaurant booth.

Mrs. Berns took the matching chair directly across from her. I landed in the recliner next to Mrs. Berns.

There sat the four phones, lying like snakes on the table between us. "The lines go live at ten sharp," Kennie said.

It was 9:59.

Bad Brad rubbed his hands on the top of his track pants. "My palms are sweating."

My *everything* was sweating, but I certainly wasn't going to admit it. I began to scratch out card club notes for the article—thirty-three attendees, bars, chips, coffee and soda provided, open to the public, ten-dollar-a-month donation suggested.

"It's now ten o'clock," Kennie said, unnecessarily. She brought her glass of wine to her mouth too quickly, clinking it against her teeth.

I continued to write. Helen Ripley was the lead organizer, but it was a volunteer position and others were welcome to apply. The gatherings rotated among church basements in town so no religion felt favored, they were held the third Saturday of every month, and maybe nobody was going to call in and I wouldn't have to do this?

A sharp trill, the hangman's whistle, answered my mental plea. The ring came from the phone nearest Kennie. She set her wineglass down with a force that sent syrupy liquor sloshing over the side. Sitting up extra straight, she made the "om" shape with her hands and drew in a deep, long breath, eyes closed. She was seeking the eye of the tiger.

The phone rang again. And a third time.

Her eyes snapped open and she grabbed it, her fake southern accent traded for a genuine Minnesotan one, long on the *o* and heavy on the *r* and *d*. "Hello der, lover. Ready for da boat ride of your life?" I sat back in surprise. She was *good*.

Before I could process how good, the phone in front of Bad Brad rattled. He whooped and snatched it up. "Minnesota Hot Dishes, how may I reheat you?"

My stomach dropped. I hadn't known he could draw on that accent at will, making Midwestern both sexy and playful. Well, maybe we'd just get the two calls, and I could write my article and drink wine with Mrs. Berns while Bad Brad and Kennie worked in the background. Kennie had promised I'd get paid either way.

Ring.

Dammit, that was Mrs. Berns's phone. She snatched it up eagerly and pressed it to her ear. "Pack your pop because you'll need refreshments, that's how far up nord I'm gonna take you!"

Cheesus. I was so far out of my league. Was my butt crack sweating? Maybe my phone wouldn't ring. That could happen, right? After all, how many people wanted to hear erotic Midwestern?

I tried not to listen to my colleagues, but I couldn't help it. Bad Brad's eyes were closed, guttural "you betchas" flowing like cream; Kennie was waving her hand animatedly and uff da–ing with the breathy sexiness of Marilyn Monroe spliced with *Fargo*'s Frances McDormand, and Mrs. Berns was going for the money shot, talking with such fervor about sliding a long, hard spoon into creamy, warm hotdish that it made me blush.

I couldn't do this. Probably I wouldn't have to. Right?

I looked at my phone, black and ugly.

It looked back at me.

Then, like a crappy, horrible brat, it rang.

Chapter 28

I scrubbed, the scent of steamy sandalwood scouring the inside of my nose.

Probably I should have used Ajax and steel wool instead, starting with my mouth.

The things I'd said the night before. To strangers.

You betcha I'll talk ishy to you.

Ja, I'll suck that like a hungry mosquito.

Heck yes, that'd win the VFW meat raffle.

Mmmmm, your Lutheran goodbye is the longest goodbye I've ever seen.

Baby, you're going as deep as the blizzard of '91, and I loooove it.

I shuddered. I'd done it willingly. Or at least, no one had forced me. I was still gobsmacked at how many people wanted to hear naughty Minnesotan. Even more astounding was how good all four of us had turned out to be at it. We'd kept on the lines until 4:00 a.m., spewing phrases I'd never thought I'd say, at least to a stranger, including "stroke that klub" and "touch my krumkake like you mean it."

And don't even ask about the things I'd promised to do to a lutefisk.

I had three takeaways from the night. The first was that the money was good. Kennie had set up the whole business through an overseas call center that handled payments and routed the incoming customers. The callers paid $3.99 a minute. The call center received 25 percent of that off the top, and Kennie took another 25 percent. The remaining

50 percent went to whoever took the call, which amounted to nearly two dollars a minute.

The second realization was that you could make *anything* sound dirty. I wasn't sure if I'd be able to apply that knowledge anywhere outside of the Minnesota phone sex industry, but you never knew.

The third and most important takeaway was that I realized I was done being single.

It wasn't just that there were weirdos out there, though boy howdy were there. More so, last night had made abundantly clear to me that I loved Johnny, deeply, truly, and forever. That might have been a strange revelation to have while exchanging Minnesota naughties with a stranger, but you couldn't choose the messenger, only listen to the message.

I loved Johnny.

I wanted to be with him forever. I knew it more this morning in the cold light of day than I had last night. I felt it in my *bones*.

I whooped right there in the shower as the force of the realization hit me anew.

I was going to propose to him when he returned from Wisconsin. Me and Johnny were going to be married.

No more games for me, just love as far as the eye could see. I'd made nearly $600 last night. A couple more evenings and I'd have enough to buy a ring and whisk Johnny away to a tropical location. I would open myself up to him completely.

I was smiling so broadly that it hurt my face. The decision made, a lifetime of stored fear fell off like old skin swirling down the drain. For the first time in my life, I was going all in.

I stepped out of the shower wearing nothing but a grin. "Luna! I'm gonna marry Johnny!"

Her tail thumped happily. Probably she heard "Luna! You are a honey!" but I appreciated the enthusiasm nonetheless. I toweled my hair, pulled on jeans and a T-shirt, and brewed a pot of coffee. Kennie wouldn't pay us until the end of the week, which meant I was dining on a can of garbanzo beans for breakfast. Maybe Ron could give me an advance against the new column. I had only two more clubs to visit, after all: a cooking class tomorrow night and yoga Friday, the same night Johnny would be returning from Wisconsin.

I glanced at the clock. I still had a funeral to attend this morning. Thoughts of Rita's death sobered my mood. I hoped there would be a good turnout.

I had two hours before I needed to head to the church, which gave me enough time to eat breakfast, play with Luna and Tiger Pop, finish planting seedlings in the greenhouse, and fantasize about a life with Johnny.

I hummed as I danced through my chores, dreaming about how nice it would be to share them. I loved cooking for other people, making a home. I could choose that life. Screw that—I would *fight* for that life. I was smiling again as I pulled on my jacket. Neither Tiger Pop nor Luna wanted to head to the greenhouse with me, so I crunched through the snow alone.

The thermometer nailed to the post outside the shed informed me that the temperature was currently ten degrees above zero. Brrr. It was a steamy fifty-five degrees inside the greenhouse, though—not tropical but enough to keep seedlings alive. I began to fill the tiny peat pots with soil, lining them up in plastic trays, enjoying the smell of earth and the delicious memories of what Johnny and I'd done on this very floor. Once I'd filled all the pots, I poked a seed into the center of each, using my pointer finger to sink it halfway down before soaking them all with water from my watering can.

Besides my usual vegetables, I would grow an army of sunflowers to remind me to choose joy and four varieties of marigolds to keep away pests. I'd plant them like an army around my garden's perimeter. I'd been saving eggshells all winter long, and those would go into the ground as well, to add nutrients as well as to repel slugs. My stomach and chest felt safe and warm at the thought of the bounty I'd create.

Once I finished, I stood back to survey my work. The pots were so neat, so organized, each of them holding the potential for a meal. My stomach grumbled at the thought of fresh tomatoes, sun-warmed, their juice running down my chin. I patted the nearest tomato pot and whispered, "You're my favorite."

I brushed extra dirt off the counter and reached for my grandma's old shears next to the barrel, where I'd left them when Johnny had surprised me. I grew warm all over again at the memory. The sensation of his hands on my body was so intense that when the door of the shed creaked open behind me, a hopeful part of me thought it might even be him.

I spun, the shears still in my hands.

"Don't kill me!" the intruder yelped.

Chapter 29

"Little D! What are you doing here?"

He kept his hands raised like an outlaw in an old Western. He still wore the army-green jacket, the name patch ripped off. Likely a Goodwill purchase, which was what his oversize blue jeans and scuffed, too-large tennis shoes appeared to be as well. "Trying to survive."

He pointed at the rusty implement I had pointed at his chest. "What is that thing?"

I leaned over to hang the shears on their hook, using the movement to calm myself. My heart was still hammering. "Something to prune rosebushes, mostly. Why are you here?"

He shoved his hands into his pants pockets, which were hung ridiculously low on his waist. "Thought I'd stop by to check in on my offer to work for you."

I squinted at him. Not much to see. He was a skinny kid. I stepped past him and looked outdoors. "How'd you get here?" I lived three miles outside of town.

He held up his thumb and then mimed walking. "A little of this, a little of that."

My eyes widened. "You don't have mittens?"

He shoved his hands back into his pockets. "Don't need 'em."

"That's true," I said. "At least, if you're trying to look like the stupidest person in Minnesota. Spring is wicked. Come on."

He followed me toward the house.

"Be careful of my dog," I called over my shoulder. "She doesn't like everyone."

But Luna sure liked Little D. She turned herself inside out trying to get close to him, licking his face and twining around his legs like I'd never seen her do before.

"Have you two met?"

He knelt down so he could pet her everywhere at once. When he giggled, his fake bravado fell away, revealing a sweet boy who was hard not to laugh along with.

"No, but I love dogs!" He caught sight of Tiger Pop and his whole face lit up. "And you have a cat? You're so lucky!"

I was about to warn him against petting my aloof kitty—she'd as soon spit on you as run away, and I meant that literally—but she leaned into his outstretched hand.

"What the *what*?" I eyed him suspiciously. "You sure you haven't been bribing my animals?"

"Promise!" He pressed three fingers to his brow, Boy Scout–style, and Tiger Pop swatted at his hand affectionately while Luna sprawled across his legs, starting off a whole new round of infectious giggling. My chuckles grew and then, in a sudden 180, morphed into tears. When Little D laughed like that, he could have been Jed's tiny twin for the pure, innocent joy.

I ducked into my bedroom so he couldn't witness my breakdown. I hadn't been able to save Jed, but maybe I could do something for Little D. I composed myself and returned to the living room, where Tiger Pop was curled into Little D's cross-legged lap while he scratched the sweet spot behind Luna's ears.

"I don't need a junior detective," I said, "but I could sure use a petsitter. Luna and Tiger Pop get lonely out here, which is the only explanation for why they're behaving like this. How about you stop by on Saturdays and the afternoons I work at the library? I'll pay you five bucks an hour to sit, as long as you OK it with your foster family and promise no more hitchhiking. I have an old bike in the barn you can borrow."

"That'd be great!" he said, his face bright.

Was it ethical that I'd be paying a kid with phone sex money? That thought was hard to hold, which, come to think of it, was a line I could use next time I worked the phone lines.

Likely I should have been more worried about Little D robbing me blind while he was here, but what the heck. We all deserved a second chance, if not more.

"You can start today. I have a funeral to go to, then I'm bringing a friend to the doctor."

The Battle Lake Lutheran church smelled like lilies, a smell that would forever turn my stomach because of the number of funerals I'd attended in the last year. It was also stuffed to the rafters. The whole town had shown up, it seemed. They couldn't all have known Rita, who hadn't lived here long and had flown under the radar when she did. They must've been supporting Doris, who sat in the first pew near the pulpit, her face gray and soft. I waited in line to hug her. It was peculiar to see her outside the Turtle Stew, like spotting a turtle without its shell. Of course she was heartbroken. She was at her sister's funeral.

Just as I was hugging her, murmuring the nothing words that you say at funerals, I was jostled from behind. I turned to see Donald, alone, wearing an immaculate suit under his black wool winter jacket.

"What do you want?" I asked. He'd budged in front of seven other people, and the service was about to start.

He stared down his weak nose at me. "Not you," he said. "I'm here to share my condolences."

The line behind him was grumbling. I wondered if I should punch him before or after church. "You knew Rita?"

Donald stepped closer to Doris and held out his hand. When Doris met the gesture, he flipped her hand to kiss the back like a courtier. "Donald Maroon," he said to her, ignoring me. "I worked with your sister at the Senior Sunset. Lovely woman. So sorry for your loss."

My eyes narrowed. On the one hand, Donald had just confirmed his connection to the victim. On the other, why in the world would he come to her funeral? They hadn't known each other for long. Had they? Frustration at what I didn't know burned inside me.

Doris smiled wanly. "Thank you."

Donald tipped his head formally, stopping just short of clicking his heels together. Then he dropped Doris's hand and left the church through a side door.

Huh. He wasn't even going to stay for the service. Doris was already getting a hug from the next person in line. She didn't seem to know Donald, or care that he had come or gone.

Strangeness.

There was no more time to process it, though, as the ushers led people to their seats. I was grateful to spot Mrs. Berns in the middle of the church. I slid in next to her. If I craned my neck, I could spot Eustace in back, head dipped, an open spot on each side of him despite the standing-room-only crowd. My heart went out to a fellow town pariah. While Battle Lake had accepted me to a certain degree—though I would forever be "not from around here"—my hometown had not. At least, that's how it had felt. Eustace had drawn the same short straw. I made a note to chat with him on my way out.

The normal pastor was on vacation, so a visiting minister performed a passable service. He stood near the casket, a large photo of Rita on an easel nearby. If I squinted, I could make out a bit of Doris in her features, though Rita's hairstyle had been more modern, her nose smaller. While the pastor spoke about God's plans and eagles' wings, my mind wandered to dark places. It still didn't make sense that Rita hadn't been working at the Turtle Stew. If I was reading Doris right, she was absolutely devastated at the loss of her sister. There had been real love there.

If the Stew was struggling and Rita and Doris were co-owners, both of them should have been working to stretch their budget.

A thought weaseled past my social filter. What if Doris was genius-level faking her affection for Rita and they actually had hated each other, and Doris had taken out a life insurance policy on her sister and then murdered her to save the restaurant? I dismissed the possibility before it stank up my brain. I'd been in this business too long. Doris wasn't faking anything. Her sister was dead, and she missed her. She was also now full owner of the Turtle Stew.

I felt a stink eye burning up the right rear side of my neck. I intentionally dropped my program and reached for it so I could shoot a glance in that direction. I found myself locked in Gary Wohnt's visual tractor beam.

He must have entered the church after me. He wore a navy-blue suit, his thick black hair impeccable. I snapped my attention back toward the pulpit, my blood pulsing uncomfortably. Gary hadn't looked away, hadn't even tried to pretend he wasn't staring at me, and his glance had not been happy. That wasn't unusual, at least not when he was looking at me, but his displeasure today appeared particularly sharp.

I decided to tell him about the argument I'd overheard between Christie and Donald. I was not in the habit of passing on gossip, particularly to Gary Wohnt, but it would be a good-faith effort at demonstrating that I had zero plans of getting involved in this investigation. Christie suspected Donald had been having an affair with someone who worked at the Senior Sunset. If he'd been sleeping with Rita, that was useful information. Plus, I didn't like Donald, so putting him in Gary's line of sight was a double-dip type of situation. It got me off the hook and cast suspicion Donald's way.

I stood as the pallbearers carried out the casket, the pastor and Doris behind them. Eustace did the same, but rather than watch his lover's body pass by, he took the opportunity to slip out the side door. I wasn't the only one watching him go. Ida, who I hadn't noticed before in the rear of the church, watched Eustace with a quizzical expression.

I leaned over to Mrs. Berns. "Does Ida know Eustace?"

Mrs. Berns yanked her eyes off the passing procession and glanced where I was looking, but she was too short to see through the crowd. "Highly doubtful."

That's what I thought. For the second time that week, I wondered if Ida was in her right mind.

Chapter 30

Maybe Eustace had reminded Ida of someone, and that's why she'd given him that intense look. In any case, I wouldn't get to talk to him at the service now that he'd ducked out. I supposed it was fine, as Mrs. Berns's doctor had only a small window of time she could check her over. We had to skip out on the church-basement meal immediately following the service, which was a sacrifice for both of us, as this church always put out the best bars.

We bundled up and headed outside, electing to walk the eleven blocks to Dr. Gunderson's office rather than warming up the car for the short drive. The temperature today promised to reach the high forties, which meant we'd likely see people wearing shorts. The impending warmth had the birds singing and the tree buds humming with potential.

We were both fully dusted with the fresh smell of spring when we strolled into Dr. Gunderson's office. I didn't know her personally, but she'd been Mrs. Berns's physician for two decades, and she had Sunday office hours, limited though they were.

"Mrs. Berns!" The receptionist's face lit up when we walked in. "How are you doing?"

"You tell me," Mrs. Berns said agreeably before taking the waiting room chair nearest the coffee machine.

"The doctor will see you in a couple minutes." The receptionist turned her smile toward me. "Mira, can I get you anything?"

"Have we met?" She was round and bubbly, wearing those kid-friendly scrubs that were covered in cute designs. I didn't recognize her.

"I met you at one of Johnny Leeson's shows about six months ago. You probably don't remember me."

I didn't, but the mention of his name made me flush. "You're good with names."

The receptionist dropped her eyes, her smile growing shy. "My husband tells me that's the only thing I'm good at." Her glance flew back up, her smile growing. In a small town, she would be accustomed to garnering laughter for that Archie Bunker–era line.

"He sounds like an asshole," Mrs. Berns said, not glancing up from her magazine.

Have I mentioned that I wanted to be Mrs. Berns someday? Not be like her, but actually *be her*?

The receptionist swallowed loudly without closing her mouth. She appeared to be considering her husband's comment from a new angle. I took the seat next to Mrs. Berns.

The receptionist was still running through a mental checklist when a patient came out from one of the back exam rooms. He had a cotton ball bandaged over the interior crook of his right arm.

He grinned at the receptionist. "I have Lyme disease!"

I took him in from tip to toe. He was definitely the kind of guy who looked like he'd had a few tick bites. His salt-and-pepper hair was feathered in a way that would have been popular when he was a teenager, and his lined face suggested a lifelong outdoorsman, probably hunter and fisher. He wore a camo T-shirt over off-brand jeans and steel-toed boots.

"Why the hell are people so proud when their tests come back positive?" Mrs. Berns muttered. "Any idiot can catch Lyme, or strep, or the flu if they try hard enough. It's more difficult to fall out of a boat."

She had a point. I touched her magazine. "What're you reading?"

She showed me the front cover of the women's magazine she'd been paging through. It featured a Photoshopped actress and big letters urging me to uncover what my man wanted in bed after I was done dieting.

"There's a quiz in here we can take," she said. "It'll tell us what our 'type' is."

I shook my head. "Our dating type, you mean? I don't have one." I'd dated all sizes and shapes and shades of men. I couldn't think of a universal running through all of them.

"Sure you do. Your type is needy guys. Just look at Johnny."

I sucked in a breath. "What? Johnny is perfect."

She pursed her lips. "I believe this magazine would refer to him as codependent. The guy puts up with all sorts of bullshit from you, with you running hot and cold every other week. He yearns to feel wanted, and like he has someone to take care of. You do that for him." She made a disgusted noise. "Wipe that smile off your face. That's not a good thing. You need a man who can stand on his own, and who's firm with you. Until Johnny can be that man, you two can't make it work, and that's a guarantee."

"Mrs. Berns, Dr. Gunderson is ready to see you."

Mrs. Berns stood, handing me the magazine. "There's an article in here about playing games when you're in love. You should check it out."

I stuck out my tongue at her retreating back. I knew relationship games were stupid, but that wasn't what I had been doing with Johnny. Was it? I tried to contain the oily feeling spreading through my gut. No, of course not. I'd been trying to protect him, was all. I now realized that had been a mistake, and if I thought too much about how horrible of a mistake it'd been, the panic would bury me. So I kept my mind positive.

I should have treated Johnny like an equal and let him make up his own mind. A healthy relationship required total honesty, and I would bring that to the table as soon as he returned from Wisconsin. He hadn't called, which I'd hoped he would after receiving the flowers, but that was OK. He was for sure busy. And hey, him not calling was as good as proof that he wasn't codependent, which was what I wanted. Someone who was independent. Strong. Healthy. Right?

I opened the magazine to an article about Morgellons. I'd never heard of the disorder and, as I read, wished I still hadn't. It was a mystery illness, and the medical community was undecided whether it was a figment of the sufferer's imagination or a real thing. The symptoms involved weird bruising and itching and, sometimes, red and blue fibers pushing themselves out of the person's skin. Sheesh. I needed to schedule some time to worry about that.

The article's ending jumped to the end of the magazine. I paged to it. It was crammed next to a nearly full-page article for a prescription medication.

I had a thought.

"Excuse me?" I asked the receptionist.

She hadn't moved since we'd entered the waiting room. "My husband is an asshole!"

Oh no. "Mrs. Berns was joking. She likes to shake up people. Kind of a hobby of hers."

"But she was right." Her cheeks were shiny, her expression pained. "My husband puts me down all the time in front of people, and everyone laughs and so I laugh, too. But I don't like it, not at all. I make good money. I'm smart."

I stared longingly at the door Mrs. Berns had disappeared through. She needed to be out here to deal with the aftermath of her remark. "You do seem smart."

"I am! I'm going to go see my husband right now and give him a piece of my mind."

I wanted to tell her that that would make her objectively less smart, but it was a lame joke.

"Before you do that, can I ask you something?" The pharmaceutical ad had triggered a recollection—the first time I'd seen Eustace, getting a prescription filled at the pharmacy. "It's about a medication, but I can't remember its exact name. It sounds like a bone, I think."

I blushed, because I had first guessed it was boner medicine, and that assumption might turn out to be right. "Femur something, like femurnib, maybe?"

"Vemurafenib?" she asked as she shut down her computer and reached for a jacket. She was actually going to go home and confront her husband. "It's a cancer medication."

I blanched as three thoughts fought for primacy in my brain: the receptionist had been right about her intelligence, and Mrs. Berns had been right about the woman's husband. Also, Rita had died of an overdose of cancer medication.

The third thought won, aided by the unexpected view of a Battle Lake cruiser traveling past the front of the clinic, a nattily dressed Gary Wohnt behind the wheel and Eustace Dickens slumped in the back seat behind the cage.

Chapter 31

"I don't care about a fight between a husband and a wife."

If I uttered the word "but" one more time, I was going to turn into one. As soon as Mrs. Berns had gotten the all-clear from Dr. Gunderson, who prescribed more water and sleep, we'd charged over to the cop shop to see why Gary had taken Eustace into custody.

Gary was not forthcoming.

"You *should* care," I said. "Donald is a lowlife; you can bank on it. Their fight might have some bearing on Rita's death. Eustace had nothing to do with it, by the way."

Gary's eyes were as black and sticky as tar. "How do you know that?"

I didn't. I knew that Eustace looked like he was about to lose his grip, though. For a man living off the grid since the Vietnam War, being imprisoned must've been a special kind of torture. He was rocking in a corner, his lips moving but no sound coming out. He had refused to look at me or respond to my asking if he was OK. Mrs. Berns was over by him, murmuring into his cell, but she wasn't having any more luck than I had.

"Look, I don't *know* anything. I have a hunch Eustace isn't involved, is all. He loved Rita. He wouldn't have hurt her."

And I don't know if he'll survive a night in jail.

Gary was standing nose to nose with me before I'd even registered his movement. "If you have something to tell me, I'm all ears. Otherwise, get out of my building."

I drew back. His anger was a blistering wave. "What have I done wrong?"

He eased back, rubbing both hands over his face. "Get out."

I sputtered. I didn't want to follow his command, but I also didn't have anything more to say. Either Gary had pulled Eustace in for questioning and was required to let him go in twenty-four hours if he couldn't press charges, or he had something on Eustace, and my instincts about the guy had been all wrong.

"Come on, Mrs. Berns."

She whispered something else to Eustace and then met me at the door.

"Gary," she said on the way out, "I got my nails done. What do you think?"

He looked. She held up both her middle fingers. His nostrils flared.

I tugged Mrs. Berns outside before he did anything more. "What'd you say to Eustace?"

Mrs. Berns glanced at her watch. "I told him that his body might be locked up, but that his mind was free, and that it should travel into the woods until you and I could spring him."

"Spring him?"

"He's no murderer."

I knew why I believed that. I didn't know why she did. I had the distinct impression that there was a whole lot more to this story than I knew. "Tell me again how you know Eustace?"

"There's no 'again.' I never told you in the first place." Her mouth was tight.

I didn't respond. We walked in silence toward my car. She finally spoke.

"You know I was married."

I nodded.

"And that my late husband died about ten years ago, and up until that point, I was primarily a farmwife."

"Right." All this had happened before I'd moved to Battle Lake, but her transformation after her husband's death was the stuff of legend.

"Has it ever struck you as odd that a woman like me could be a submissive housewife for the better part of a half century?"

Come to think of it, it had.

"Eustace Dickens is the only person alive who knows why."

It took a moment for the enormity of that statement to sink in. Mrs. Berns collected herself while it did. When she finally spoke again, her voice was deep.

"My husband was a farmer—that much of my story is true. Pretty much everything else I've told you and others about him isn't, though. He was the kind who took his displeasure out on his animals and his wife. Eustace worked odd jobs for him after the war, milking cows for cash, cleaning out the barns in trade for cheese, that sort of thing. One day he saw Xavier smack me. It was over something stupid, always was. I was outside hanging clothes on the line. Maybe I hadn't gotten a stain out of his favorite shirt. In any case, it had happened a hundred times before, the hitting, so much that I had come to expect it."

I'd stopped walking. I found myself trembling, my eyes hot.

Mrs. Berns turned to me. "Eustace Dickens put an end to it right then and there. Xavier wasn't a big man, but he was bigger than Eustace. Still, Eustace beat him to just this side of consciousness and said if he ever saw Xavier hit me again, he'd make sure he never woke up. Xavier didn't hire Eustace any more after that." She drew in a breath. "He didn't hit me again, either."

I wrapped her in my arms. She was stiff and unyielding.

"You want to know why I didn't leave after that, don't you? Why I stayed with Xavier for another ten years?"

I squeezed her even tighter. I didn't care why she hadn't left. I was happy she was here to hug. She wanted to tell me, though. "Why didn't you leave after that?"

She finally melted into my arms. "Damn if I know."

"I love you," I whispered.

"You got that right," she said, pushing away from me. Hug done. Her made-up eyes were fierce, her drawn-on eyebrows accenting her warrior anger. "So you understand that we have to find out who killed Rita Theisen so I can pay off my debt to Eustace."

"OK." Her confession had left me emotional.

"Just like that?" She studied me suspiciously. "You're not gonna put up a fight, tell me you don't want to get involved and blah de blah?"

"Nope." I was drained. The only action that offered relief was to do right by the man who'd saved Mrs. Berns.

"All right then," she said, nodding. "Where do we start?"

The Turtle Stew was across the street. "How about you go in there and ask around about Rita? I'll go grab the car, and after we interview people at the Stew, we'll drive out to Eustace's place and see if there's anything there that we can use to exonerate him."

She clapped her hands. "Now we're cooking with Crisco!"

She was almost skipping as she hurried across the street. Watching her put a sad smile onto my face. I guessed we were back in business. The melancholy smile stayed there until I reached the library parking lot, where the church's overflow parking ended up on Sundays since the library was closed.

Seeing Donald sitting in my car erased my faint grin, though.

I recognized his white shock of hair; his rich man's clothes, the same ones he'd had on in church two short hours earlier; the pompous way he sat there, his hands on the wheel of my beloved Toyota. What the hell was he doing in my car? If he thought he had any chance of weaseling his way into my pants because he and his wife were contributing to the library, then his thinker was messed up, particularly considering how rude he'd been at Rita's funeral.

My rage grew as I jogged toward my Toyota in the otherwise empty lot. My blood was pumping purple. I reached the driver's side door and yanked it open.

"I don't know what the sweet hell you think—" I choked on my own words as Donald's body toppled toward me, my grandma's rusty garden shears protruding at an angle just below his rib cage.

Chapter 32

The handcuffs were overkill. Plus, they hurt.

"OK, I get it," I told Gary Wohnt. "You're serious. You don't want me to get involved in the investigation into who killed Donald and stuffed his body into my car. I won't. I promise."

Gary began reciting my rights by way of response. He was a hard man to read under the best of circumstances, but he'd been downright monolithic since he'd arrived on the scene in response to the terrified 911 call I had made from the library's phone.

My mouth went dry and the world swayed. "You're seriously arresting me? For what?"

He pointed at the corpse and finished the Miranda warning, which was a funny name, I thought, somewhat hysterically. *Miranda getting her Miranda rights read to her in Battle Lake, Minnesota.* A small throng had gathered, but they were keeping their distance as a polite Minnesotan response to deviance. *Stare, don't crowd.*

The far-off wail of the ambulance Gary had called cut through the spring air.

"You can't possibly believe I murdered this man." My nose itched, but my hands were cuffed behind my back. "I was standing in front of you at the police station fifteen minutes ago!"

He led me to the rear of the police car, grasping the back of my neck with his hot hand and ducking my head so I didn't bump it as he shoved me in. His skin was rough against my icy flesh. I jammed my knee going in and bit my lip so I wouldn't cry.

This couldn't be happening.

I closed my eyes and tried breathing through my nose to keep from hyperventilating. It wasn't working. Donald's corpse had splayed onto the pavement when it hit the ground, which meant he hadn't been dead long enough for rigor mortis to set in.

Wait. I knew exactly the ballpark in which he'd been murdered because I had held those shears myself not four hours earlier. My heart froze. Little D had seen me with my grandma's rusty garden tool, too. Had he gone back to the house to steal the weapon and murder Donald with it? If so, what in the world was his motive? More importantly, how could he have pulled it off? He was small for his age, and it must have taken some force to wedge those blades under the rib cage and into the heart of an adult man.

I swallowed the bile rising in my throat.

One of the Battle Lake deputies arrived, finally, followed shortly by the ambulance. Mrs. Berns appeared on the scene and tried to fight her way to the police car where I was being held, but the deputy kept her back. After he'd handed off the scene, Gary slid in behind the wheel and put the car into drive. I could smell his cologne again.

"Gary." When had I started crying? "I don't want to go to jail. I didn't kill that man."

It was all a mistake, I knew it. It would be cleared up in moments.

"That's the man you told me to question in Rita's murder?"

I squeezed my eyes shut. "Yes," I whispered.

"You didn't seem to care for him very much."

No, I sure hadn't.

"Is there anything else you want to tell me?"

Tears were stinging my eyes, making it impossible to see. The bump of the car informed me that we'd pulled into the police station's parking lot. I felt like throwing up. I couldn't think of any words to defend myself, nothing that would help. For the first time since we'd met, I wasn't hiding a thing from Gary, but it didn't change anything.

He helped me out of the car more gently than he'd stuck me in, then led me to a jail cell on the opposite side of the station from Eustace's. He undid my cuffs before sliding the door shut behind me. I fell onto a cot, the only furnishing in the cramped space other than a sink and toilet, and rubbed at my sore wrists, my head between my knees. My brain offered only sheets of gray.

That's the position I was in when Mrs. Berns and Kennie stormed into the station. I couldn't see them, but boy could I hear them.

"Are you serious, Gary?" It was Kennie speaking. Yelling, actually. "You know she has nothing to do with any of this."

"A murdered man was found in her car. She identified the murder weapon as belonging to her. What was I supposed to do, Mayor Rogers? Let her go?"

Mayor Rogers. He was being very formal.

"Yes, Chief Dumbshit." This was Mrs. Berns. "You were supposed to let her go. She's been with me in church or you in this very room for the past three hours. I poked that dead body back in the library parking lot, and it had a lot of give."

Oh dear.

"So I'm her alibi, as is most of Battle Lake."

The gray slate of my mind gave way to firmer thoughts. It was true that most of Battle Lake had attended and stayed for all of the funeral, Eustace, Ida, and Doris included. If Donald's murder was in any way connected to Rita's, that meant those three were most likely clean.

"We'll have to let the ME examine the body before we have a time of death, Mrs. Berns." Gary's voice was surprisingly calm, but not a peaceful calm. It was more of a quiet-before-the-storm-that-rips-off-your-face kind of calm. "And we can't rule out accomplices."

Mrs. Berns and Kennie argued and cajoled for another ten minutes. They would have kept it up all afternoon, I think, if Gary hadn't offered to arrest them, too, if they didn't get the hell out of his way. Mrs. Berns hollered in my direction that she'd take care of Tiger Pop and Luna before I heard the police station door open and shut and smelled the fresh waft of air signaling that they had left.

I sat up. Had Gary gone with them? A clang of a cell opening on the other side of the building informed me that he was still inside and opening one of the two lockups on the other side. I hoped he was releasing Eustace. If he was, that meant he'd either been using the man as some kind of bait or realized he had no reason to keep him.

My mind ping-ponged to a more personal concern. Oh god, what would Johnny think of this? I certainly could not propose to him if I was in jail. I had to get out of there, and fast. I shouldn't be in custody for more than twenty-four hours, right? Sure, I'd confessed to Gary that I didn't like Donald, and then I found the man murdered in my car with my rusty garden shears sprouting from his chest, and I'd been the one who discovered Rita's body in the doll, and I'd been connected to, oh, ten or so other corpses in the past ten months. But besides that, he had no reason to hold me, right?

My head dropped into my hands, and I groaned.

I was sunk. I might as well pick up a useful prison trade, like tattooing or cigarette smuggling.

I felt a tickle on the back of my hand and lifted my head. A spider! I squealed and brushed it off. Spiders were the devil's spawn. In hell they dressed as clowns. It turned out that, when in jail, you should never ask yourself how things could get any worse, because all of a sudden, I felt like I was crawling with them. I rubbed my arms and hands, shaking myself. I tried to search everywhere at once. I couldn't find any more, despite the creepy willies tickling my body.

I needed to calm the hell down.

I lay on the bed and closed my eyes. I would get out of here, and soon. I was no murderer. Once I was released, I'd find the real killer before Johnny returned. Then I'd sweep Mr. Leeson off his feet, carry him away to a tropical paradise with water the color of a blue slushie, and we'd dig our toes in the white sand as we held hands and skipped.

I felt myself relax slightly. And then slightly more. Panic gave way to exhaustion as heavy as gravedigger's dirt. I slipped into an uneasy sleep, where I dreamed of a giant cat licking my face. Its tongue was scratchy, its fur soft. I liked it. I reached out to pet the kitty, and it jumped away.

I followed, but the kitty ran.

So I ran after it, moving so fast that I knocked a pan off the counter. It fell to the floor with a clank, loud enough to wake me up.

I blinked into the dark. Where was I?

Jail.

The realization was suffocating. How much time had passed? I listened. The cop shop sounded empty. It was definitely after hours. What had woken me?

"Psst."

Chapter 33

My intestines clenched. I sat up slowly, disoriented, underwater, alarmed. I didn't know people actually said "psst." Had I imagined it?

"Hello?" I said tentatively.

"Mira?"

"Mrs. Berns?"

"Don't forget Kennie Rogers," came a southern purr from the darkness on the other side of my cell door. "We're busting you out of this pop stand."

My eyes were beginning to adjust. I could make out their forms. Still, I felt like I was floating, endless space above, bottomless black below, me a softly twirling balloon between. How on earth had I slept the day away? I was the fainting goat of humans. "You're breaking me out of jail?"

I heard the clean metal *slick* of a key sliding into a lock. "Sort of," Kennie said. A tumbler fell into place. "As the mayor of Battle Lake, I'm the head constable to which all others report."

"Constable?" I couldn't track what was happening to save my soul.

"It's an 1887 city ordinance," Mrs. Berns chimed in. "All they had back then were constables. Nobody has used the law since then, so there's been no reason to update it. I think that will change after tonight."

The jail cell door squeaked as it opened. "It's true," Kennie said. "I was hoping to save this nugget for a conjugal visit, but nobody I've wanted to sleep with has been locked up here, so I guess I'm cashing it in on you, Mira James."

The reality of what was happening outside the cell finally synced with what was happening in my head. Mrs. Berns and Kennie were springing me from the clink. That was the definition of true friendship. It was also as stupid as dirt. "I can't be on the run!"

Mrs. Berns was first in the cell. She patted my cheek. "Prison has changed you."

"I'm serious. As of right now, I haven't committed any crimes. If I walk out of here, that all changes."

"Haven't you been listening?" Kennie helped me up off the bed. "Since you haven't been formally charged with anything, you can only be held for questioning for a limited period of time. Did you kill Donald?"

"No!"

"There. Questioning done. As head constable, I declare you free on your own recognizance. No harm, no foul. Now go find the real killer, and quick. I estimate you have twenty-four hours to figure out who iced Rita and Donald, less if you manage to tangle with Gary again."

My brain stopped spinning and focused. Where would I start?

Kennie slipped something black and cool into my hand. "It's a burner phone, untraceable. You can use it for research, and to keep me and Mrs. Berns updated."

The phone vibrated in my hand, a tiny electronic fart.

"And to make two bucks a minute," Mrs. Berns said, chortling. "It's one of the Minnesota sex phones."

Kennie pushed me toward the cell door. "A woman has to be business savvy and money wise in this world. No shame in working two jobs at once."

I let them shuffle me toward the station's main room, which was dimly lit by recessed lights. We held our hands out to avoid bumping into desks. "Is Eustace free?"

"Yep," Mrs. Berns said. The smile was clear in her voice, even in the murky dark. "Gary must think the same person killed Rita and Donald. That, or he didn't have anything to hold him on."

That was a relief, not only for Eustace's sake but also because that meant I could talk to him at his home rather than in his cell, which would have been impossible given my current almost-status as a jail breaker. As soon as I stepped outside of the front door and into the inky ice of a March night, there was no going back.

I created a mental checklist.

I needed to speak with Eustace, Ida, Doris, and Christie, plus get to a computer so I could access my database and research all four more deeply than I had earlier in the week, back when I was only curious and it wasn't my ass on the line.

"What time is it?" I asked.

Kennie answered. "A little after three in the morning."

"I wanted to break you free at midnight. Thought it'd be a nice touch when they wrote a country song about tonight's escapades," Mrs. Berns said. "But Kennie said we best wait until after bar close in case they needed to bring someone in." She began to hum "The Gambler" while Kennie peeked out the front door of the police station.

I didn't have long enough until dawn for my liking. I needed to hole up somewhere until I could interview everyone. Not my place, Mrs. Berns's, Kennie's, or Johnny's. Those were the first spots Gary would search once he realized I was gone. Too bad Kennie and Mrs. Berns hadn't brought one of Ida's dolls to put in my cell bed. It might have bought me a few more hours.

Ida. The nursing home. *That's* where I could hide out. Gary wouldn't look for me there, and no one inside would know I was on the run.

When Kennie gave me the OK, I stepped into the crisp-apple air, my cheeks stinging from the cold.

I had to be the first person in history who'd broken out of jail to enter a nursing home.

Chapter 34

I reached the Battle Lake Senior Sunset at 4:07 a.m. A sleepy front desk worker buzzed me in and blinked once, long and slow, when I told him I was the new CNA.

After he processed my words, he pointed at the clipboard in front of him. "Sign here. Next time, come in through the back entrance."

"You got it. Sorry." I signed illegibly and scurried through the pneumatic entrance leading to the residents' rooms. I stopped at Ida's first and found her sitting in front of her window, hair swept up in an immaculate, swirling bun, hands busily knitting.

"Mira!" Her face lit up. "What are you doing up so early?"

"What are *you* doing up?"

"We all wake up before the sun here at the home, at least those of us who can. It's the curse of growing old that you are more awake at the same point in your life when there's less to do."

She seemed a little sad. It could have been the hour, or my sleep fuzziness.

I closed her door behind me. "Can I talk to you about Rita a little bit?"

She patted her hair. "Of course, honey, but I don't know that I have anything new to add."

"You might now. Did you hear that Donald Maroon was murdered?"

Her eyes grew wide. "That's horrible. Who is Donald Maroon?"

"That new volunteer? The rich one from the Cities? A thick head of clownish hair and a mouth shaped like a cat's behind? His wife was assigned to the library, and he was working here."

She tapped her chin, searching her memory. I recognized it when it landed. "The one who was hitting on Rita! Of course. I saw her brush him off more times than I care to count. She definitely did not like him. It makes sense, if she was dating Eustace. Although I don't think a single woman would like the way he was grabbing at her any more than a committed one."

I clutched the footboard of her bed to steady myself. I struggled to keep my voice level. "When we spoke earlier, you mentioned that you'd never seen Rita before."

She returned to her knitting, a dreamy smile on her face. "Did I? That's another of the gifts of growing old. You don't remember as much as you used to."

That could've been. Or she could have been hiding something and passing it off as memory loss. I shook my head, not wanting the morbid, mistrustful thoughts to creep in. I knew Ida. She was sweet, and honest, and definitely not a murderer or even an accomplice to murder. Dealing with so much death had made me suspicious. I needed to stick to my instincts. "Do you know Doris?"

"Owner of the Turtle Stew?" Her needles clacked as she knitted without looking up. Her pink scalp shone through her white hair. "I do, though not well."

"Did you know that Rita and Doris co-owned the Turtle Stew?"

She nodded pleasantly. "I knew that the previous owners passed it on to their daughters, and of course I knew that one of the daughters was Doris because she's been working there every single time I've stopped in. It stood to reason that her sister, Rita, was the other co-owner."

I perched on the edge of Ida's bed, the only other option besides the chair she currently occupied. "Any idea why Rita worked here rather than the Stew?" It was a long shot that Ida would know anything about that, but I was on the lam. I couldn't afford to leave any stone unturned.

Ida's shoulder twitched. Her eyes lifted toward me and then dropped. "I don't like to gossip."

I stood up again. "This isn't gossip. It's an investigation." Sort of.

She pressed her lips together. "All I know is that there was some talk of a fight over a man a long, long time ago that split the sisters apart. Some of the hens were cackling about it at the funeral buffet. It would be a shame if it were true, to lose time with family over something temporary, don't you think?"

I did.

It wouldn't have surprised me if it were factual, though. Love made people foolish. I didn't know if a fight about a guy years ago had any bearing on what was happening now, but it was worth adding to my list of threads to follow.

I opened my mouth to ask if she still planned on making a doll for Kennie but noticed she was nodding off in the middle of her knitting. Another perk of old age? I reached for the afghan at the foot of her bed and was moving to wrap it around her when a terrified scream echoed down the halls.

Chapter 35

I charged out of Ida's room, following the sounds of commotion. An intern and two nurses had gathered outside Abraham's room, scuffling and grunting, their crepe-soled shoes squeaking on the institutional floor. They were trying to restrain someone. I soon realized who.

"Little D! What are you doing here?"

One of the nurses stepped back, her hand diving into the pocket of her blue scrubs and coming out with a phone. "You know this kid?"

His face appeared smudged, like he'd been crying.

"I do. What's going on?"

She jerked her thumb over her shoulder, toward Abraham's peaceful form. "Caught him trying to strangle Abraham."

The world lurched underneath me. I grabbed the wall, feeling green from head to toes. Little D had been the last one to see me with the shears before they ended up in Donald Maroon's gut. Now he'd been caught trying to murder Abraham. I didn't see how he could have possibly lugged Rita's corpse onto the stool in the Turtle Stew, but what did I know? He might've been a true psychopath, or working for one.

"What are you doing here?" I demanded.

He refused to look me in the eye. I didn't have the stomach to push it. I didn't want to see the guilt written there.

"Make sure someone keeps an eye on Abraham's room," I said to the nurse. "The kid might have an accomplice."

I felt his eyes burn on me then. I would never know if they raged with betrayal, or insanity, or a plea for help because I turned and walked away. I had a million questions, but I wasn't going to do him any good if we were both behind bars. If he was involved in all this, I had to find out how so I could help him, and I had to be free to do that.

I needed to interview Doris at the Turtle Stew.

And I would most certainly need a disguise to pull off my plan.

Chapter 36

The wig itched.

Or it was the delicate, poisonous trace of a nervous breakdown working its way from the top of my spine down.

Nope, it was the wig.

It was funny, really, that I was dressed like what I most feared in this world: a human doll. I'd had nowhere to go for a disguise except Ida's room. I'd tiptoed to her closet, where I discovered a shelf full of wigs that she'd purchased and outfits she'd scavenged or sewn before her doll-crafting venture came to a screeching halt.

I grabbed a wig styled in a blonde bob, a pair of nerd-size prescription-less glasses, a FLORIDA IS FOR LOVERS sweatshirt, mom jeans, and a pair of slightly used tennies. I tugged it all on as Ida slept, straightened my wig in the full-length mirror, and decided all I needed was a minivan to drive and nobody would ever recognize me.

Still, I kept the glasses crammed tight to my face as I walked down Battle Lake's Main Street, ducking my head when the police cars raced past in the direction of the Senior Sunset. I even altered my walking rhythm, slowing my normal speed racer pace and adding a loose hip wiggle that I imagined someone who'd pushed a child through their loins would possess.

No one glanced my way twice.

I was surprised at how uncomfortable that made me. I considered myself a feminist who wanted to be recognized as a person rather than a collection of body parts, and I certainly did not want to be catcalled. Still, I'd grown used to getting a second glance here and there—more accustomed than I'd realized. Now that I was dressed like a mom, I'd become invisible. Talk about a shitty superpower.

Thanks for that one, society.

I supposed it was working in my favor. I dropped my ego outside the Turtle Stew and entered, happy that only a few tables were filled at this hour, and that Doris was back on the clock, standing behind the counter. She appeared to be training a new waitress, though I couldn't see who she was because she had her back to me.

I slid onto a stool, wondering how well my disguise worked up close. "Coffee, please."

Doris and the waitress broke apart guiltily, and I realized it wasn't a waitress at all. It was Christie Maroon, wearing a grim expression, more business than grief despite the recent loss of her husband.

"Coming right up," Doris said in my direction. She whispered something more to Christie, who nodded sharply before disappearing into the kitchen. Doris grabbed a white porcelain mug from the stack, flipped it open side up, and poured me a rich, dark cup of coffee. "Cream?"

"Yes, please." So far, so good. "How's life going?"

She slid over a serving bowl full of tiny cream tubs. "Almost fast enough."

"Doris, it's me. Mira."

She studied my face, her eyes wide. "Holy hell! I heard you got arrested."

I opened a creamer and poured the liquid into my coffee, stirring the clouds with a smooth silver spoon. "I was brought in for questioning. They didn't have anything solid to hold me on."

Her eyebrows narrowed. "Then why are you dressed like you've given up on life?"

"I take offense at that. But this isn't about me. You heard about Donald?"

She stopped herself from looking toward the door Christie had just left through. "Terrible tragedy."

I shrugged. The only misfortune that came to mind was that his fresh corpse had been tucked away in my car. "I think whoever killed him murdered Rita, too. I need to ask you some questions, but they might be touchy."

She set the coffeepot down. "Shoot."

"You and Rita both own this restaurant. Why didn't she work here?"

"We were oil and vinegar." She studied her nails. "We loved each other, of course, but we've never been able to be in the same room for long."

"I heard you two once fought over a man."

She began to straighten the condiments on the counter, fidgeting until they were all perfectly aligned. "Who told you that?"

"Small-town gossip. You know how it works."

She grabbed a washrag, set it down, and sighed, aging ten years right in front of my eyes, a gloomy dust falling into her wrinkles, dimming her. "That's old news. Thirty-three years old, to be exact. We both fell for the same guy. Rita got him."

"Who was he?"

Her eyes flickered. "No one you'd know. He moved out of town shortly after. Rita followed, but they couldn't make it work. The end."

"You're not still mad after all these years?"

She snorted. "Not even. She did me a favor. The guy ended up in Phoenix, last I heard, selling water-damaged cars to snowbirds. Rita and I kept in touch, but we were never close, before or after. When she came back to town this last time, she chased after Eustace and landed him. Good for her, I say. This restaurant is my only love."

"What would you say if I told you that Rita had been cheating on Eustace?"

Rita actually laughed, the kind from the belly, with authentic humor. "I'd say you were high. You can think a lot of bad things about Rita, and I have, but she was as loyal to her men as the day is long."

I studied her for any sign of deception and found none. She was revealing her whole hand. "Then why didn't she help you out by working here once she found out you guys were losing the Stew?"

Her eyes narrowed. I saw her gearing up to argue, and then the fight drained out of her like water from a tub. "Rita never liked the restaurant business, and so we came to an agreement we both could live with long ago. I run the place, and I send her ten percent of the profits. It worked great at first. Since then, I may have developed an interest in online gambling."

She put her elbows on the counter and dropped her head into her hands. "I asked Rita to sell me her half of the restaurant because I couldn't get a mortgage without her permission. She figured out what I needed the money for and refused. It was the kindest thing she could have done."

Doris swiped at her face. "I haven't been back online since she died, and I won't gamble again. It's a promise I made to her spirit, and I will honor it."

My heart broke for her. Their relationship had been mended, but too late. "You don't think Rita killed herself?"

Doris puffed up. "I'm positive she didn't. She never did a drug in her life, hardly touched liquor, even. She was murdered."

"Any idea who killed her?"

"None, but whoever did it better hope the law gets to them before me, because I will destroy them."

I thought of the body's placement at the counter. "Who has keys to this place?"

"Me and Burt, the morning cook." She nodded toward the kitchen. "And anyone else who knows I keep a spare key in a crack in the siding near the back door. That means a series of past waitresses and cooks, and maybe some customers who like to start the coffee extra early."

So, pretty much all of Battle Lake. I'd dead-ended. Again. *Unless.* "Do you know Little D, by chance? He's a foster kid here in town, smallish for his age, always wears an old army jacket?"

Doris closed up like a morning glory at dusk. "Seen him around, I suppose. It's a small town. I better get back to work."

"Wait, what is it?"

She shrugged, but it was forced. "He's a kid, always seems to be in trouble. What's to know?"

She grabbed the coffeepot and rushed onto the floor even though there weren't nearly enough tables to justify bustling. She clearly did not want to talk about Little D, no matter how hard I tried for the next half hour.

I prayed for better luck with Eustace. Time was running out.

Chapter 37

Doris let me borrow her car to drive out to Eustace's. The black burner phone rang two different times on the drive, but I was not in the mood for a Minnesota sexy chat. I had two murders to solve, and the main suspect was a young boy, a kid I happened to be growing fond of. Eustace, Doris, and Ida were also potential suspects, though I didn't figure any of them for it. Christie was the only one with motive to murder both victims. She could have killed Rita if she thought Donald was sleeping with her, then offed Donald for being that campfire's poker.

Could she have hired Little D to help her with her dirty work?

The more I thought about that possibility, the more sense it made. Little D had told me he was looking for work. Maybe he'd approached Christie, too, and she'd taken him up on it, getting him to help her murder her husband's alleged lover and then her husband. Though that wouldn't explain Doris's hinky reaction when I asked her about Little D, or the fact that Doris and Christie had been conferencing when I slid into the Stew. And it certainly didn't jibe with Little D trying to strangle Abraham, who wasn't connected to anyone else in this poopnado, as far as I could tell.

This was my messiest case yet.

The one person who might be able to shed light on it all, Little D, was likely by now in the one place I could not go: jail.

Blergh.

I eased Doris's car down the rutted minimum-maintenance road toward Eustace's property, not wanting to jar her shocks. I wondered what would become of my beloved Toyota. After Donald's corpse had plopped out, I'd statued there for a good two minutes. The driver's seat had been dirty brown with blood, the gamey smell of fresh death turning my stomach even now, just thinking about it. I'd run into the library to call the police. For sure my vehicle had been impounded. Probably it would need to be destroyed. I'd relied on my chariot for more than ten years, and it had served me well.

Damn Donald, dying in my ride.

Eustace's cabin broke into view, appearing exactly the same as the first time I had pulled in, minus the chimney smoke. I parked in front of his home and stepped out of the car. Today would be another warm day. It featured the unique smell of warmth wrapped in cold, the bud of spring ready to bloom.

"Hello?"

No answer. I called again, this time louder. "Hello! Eustace, you here?"

Nothing.

I walked to the window and pressed my face against the glass. Everything was in order, all furniture in place, the fireplace still. I headed to the rear of the cabin, where a bed and mattress leaned against the outer wall. They hadn't been there for long—no rust, no stains on the mattress, only the lightest of snow cover on them. I returned to the window to double-check and noticed that Eustace's single bed was still inside. Was the mattress stashed behind the cabin Rita's, propped outside after her death so that Eustace didn't have to think about her?

I made for the shed. The deer hide was still strung out front, two rabbit pelts drawn flat next to it. The knife was no longer stuck into the butcher bench. I walked over to the tractor tire and kicked at it, releasing a delicate chime of icicles. Eustace definitely wasn't on his property, and without a new snowfall, there'd be no way to tell by his tracks if he'd returned since he was released from jail. I settled for jotting down a note and tucking it into the jamb of his door.

We need to talk. I'll stop back. —Mira

I also wanted to speak with Christie but couldn't risk that move. For all I knew, she'd as soon turn me in to Gary as tell me what she knew. Until I figured out a work-around, that left only one task for me to complete, and that was to pop into my database and research. I could use the library computer if all was clear.

I texted Mrs. Berns, who should've been at the library right then:

I need a computer. Who's there?

She texted back within minutes, her message a cacophony of words and symbols:

Christie. :<> She's being hairogant again. :-|| She leaves at 4 :-O Come back then. :-*

I texted her back a quick confirmation: OK.

She responded: 0:-)

I took that to be her version of "sounds good."

I slipped into drive and pointed toward the Turtle Stew. Doris needed her car back, but then what? I was a wanted woman with nowhere to go, as aimless as a kid with pot to smoke.

That sparked a thought. When I was a teenager and wanted to hide after hours, me and my friends met up at Nordland, a country church surrounded by fields and farmhouses. It was never locked. We'd drink pinched wine in the choir rehearsal space and eat pickles out of the fridge.

I didn't need the condiments or liquor, but maybe the Battle Lake Lutheran Church could offer me sanctuary. As soon as the thought occurred to me, I realized I was exhausted. It must've been stress because I'd slept nearly twelve hours in jail already.

I parked Doris's car behind the restaurant and left the keys in the ignition like she'd asked. Then I humped it to the church.

Just like before, no one on the street glanced my way twice.

I was nothing but a blonde mom, used up and out to pasture, walking in Battle Lake.

The church was unlocked. I made straight for the upper level of pews, which were deserted this time of day. I tucked myself on the floor in the far corner, a place where I'd be impossible to spot unless a person walked over looking for me.

I folded my jacket under my head and fell immediately into a dark and dreamless sleep.

A text from Mrs. Berns woke me.

All clear. :-))

Chapter 38

"Did you find out anything?" Mrs. Berns asked, meeting me at the library's front door.

I filled her in on Little D, Christie talking to Doris, and Doris's gambling problem.

"No Eustace?"

I shook my head. "I couldn't tell if he'd been back yet or not, either. I'm going to dig into the database and see what I can find." I could feel Mrs. Berns's stare piercing my neck as I headed to one of the public computers and began typing, my back to the door.

"You know," she finally said, "I can see you as a mom."

I didn't pause my typing. I was still wearing the clothes I'd sneaked out of Ida's closet, and Mrs. Berns had yet to comment on them. "That's because I am literally sitting in front of you dressed like one."

She walked over and pinched the soft spot on the back of my arm. "Ouch!"

"Learn from the pain." She tugged out the chair next to me and dropped into it. "I meant I can see you having kids. Ever considered it?"

"Nope." I kept my face glued to the screen, even though it was hard to focus with her words stirring up my guts. I was twenty-nine years old, and I loved other people's kids for short periods of time. I told myself that they seemed so sweet because I wasn't required to do any of the hard work of raising them. I'd even told myself that at the Fords' when I'd seen all the tots at her day care, but I knew the truth. I was afraid I'd be a lousy parent like my own dad, and I didn't want to inflict that on a kid. I knew the cost too well.

Besides, when had I ever been in a relationship stable enough to consider having a child with the guy? But now that I was going to ask Johnny to marry me . . . Probably I should clear my status as a loser on the lam before I let my brain follow that train.

"Do you want to talk the domestic arts with me, or do you want me to find out who killed Rita and Donald?"

She pinched my arm, harder this time, as she walked away. "I warned you."

She had. I rubbed the spot. There'd definitely be a bruise there, one to match the black-and-blue stripes the rock wall climbing harness had left. But there was no time for self-pity. My suspect list stared at me from a spot next to my computer: Eustace, Doris, Rita, Christie, Donald, and Little D, whose real name I did not know. Maybe I could backtrack that information based on who his foster parents were. I scribbled Abraham's name on the sheet of paper as an afterthought. He seemed like an outlier in this whole mess, but there was too much at stake for me to cut corners.

My fingers flew like hummingbirds.

A search on Eustace Dickens dug up scant information no matter which direction I came at it: cross-referencing his army division and the men he'd served with, searching for phone or credit card records and marriage certificates. The closest thing to a hit I discovered was when I examined the property records for his current home. It was registered to E. M. Dickens, presumably Eustace, who'd inherited the land free and clear from his parents.

It appeared that land taxes were paid out of a bank account, also registered to E. M. Dickens and set up shortly before he went off the grid. My guess was that he'd arranged his finances so the government wouldn't bother him. Other than those two thin records, there was only the single newspaper article. A second reading of it yielded no new information.

A search on Doris and Rita didn't offer any fresh insights, either, though the fact that Doris had been operating at a loss for the last two years made more sense now that I knew about her gambling problem. I hoped she was being honest with herself about never betting again. She'd been paying Rita a portion of the profits for years. With Rita gone, she'd have more money coming in. Not a lot more—it was a small-town restaurant, after all—but maybe enough to recoup the deficit of the last few years and live comfortably if she stayed straight.

I closed out the screen on the sisters and began a new hunt on Donald and Christie Maroon, overwhelmed anew at how many articles there were. Even more appeared now. Donald's murder had made the *St. Paul Pioneer Press.*

Philanthropist Donald Maroon Stabbed to Death

Donald Maroon, lifelong resident of St. Paul and philanthropist best known for generous contributions to organizations such as the Minnesota Chamber Orchestra, Minneapolis Museum of Science, and the Boys & Girls Club of the Twin Cities, was stabbed to death in the northwestern Minnesota community of Battle Lake, where he and his wife, Christine Maroon, were completing volunteer work. The police have no suspects at this time. Despite a recent rash of murders this past year in this central Minnesota region, police chief Gary Wohnt calls Maroon's death "an outlier occurrence that will soon be solved." Maroon has no children and is survived by his mother, Lisbeth Maroon, and sister, Wanda Maroon, both residents of Denver.

Christine Maroon's family, the Latchviks, are famous for founding Assurist Medical Research, a Fortune

500 company. Mrs. Maroon was not available for comment at press time.

Huh. The money had been Christie's, not Donald's. I blamed cultural stereotypes for my assumption otherwise. Also, Christie wasn't commenting, not even a PR-ish, superficial "please respect my privacy at this difficult time." And even more telling, if I was correctly reading between the lines, the paper hadn't gotten anyone else who knew Donald personally to issue a statement about him.

Apparently the late Donald Maroon was exactly as much of a dink as he appeared to be.

I kept burrowing, just to be sure. That doggedness didn't always work, but this time, I hit pay dirt twelve screens deep, where I discovered a record of a civil court appearance filed by Carver McPherson of the Carver McPherson Private Investigations firm. According to the court filing, Christine Maroon had failed to pay Mr. McPherson for services lawfully rendered. If Christie hadn't paid the guy she'd hired, he might be just sore enough to tell me what he'd been brought on board to discover.

I googled his contact information. His phone number popped up. I called. After five rings, I left my name and number on his voicemail and asked him to return my call as soon as he could.

Something was nagging at me. I tapped my pen on my list. The tip kept landing on Abraham Nillson's name. Might as well search there next to see if I could find out why Little D had tried to strangle the guy.

Click clack.

I hadn't really expected to find anything.

My mind was actually wandering to thoughts of Luna and Tiger Pop, and how I looked as a blonde, and when I'd last eaten.

I wasn't prepared when the first hit popped up on my screen, chilling me to my core.

Chapter 39

Abraham Nillson had fallen into a coma nearly one year earlier, when his heart machine had failed. That I had known, thanks to Curtis Poling. The chilling news? That Assurist Medical Research had created the defective machine and was on the hook for Abraham's ongoing medical care, in addition to a $5 million settlement currently being held in trust against Abraham's recovery. A quick internet search showed that a coma could last for decades, and that full-time care for a comatose patient cost thousands of dollars a day.

My heart raced.

My fingers flew as I dug down to unearth the executor of Abraham's estate. Mr. Nillson was a sitting duck, every one of his inhalations keeping his multimillion-dollar trust out of the hands of whoever stood to inherit it at his death.

Except he had no living relatives.

That meant the only one who would benefit from him reaching an early grave was . . . Assurist Medical Research.

It would save them the cost of his ongoing care, though they wouldn't be able to recoup the $5 million settlement. A bank was managing his trust until such time as he awoke, and in the event of his death, Minnesota's intestate succession law required that any of his money escheat into the state's coffers.

I was no math whiz, but the cheddar Assurist would save by not paying for Abraham's ongoing care would eclipse the cost of the settlement within a few years. That pointed the attempt on his life squarely at Christie. Murdering Rita and then Donald had merely been her warm-up, housekeeping detours on her way to the money shot.

I began to glow with the confidence of a puzzle solved but soon realized that my leaps of fancy didn't make any sense. That knowledge settled like a cramp in my back. Surely Assurist was insured up the ying-yang—Abraham's settlement wouldn't come out of Christie's pocket. There was something I was missing, something right in front of my eyes.

I drew in air through my nose to a count of three, forcing myself to calm. If I chased a mental lead too intensely, it would only slip farther away. Instead, I thought of dry red wine, and kissing Johnny's sweet lips, and dark chocolate. As soon as my shoulders loosened and my breathing relaxed, there it was.

The memory I'd been hunting.

I returned to my computer screen, scrolling to the first page of hits, and found it immediately, now that I knew what I was looking for. Assurist was poised to go public in April. Abraham's settlement might not cost them money up front, but a comatose patient, made unresponsive thanks to their celebrity heart machine, certainly wouldn't do them any favors on the IPO front. Abraham Nillson was an incredible liability for Assurist, not so much in the cost of keeping him alive as in the bad publicity he represented. As long as he lived, he was Assurist's human Edsel.

This was all coming together.

Christie had hired Little D to kill Abraham so that her company's public offering went smoothly.

Poor kid had probably walked himself right into that. A rage began to bubble in my chest, creating deep lava gurgles. Christie had no right to involve a child in her dirty scheme. I rolled my shoulders and my neck, trying to mellow myself. I was angry, but maybe unnecessarily. After all, without a confession from Little D, all I had was speculation.

I drummed the keyboard. I could dig some more, find out if Little D had a file or some other information in the database. I almost didn't have the stomach for it. The boy was in foster care. Life had not treated him well, and it appeared to still be kicking him, this time with steel-toed boots. Still, I couldn't be squeamish, not if I was going to help him.

I input the Fords' name and address.

My computer informed me that the Fords ran a licensed day care. Also, they had fostered more than two dozen kids in the last five years, but currently were home to only one.

David Dickens.

I clicked on the link guiding me to his birth certificate, reading and rereading the information I found there, blood thudding in my veins. No matter how many times I read it, I couldn't make room in my head for the information.

His mother was unnamed. His father was E. M. Dickens.

Eustace was Little D's father.

Chapter 40

"It doesn't make any sense."

"You keep saying that," Mrs. Berns said. She was behind the wheel of a borrowed pickup truck. She'd insisted on being the "getaway driver," even though we had to wedge two never-checked-out encyclopedias under her rear to get her tall enough to see over the steering wheel.

I would have put up more of a fuss if I knew how to drive a three-on-the-tree, or if there weren't something so life-affirming about seeing my best friend behind the wheel, handkerchief tied to her head gangsta-style, white-and-blue hair poking out around the edges, cat-eye sunglasses guarding her eyes, a fierce smile on her coral-colored lips.

We had closed the library as soon as I'd discovered who Little D's dad was. Now I really needed to talk to Eustace.

Mrs. Berns continued. "But I think it makes all the sense in the world. Eustace is a private guy. If he had a kid, he could easily keep him under the radar, homeschooling him, getting his clothes at garage sales here and there, teaching him to live off the land."

I thought of the snow-buried tractor tire sandbox in the yard and the single bed recently moved out of Eustace's cabin. It hadn't been Rita's. It had belonged to Little D. "But why give him over to foster care? Why now, if he's raised the kid on his own just fine for a dozen years?"

Mrs. Berns steered the pickup into Eustace's front yard, the truck's old shocks nearly bouncing her off her encyclopedic perch. She pointed toward the cabin, the fading evening light creating shadowy pockets of mirage and truth. "Why don't you ask him yourself?"

Eustace was cleaning another pelt. He hadn't flinched or even glanced our way as we parked the truck and crunched through the icy crust of snow. As we neared, I realized I didn't recognize the animal it had been, not from the underside, but it appeared remotely piggish. I made a note to not examine it any closer as well as to avoid the forest.

Eustace kept scraping the hide, finally shooting us a cursory glance as we came to a stop behind him. The smell of animal gut was hot and primal.

"Eustace?"

He spoke into the animal hide. "You got out of jail."

I'd forgotten that was the last place I'd seen him. "Yes and no. A friend sprang me. I'm here because I need to figure out some stuff, quick, or they'll arrest me again."

This got his attention. He turned, resting his scraper on the butcher bench. "You were arrested for the murder of that rich guy from the Cities?"

"I found his body in my car."

He reached for a rag and wiped his hands thoughtfully. His lesions were invisible in the waning light, and I caught a glimpse of what a handsome man he had once been, his jawline strong, cheekbones high. He had a good German face.

Mrs. Berns stood beside me. "Eustace, we know he's your boy."

The hand wiping became more intense. "I didn't hide it from anyone, not any more than I hide anything. I live my life in private, that's all. I gave him all the schooling he needed out here. We had a good life."

"Why'd you put him in foster care?"

The rag dropped from his grip. "They say I have one year to live. It's the cancer. I can't afford the drugs to keep it in check, not regularly, like I'm supposed to. When I can pay for them, the side effects are almost worse than the disease." He tugged off his hat and angled his scruffy head to catch the last of the light. He pointed at the angry lesions, the worst of them under his cap, weeping.

I burned with shame at judging him when I'd first seen him in the apothecary.

Eustace crammed his hat back on his head. "I didn't want the boy to see me die. Simple as that. He deserves a family that would love and care for him. His mom disappeared right after he was born, and I'm all he has. That's no good, no good a'tall. I'm hoping the Fords adopt him. I chose them myself. They're good people, and he's a real nice kid. He might be having a hard time adjusting to being without me, and that sometimes looks bad to others, but deep down, he's good."

Could Eustace hear my heart breaking?

"He tries to come back here now and again, but I have to shoo him off." Eustace made the purest sound of pain I'd ever heard, a sob thin as ice cracking, but he kept talking. "It's the best thing for him."

Both Mrs. Berns and I hurried forward to offer comfort, but he made a halting motion with his hands.

"I don't deserve anything from anyone. I made all this happen, for better or worse, and now it's worse. If you want to assist me, help my boy make a new life."

He didn't know. Good lord, *he didn't know* that Little D was being held for attempted murder.

"Eustace?" I would have rather sliced off a chunk of my own skin and had Eustace turn it into a wallet than finish my sentence, but that choice wasn't on the table. I had to do the right thing. "Little D tried to strangle a man at the Senior Sunset this morning. I was there. The cops took him away."

Eustace's face collapsed on itself. "My boy wouldn't do that. That's not my boy."

I wondered how well he knew who his boy had become, the child who'd been forced to live with strangers.

Chapter 41

Driving down the highway after leaving Eustace's cabin, the pickup cab was funereal. Eustace had disappeared into the woods before we'd even left the driveway. We'd offered to help him any way we could, but he was inconsolable, and who could blame him? He'd tried to do the best he could by his son, making an unthinkable sacrifice. Yet Eustace's heroic act may have unbalanced his child to the degree that Little D viewed murder as a moneymaking option.

Maybe he'd thought he could make enough money to save his dad.

I began to seethe on the drive to town. Scratch that—I was on fire, a raging wall of anger. If Christie had set up Little D for this heinous crime, I would burn every hair on her body before dropping her into the wilds of Minnesota, naked and rolled in honey and then sand, to fend for herself. And that was just the start.

"I need to talk to Christie," I told Mrs. Berns.

I didn't even wait for the truck to come to a complete stop in front of the Battle Lake Motel before jumping out and darting to Christie's room, the number of which she'd shared along with her cell when Kennie had initially introduced her at the library.

Christie didn't answer the door, but I'd been boning up on my lock picking, and Mrs. Berns had had the foresight to grab my pick kit from the house when she checked on Luna and Tiger Pop. It took several minutes of wiggling and jimmying while Mrs. Berns kept an eye on passing traffic, my attempts made worse by the rage-trembling in my hands, but the tumblers finally fell into place. I turned the knob and stepped inside, Mrs. Berns on my tail.

Vegan was the only living creature in the room, and he was squirming to beat the band in his tiny kennel. Mrs. Berns took him outside to relieve himself while I ransacked the closets and dressers, two of each. They were clearly divided, with Donald's clothes and toiletries in one and Christie's in the other. The police had surely already been here, but I searched every pocket and drawer just the same.

Mrs. Berns returned, holding Vegan in one hand and a gnarly, gristled bone in the other.

"What the hell is that?"

"Deer femur, I think. Bill had it rolling around in the back of the truck." She set the bone down, along with Vegan, who pounced on it, his entire body trembling with joy.

"That bone is bigger than the dog, who, by the way, does not eat meat."

She shrugged. "Looks like no one told him that. Have you searched in the bathroom yet?"

"It's all yours."

We spent the next half hour lifting the mattress, turning lamps upside down in search of hidden wads of money, and peeking inside the toilet tank for a taped weapon. A big part of me hoped Christie would return and find us so I could let loose on her. She didn't, and we also didn't discover anything more scandalous than face lotion that cost more than my car, receipts from a variety of Battle Lake businesses, and a power cord that suggested Christie owned a laptop that she must have taken with her.

Desperate for any information, I rang up Carver McPherson, the private eye who'd sued Christie for nonpayment. He was the only potential lead I'd yet to make contact with in this steaming pile. No answer. I left another message.

"Dammit!" I said, pacing. "We've dead-ended. Until I talk to Christie or hear back from the PI, there's nothing we can do."

Mrs. Berns dropped onto the bed. We'd yanked the shades tightly shut, but the lurid yellow glare of the parking lot light leaked in around the edges. Outside it was full evening, most everyone home from work and puttering in their living rooms or kitchens, the Battle Lake traffic light as it rumbled past. The normal world felt far away yet close enough to touch. How to break out of this weird bubble I'd found myself in and return to a life where people worked during the day, watched TV at night, and headed to the movies when they craved a little excitement?

Mrs. Berns jerked a black phone out of her pocket. "We could make some money."

I snorted. "Pass. I don't have the energy for phone sex."

"Not phone sex, the cooking class in Urbank. The one you're supposed to audit tonight for Ron, who signs your paycheck? I can call them and see if they have two open spots left. If they do, I'll reserve them under an alias."

"Are you serious? You broke me out of jail this morning. There must be an APB out on me."

"Nope. Kennie's been listening to the police scanners. They're not looking for you, or at least not advertising it. We think it's because Gary doesn't want people to know you broke out. He must be humiliated that someone jumped the fence on his watch." Mrs. Berns cackled at the thought.

"That means that Gary and his deputies will be doubly invested in finding me."

She began dialing. "All the more reason to get the heck out of Battle Lake. We can kill a couple hours and then come back and check on Christie. You have any better ideas?"

I did not, no matter how I tried. I'd exhausted every other option and had nowhere else to hide.

Besides, it was just a cooking class. What could possibly go wrong?

Chapter 42

Urbank was twelve miles from Battle Lake as the crow flew, but because of the thick cluster of lakes separating the two towns, you had to drive ten miles south and then ten miles east to get there, a perfect ninety-degree angle of forest-lined roads.

The community center was constructed of sheet metal and windows, which wasn't unusual in the area, though Urbank's commitment to the pole barn look for a structure this size was impressive. I studied the outside as Mrs. Berns ducked in to make sure no one who would recognize us was taking the class. I was still in disguise as Invisible Mom, and we were one town over from home, but we wanted to at least wear the gloss of common sense.

"All clear," Mrs. Berns said when she returned to the pickup truck. "For tonight, you're answering to 'Tammy.'"

Fine. It went with my disguise.

"Last name: Sackrider," she finished.

I scowled. "You couldn't leave well enough alone, could you?"

"I don't know what you're talking about. I graduated high school with a Sackrider."

Probably we all did. "What name did you give yourself?"

"Anna."

"That's surprisingly low-key for you."

"Last name: Conda."

There it was. "Are there a lot of people inside?"

She pulled out a tube of lipstick and freshened up her mouth, drawing well outside the lines. "It's packed to the rafters, but no one I recognize. It'll take us an hour, tops, to nail the info you need for your article, and we'll head back to track down Christie. Your phone turned on?"

I held up the cell phone.

She made a scolding sound. "Your battery is dead."

I turned the phone to face me, my stomach dropping. "No! I don't have a charger." What if I'd missed the call from Carver McPherson?

"You can borrow my portable charger." She dug it out of her purse and handed it to me. "Come on."

I plugged the phone in as I walked and dropped the unit into the inside pocket of my borrowed parka, the movement distracting me from the dawning awareness that an octogenarian was more tech savvy than I was. I'd check the phone for a call from McPherson as soon as it had enough juice.

The community center's foyer was essentially a hallway. Mrs. Berns led me to the first room off to the left, the noisy one. Inside was a surprisingly well-lit and well-stocked kitchen-classroom combination. Four counters, each with their own sink and four-burner stove, were arranged like desks, with a larger stove and sink at the front of the classroom. Two enormous refrigerators and a standing rack of spices lined the back wall. An open doorway led to a small pantry stocked with dried goods. A couple dozen people bustled about. They weren't cooking yet, but the smell of frying hamburger and something spicy and powdery, like curry, hung in the air from past classes.

I rummaged in my pockets for a pen and paper so I could take notes. "This is much better equipped than I would've guessed. How long has this place been here?"

"You got me," Mrs. Berns said. "I'd have come here earlier if I knew."

"Let's move up front so I can ask questions."

"Don't forget that you're undercover."

I raised an eyebrow "Thanks for the reminder to fly low, Anna Conda."

She nodded smugly. "My pleasure."

She still had the handkerchief tied around her head, her sunglasses perched on top even though the sun had set a couple hours ago. She looked tough, and so it wasn't out of place at all that she began humming "Baby Got Back" as we made our way to the workstation nearest the front and introduced ourselves to the foursome already situated there.

I let Mrs. Berns take over the chitchat, something I wasn't particularly good at. That allowed me to scour the classroom, looking for eyes that lingered on me a little too long. My wig and clothes—the mom invisibility cloak, as I'd come to call it—had grown surprisingly comfortable, but I couldn't let down my guard.

Mrs. Berns was trying to rope me into the small talk when the instructor, a sweet-looking woman in her sixties, walked to the front of the classroom, clapped her hands, and ordered us to move so we weren't working with the people we'd come with.

"You'll leave tonight with recipes *and* new friends!" she warbled as she tied on an apron with HOT STUFF COMING THROUGH! hand stitched on the front.

I grumbled, staying put. I'd never liked making new friends. I wasn't good at it. I preferred loyalty and consistency. Mrs. Berns happily ditched me, however, not even bothering to say goodbye as she made her way to the back, a grin planted on her face. I found myself joined by four bachelor farmers, all of whom swore they hadn't come together but coincidentally wore the same uniform of overalls and feed caps and all had the same last name—Hollermunn. They also all smelled of engine oil and looked to have used their fingernails as makeshift screwdrivers at one time or another.

"Is this your first cooking class?" I asked Matt, the farmer closest to me. I put his age in the low fifties, and guessed him to be the youngest of the foursome.

"Yep," he said agreeably, adjusting his Carhartt overalls as he pointed to the other three. "My b—these *strangers* and me thought it'd be best if one of us learned to cook."

"I get it," I said. "You're brothers, and you're already uncomfortable enough being here. You don't want to make it worse by splitting up. I won't tell."

A sheet of identical relief fell across each of their faces, momentarily erasing some of their lines.

"Thank you," Matt said. "Really appreciate that."

I nodded, checking my phone as I folded my coat over a stool.

No messages and battery at 20 percent.

The instructor clapped her hands again for our attention. "Most everyone is here. We still have one no-show. Please make room at your workstation if he arrives late. Now, let's get an idea of what we're cooking today."

She held up an industrial-size roasting pan, her arm muscles straining. "Inside here I have a triple batch of spaghetti hotdish, a perfectly balanced meal. I'm going to pass it around for you to taste so you know what you're aiming for. Please use a clean fork and take only one bite."

She stopped at our table first. The four brothers used their forks like shovels, balancing as many wormy noodles in a single bite as they could. I dipped in more delicately.

"Don't be shy," she encouraged. "Get a little of everything!"

"Are there any almonds in here?" I asked. "I'm allergic."

She tipped her head toward the pantry door. "This spaghetti hotdish is nut-free. We do have almonds in the dry-goods room, but the container is clearly marked. I'll make sure no one uses any in their meals tonight." She smiled perkily. Too perkily. I had a hunch that was how she did everything.

With her staring at me, I had no choice but to dip back into the hotdish. I brought the "perfectly balanced meal" to my mouth, the smell of sautéed hamburger reminding me that I hadn't eaten all day. I chewed as she listed the ingredients.

"This dish is made of spaghetti noodles, corn, and turkey burger, topped with breadcrumbs."

I munched. There was no sauce. No flavor. No warning. Just textures and temperatures without taste, churning around in my mouth. I would definitely include this ultimate Minnesota food in a future Battle Lake Bites column.

My readers would *love* it.

Once everyone had tried the flavor-free dish, she returned to the front of the class. "Along with the spaghetti hotdish, you and your fellow chefs will be creating a gelatin salad using a mold, a taco salad that's perfect for bringing to potlucks, and if there's time, we'll briefly touch on refrigerator pickles."

That all worked for me.

As we dug into our tasks, I welcomed the familiar soothing power of cooking. It worked like gardening on my frayed nerves, calming them with the repetitive, healing actions of tending home and hearth. I even began to enjoy working with my cooking group. The bachelor farmers were not a sanitary group, but they were willing and easygoing, and that counted for a lot. If I weren't wanted for murder and hadn't accidentally broken up with the love of my life, I'd have rated this night a good time.

I ran into Mrs. Berns when we both found ourselves at the main refrigerator.

"How's it going?" I asked her.

She scowled. "I want to stab everyone in my group in the eye."

I glanced over her shoulder. They seemed fine—a group of married-looking couples who appeared to be enjoying a night out away from the kids. "Why?"

"See the tall blond guy?"

I nodded. He was whispering something to the woman he'd come with.

"He slipped a pubic hair into my cottage cheese. It's like cooking with Clarence Thomas over there."

I gagged. "Why would he do that?"

She shrugged. "Some people are weirdos."

"What'd you do when you saw it?"

"Nothing right away. I just keep farting when he gets close. It's amazingly effective, because ever since I sampled Ms. Perky's spaghetti helldish, it smells like a stranger has crawled into my intestines and is burning rubber bands to keep warm."

I coughed on my own spit. "You could have just tossed the pubic hair."

"Where's the fun in that?"

Indeed. I leaned into the industrial fridge to rummage for the cheese blend I'd come for. I located it in the back, where it'd fallen behind an enormous bag of parsley, Minnesota's state herb. I had it in hand when Mrs. Berns pinched the back of my arm so hard that I dropped the cheese.

"What was that for? I didn't say anything about the farting. In fact, I think it's a fine survival mechanism. You're like a human skunk, cute on the outside, stinky inside."

She wasn't responding.

Her face had gone white, the contrast stark against the deep-red handkerchief perched on her head.

I followed the direction of her eyes.

She was staring at the front door, where an out-of-uniform Gary Wohnt had entered the cooking class.

Chapter 43

The lump of spaghetti in my stomach lurched.

Curse words!

What was the man doing at a cooking class of all places? I ducked into the pantry next to the fridge, Mrs. Berns at my heels. Gary hadn't glanced in our direction, but it was only a matter of time before he spotted us. The room wasn't that large. My disguise might stand up from a distance, or in passing, but not in close quarters, and especially not with Mrs. Berns at my side.

"I'm going back to jail," I whimpered. We both knew Kennie's "chief constable" argument wouldn't hold up in court. I'd been legally detained, and I'd illegally broken out, adding gasoline to my crime fire. I scoured the pantry for an escape route. The only way out was the way we'd come in. We were trapped. It was difficult to draw a full breath, and a trickle of sweat rolled down my back.

"Not on my watch," Mrs. Berns said, scanning the list of dry goods.

I groaned. It was hopeless. I was going to jail, at least temporarily, which meant that no one was looking out for Little D and a double-murderer was walking free. "Unless you plan to disguise me as a cupcake, I can't possibly see what will get us out of here."

"Not us," she corrected. "*You.* I haven't done anything wrong."

At least as far as Gary knew.

"Aha!" She grabbed a plastic container off the shelf and shoved it into my hands. Its label read ALMONDS.

I pushed it back toward her. "I'm allergic, remember? My face swelled up like a puffer fish last time I had them."

"I know. You told me."

My brain felt thick. Why in the world would she want me to have an allergic reaction? While I did not have a severe allergy, eating almonds made me itch, gave me a headache, and distorted my features to the point that . . . *Oh*. The ball finally dropped into place. "You want me to use my allergies as a disguise."

"Unless you have a better idea."

The instructor moved to the front of the class, a straight sight line from the pantry door, and coughed loudly to get everyone's attention. "We have a late arrival. Please welcome Gary Wohnt of Battle Lake!"

I flipped the lid on the almonds and chucked a handful into my mouth. I chewed, almost moaning. It wasn't just that I was starving—I'd genuinely forgotten how delicious almonds were. Nutty, sweet, clean. I had only a moment to process the flavor before my tongue turned fuzzy and my eyes and palms began to itch.

"Wow," Mrs. Berns said, genuine respect in her voice. "That's quick."

I kept chewing. "How do I look?"

"Like you blew a garden hose. How do you feel?"

"A little exhilarated, actually. My heart is racing. I might be able to fly."

She patted my arm. "I'd keep my sights on breathing for now."

"Sounds good." I was having trouble organizing my thoughts. "We can't leave at the same time, right? I look less like me without you at my side."

She grimaced. "Kid, you hardly look human. I'm going back to my station to tell those losers that I left something in my car. If I can sneak out without Gary seeing me, I'll do it, and you follow. If Gary spots me, I'll make a scene, and that's when you'll duck out. I'll be right behind you. Got it?"

"Whee!" Honest to god, I hadn't felt this great in a long time. My head had become a balloon tied to my neck, and balloons meant parties. I was a walking party!

Mrs. Berns muttered something under her breath that sounded like "What fun," or possibly "What have I done?" She set her shoulders before turning from me and striding toward her table. I began organizing the dry goods so I could look busy while keeping an eye on the main room. Well, a sliver of an eye, as that's all that was left since they'd started to swell shut.

Mrs. Berns made it halfway across the room before Gary intercepted her. Normally, my heart would've started thudding extra hard at spotting something like that, but it couldn't beat any faster.

"Gary Wohnt!" Mrs. Berns yelled as he charged toward her. "Are you still doing that undercover work for the health department?"

The room grew quiet, all eyes on Gary. He drew back, his expression quizzical. I was struck by how handsome he appeared in his button-down shirt and slacks. Didn't matter. I was going to marry Johnny! Whee!

"What is that?" Mrs. Berns covered the distance between her and Gary, holding her ear up to his mouth. "You're here at the Urbank Community Center secretly checking for code violations?"

The instructor blanched at the front of the classroom, a realization that made me giggle because I had just eaten almonds, which also sometimes blanch. My brain was so good at thinking things!

And unable to stay on a single thought for long.

Still, I was pretty sure I was the only one who saw the instructor surreptitiously slide the spaghetti hotdish off the counter, moving only her hand as she dumped it, pan and all, into the trash. She needn't have been secretive. All eyes were on Mrs. Berns and Gary, which was my cue to make like a tree and leave.

I decided to slip out the back quietly but confidently because that would draw the least amount of attention. Unfortunately, I'd lost all peripheral vision and so knocked a pan off the counter halfway to the exit. It fell to the floor with a clatter. I risked a glance toward Gary.

He was looking straight at me. He squinted.

An expression crossed his face. Was it recognition? Anger?

Nope, it was pity. I tamped down the momentary, out-of-place thought that it hurt to have Gary look at me like that. He removed his gaze with a deliberateness that suggested he hadn't meant to stare. I must've looked hideous, some sort of blonde pencil troll darting out of the pantry in jeans so high-waisted they served as backup birth control. Ah well. Whatever worked.

I skedaddled outdoors, the cool night air a balm on my swollen flesh. I snapped a relatively clean-looking icicle from the community center's mailbox and sucked on it, relieved that I could still swallow. My allergy had never been severe, but that didn't mean it couldn't get worse. The pickup truck's side mirror winked enticingly at me, but I refused to heed its siren song. I did *not* want to see what I looked like.

The front door of the center whipped open. It was Mrs. Berns. She tossed me my coat. What a smart woman.

"In the truck. Now," she said.

"Okey doke." I followed her lead, slipping the jacket on as we speed-walked. We both slid in and she started the truck. We lurched out of town, with Mrs. Berns checking her rearview mirror every ten seconds.

She reached under her seat and pulled out a first-aid kit. "There should be some Benadryl in here. We'll get you some water at the gas station on the corner. We have to flush your system."

"Thanks. Hey, how'd you get out of there?" My hands were so swollen that I could no longer make a fist. I needed to locate that Benadryl, and fast.

"I said I didn't want to be party to any hairy hotdish sting, and I stormed out."

Fair enough.

My phone warbled inside my pocket. I yanked it out. I recognized the number.

Carver McPherson was returning my call.

Chapter 44

Once I explained who I was, what I wanted, and how it would be a professional courtesy that I'd be sure to repay one day, Carver McPherson was amazingly forthcoming. It didn't hurt that he was still sore from being forced to sue Christie for money owed.

"It's exactly what you think," McPherson said, his voice high and nasal. "Wife wants to find out where husband is dipping his wick. When you deliver the bad news, she doesn't want to pay, like her screwing me over can suddenly transform her husband into a decent guy."

I was grateful for the piercing pitch of his voice. It kept me from getting too sleepy from the Benadryl I'd swallowed dry. "So Donald was cheating."

"Like it was his job." I heard the clicking of keys on the other end. "He was worse than most, though. Preferred teenaged girls, possibly underage. After Mrs. Maroon refused to pay, I sent that info on to the Minneapolis PD. He got caught in a sting, made some sort of plea deal. Turns out that if you have enough money, you can buy your way out of anything."

"Gross."

"I imagine that's why he got out of town."

"This was recent?"

"Not the interest in young girls, but it took them a while to catch him."

"Did the sting make the papers?"

"Nope. The guy had to take a set of shears to the chest for that. You know anything about his murder?"

My eyelids grew extra heavy. "I read the same article you did. No suspects." *Except me, but whatever.* My rapidly slowing thoughts wandered to Rita, who had been nearing retirement age at the time of her death. "Donald ever go after older women?"

"He's what we call an opportunity predator. There's the meat he prefers, but he'll eat anything."

I blerghed. "Why didn't Christie just divorce him?"

"You got me. The money was all in her name. She could have lanced him off anytime. Maybe she loved him?"

I'd heard of weirder things. "Did you ever get paid?"

He chuckled. It sounded like a wheeze. "Yep. It was court-ordered. And then I got a bonus to stay quiet with the press. You're not press, are you?"

I was beginning to think Carver McPherson was a crap detective. "I told you at the start of the conversation that I'm a private investigator." The best lie is the truth that misdirects. Always.

"When you're not offering Minnesota phone sex?"

I felt my throat close up, and it wasn't allergies. "What?"

"I backtracked this phone number."

Maybe he wasn't so lame after all. "It's a side job."

"Speaking of *jobs*," Carver McPherson said, his whiny voice dropping an octave, "don't suppose you can give me a phone freebie? In exchange for all the information I just gave you. I do get turned on by a strong Midwestern girl. You could say anything to me."

"You got it." If he could see my glower, his blood would have had the good sense to speed northward. I adopted my thickest Minnesota accent. "Ever see the wood chipper scene from *Fargo*?"

Click.

I filled in Mrs. Berns on the scant new information, which essentially verified that Donald had been every bit the creep he'd seemed and more, and that it was in Christie's best interest that her husband disappear. By the time we pulled up to the Battle Lake Motel, my eyes no longer felt glass-lined when I blinked, and I could take full breaths. I risked a peek in the mirror on the back of the sunshade.

"Yikes! I look terrible."

Mrs. Berns parked on the far side of the lot. Five of the units had lights on. Christie's was one of those, and a sleek black BMW was parked in front of it. "You look like a supermodel compared to the marshmallow shitshow your face was before." She unsnapped her seat-belt. "There was so much swelling I figured either the Benadryl was going to save you, or your face was going to pop and I'd have to wipe it off the inside of the windshield."

"Thanks for the perspective."

"You bet. What's the plan with Christie?"

"We knock on her door. When she opens, we ask her how many people she killed this week."

Mrs. Berns nodded. "Good plan."

Chapter 45

"I most certainly did not."

Christie's response didn't surprise me. Usually, murderers didn't like to cop to it right away. It slowed their game. What I was hoping for was some truth hidden behind her eyes or in her body language, something that tipped her hand. Other than a recoil when she saw my swollen face, she'd been impossible to read.

"You didn't even kill him a little bit?" Mrs. Berns asked.

She and I sat on two stiff-backed upholstered chairs. Christie was poised on the edge of the bed, two packed bags next to her. Vegan lounged behind her. His bone was nowhere in sight, though his distended belly suggested he'd found a place to hide it from his mistress.

"I don't miss him, that's for sure." She reached into her purse and pulled out a pack of cigarettes. "You mind?"

I pointed at the No Smoking sign nailed to the far wall. She sighed in resignation and tucked the pack back in her bag. The self-righteous health nuts were always the first to slide when the going got tough.

"But loathing the predatory, cheating bastard doesn't mean I killed him. What would be the point?"

"To keep from causing a scandal just before your company goes public?"

She laughed. It was a startlingly Cruella de Vil sound. "You don't know much about corporations, do you? As long as we're making a profit, and we are most definitely profitable, the investors will continue to line up. Donald was an embarrassment to himself, but he and I stopped sleeping together years ago. We were friends. Travel companions. It was easy enough to keep him around. It kept me from having to pay out on the prenup, and he could be funny. I don't mind that he's dead, but I didn't want it bad enough to risk a prison sentence." She looked down her nose at me, not so much haughty as confident in her truth.

I decided to switch tacks. "What can you tell me about Abraham Nillson?"

She appeared genuinely puzzled. "Nothing."

Now I was confused. "Do you know a foster kid named Little D?"

She shook her head, almost looking bored. "Never heard of him. We haven't met any children since we've been here."

"How about Rita, the woman your husband was hitting on at the nursing home?" Mrs. Berns asked. "We heard you fighting about her outside the library."

Christie pulled out her cigarettes again. She didn't ask this time, just lit one up. "Donald and I were indeed fighting outside the library, but I could not care less who he sleeps with. I was mad because I actually believe in the SLUMN program. I wanted to immerse myself in the small-town experience, and Donald was going to muck it all up by drawing attention to our marriage."

Her acrid smoke curled up my nostrils. "But you didn't care that he was cheating?"

She shrugged. "Our rule was that if I didn't hear about it, I didn't care about it."

Some people's kids. "But I saw you and Doris at the Turtle Stew yesterday, whispering. What could you have possibly been scheming about if it wasn't Doris's sister's connection to your husband?"

Her eyebrows drew together. "We weren't whispering. We were talking business. I might want to invest in the restaurant."

Mrs. Berns and I exchanged a puzzled glance. Something wasn't adding up here, but I didn't know what it was. I went for the obvious to stall. "Your bags are packed. You're leaving?"

She sucked deeply on her cigarette before standing to open a closet, stepping aside to allow us to look inside. It was full of women's clothes. Same with the dresser drawer she opened. "The packed bags are Donald's things. I don't need them anymore, obviously. I was going to donate them to a secondhand shop as soon as I had the OK from the police."

She arched an eyebrow, her eyes walking the length of me. "Speaking of police stations, aren't you supposed to be in one?"

Mrs. Berns jumped to her feet and peered at her naked wrist. "Would you look at the time! We have to be going. Thanks so much for talking with us."

Christie watched us through a haze of smoke as we scrambled out of her room. Her gaze was more curious than calculating, which meant I was more baffled than ever. This entire investigation was turned inside out, leaving me no idea who had done what to whom.

The only person left who could shed some light on all this was Little D, and he was in jail, probably juvie.

Only a parent would have access to him.

The truth weighted me down like a yoke: we needed to get Eustace involved. He needed to go to jail and talk to his son.

Chapter 46

We agreed that it'd be best if I hid out at Eustace's while Mrs. Berns drove him to the juvenile detention in Fergus. The waiting killed me. Eustace had pointed me toward a stash of books he kept in one of his cabinets, but they were all of the Grizzly Adams variety, containing information on canning, processing meat, building survival structures, cleaning guns.

By the time I heard the pickup crunching up the driveway's icy gravel three hours later, I felt confident I could construct a halfway decent yurt if required. I was equally confident that I liked the grid. *Loved it*, in fact. Running water, heat you could turn up with a dial, dill pickle potato chips? Good, good, and good.

I ran out to meet the truck.

Both Mrs. Berns and Eustace appeared grim when they stepped out. "What did you find out?" I asked.

Eustace stormed past me into the cabin.

I looked at my friend. "Mrs. Berns?"

She shook her head. "It was hard on him, seeing his boy locked up."

I blinked back tears. Of course it must have been agonizing for both father and son. Eustace wouldn't have visited him if it weren't desperate times. "Did Little D have any information?"

Mrs. Berns stared past me, toward the front door of Eustace's shack, which he'd slammed behind him. "Little D was too mad to say much.

He just kept repeating that the 'old guy at the nursing home' is a liar if he said Little D tried to hurt him."

"Liar?" I said, my heart dropping. "If he was talking about Abraham, try 'ventriloquist.' The guy's in a coma."

"I told Little D that. I also informed him that you'd go to jail for Donald's murder if we didn't find out what was going on. Eustace pretty much repeated my words, but Little D wouldn't talk. He was so furious he was shaking. Or maybe he was scared."

I sat down heavy on Eustace's front stoop, ignoring the coldness of the wood. "So we're right back where we began. Maybe even farther from our starting point, if Little D didn't know who he was strangling or why."

Mrs. Berns dropped next to me. "The police said they found items on the kid that they thought were stolen—some electronics, candy, jewelry."

I latched on to the only solid information she'd offered me. "Electronics and candy he could pick up at a few stores in Battle Lake. Who sells jewelry?"

"I'm thinking he lifted it from the Senior Sunset. The officer who told Eustace about it said it looked like antique stuff, monogrammed rhinestone buttons, tchotchke crap."

Rhinestone buttons. Ida and her dolls.

I'd come full circle.

"Can you drive me to the nursing home?" I asked Mrs. Berns.

"Are softballs hard?"

I blinked loudly. "Are you really asking, or is that a rhetorical question?"

"I'm really asking." She stood, wiping off her behind. "I was thinking of joining a league this summer."

"I'm pretty sure they're hard."

She nodded thoughtfully. "Good to know. And yeah, I can drive you to the nursing home. Let's go."

◆ ◆ ◆

Dusk was laying its glittery cape across the atmosphere, turning it not quite dark, almost foggy. Mrs. Berns dropped me off behind the Senior Sunset. The plan was for me to check on Abraham and Ida while Mrs. Berns made sure that Luna and Tiger Pop were doing OK. If I didn't discover the killer by tonight, she'd bring my babies to her apartment. It was technically against the rules, and they'd hate living in town, but I couldn't leave them isolated for much longer, and my previous petsitter was in juvie.

I shoved those worries from my head. I needed to identify Rita and Donald's murderer tonight, and it most certainly would not be Little D. That was all there was to it.

I hid in some bushes for the third time that week, timing my entrance into the Sunset for when the front desk worker took a bathroom break. When she disappeared through the door behind her desk, I marched inside and strode self-assuredly toward the nursing home section. I was confident on the outside, but inside, my heart was thudding, my belly quivering. What if someone recognized me?

I still wore the wig, and my features remained mildly distorted from the almond attack, but I was a regular.

I was relieved to reach Abraham's room without confronting anyone I recognized. Mrs. Berns's mention of the monogrammed buttons found on Little D had reminded me of the jewelry I'd first seen in Abraham's room. When it had fallen under his bed, I'd thought it was a rhinestone pendant inlaid with a golden *M*, but it might have been a button. Something about that piece was nagging at me. If Little D had since stolen it, then I was out of luck. If it had been tucked inside one of Abraham's drawers, though, or stored wherever the rest of his altar offerings were placed, holding it might wiggle loose a connection in my brain.

I was relieved to find no staff or supplicants in Abraham's room, leaving me alone with the unconscious patient, the smell of lilies still overwhelming. Who kept bringing them? "Hi," I said, adopting the church whisper his coma seemed to demand. "Don't mind me. I might have left something here, and I wanted to stop by and look for it."

I dropped to all fours, searching every corner. Nothing—not even a dust bunny. Score one for the Sunset's cleaning staff. "Sorry, but I need to look through your drawers, too. Scout's honor I won't take anything."

He didn't stir, but the lamplight fell just so on his right side, illuminating the dreadful bruises circling his papery neck. I didn't want to believe Little D made those ugly marks. I tore my eyes away and focused on his nightstand drawers, followed by his dresser drawers and the boxes stored in his closet. He owned only one other set of clothing, which made sense, since he didn't leave his bed.

Trinkets, notes, religious pamphlets, and more notes had taken over the rest of his storage space. It was an impressive stash. I wondered what the nursing home would do with it once there was no more space to store it all. They might have to put a stop to the Abraham altar.

But the rhinestone jewelry I was searching for was nowhere to be found. I finally had to admit defeat, my chest pained. I really thought I was onto something, but I needed a closer look to trigger the connection. Oh well. The button I was looking for simply wasn't here.

I whispered goodbye to Abraham's still form before slipping into the hall, hoping Ida might have some insight into the situation. I scurried to her room, avoiding eye contact with the handful of nurses' aides and residents I passed. Given the velocity of small-town gossip, it wouldn't have been news to anyone here that I'd been arrested. Since Gary hadn't let it be known that I'd escaped, it was my fervent desire that anyone who saw me would either not recognize me or, if somehow they did, would assume I'd been released.

Still, the relief I felt when I reached Ida's room unaccosted left me weak-kneed. That reprieve lasted right up until I spotted the huge Dolly Parton–esque doll propped on her bed in her otherwise empty room. "Holy flying monkeys, what is that?"

Ida backed out of her closet with an armful of clothes. Her hair was mussed, and it appeared to take her a moment to recognize me, and then to realize what I was referring to. "Mira! Isn't she lovely? It's Kennie's doll."

I pushed my stomach out of my throat and stepped closer. The doll's face was overly made-up, her hair huge and blonde, and she sported at least an E-cup under her Western wear. I reached gingerly to touch her face and recoiled when I felt the smooth, cool plastic. "Is that one of Kennie's actual outfits?"

Ida set her pile of clothes on the foot of the bed and began folding. "Kennie donated a set of Modern Cowgirl clothes to the project. She wanted the doll to be as realistic as possible."

Mission accomplished. If you tossed the doll a quick glance, she looked like a sleeping country singer. For the first time, I noticed the plastic Barbie hat perched in her hair and the plastic Barbie boot earrings dangling from her plastic ears. It was the outfit I'd seen Kennie wearing the same day I'd discovered Rita's body at the Turtle Stew. "Doesn't it creep you out to make another doll?"

Ida snapped a shirt in the air before putting tight creases in it. "I loved making the dolls. I can't put them in public anymore, but this is a nice compromise."

I put as much space between me and the Kennie doll as I could in the small room. "You've got a knack for this, that's for sure. She looks real." I shuddered from top to bottom before continuing. "Hey, can I ask you something? A couple days ago, when I was visiting Abraham, I saw a pendant or maybe a big button in his room. It looked like an antique."

Ida's glance darted toward her closet and then back onto the clothes she was folding. "Probably just an offering. We're not allowed to go back into his room, you know. Not until this whole business with the murders and that strange boy is cleared up."

Made sense. I was willing to bet some of the residents would still sneak into his room just as I had, though. "Probably. But there's something about this specific piece. I've seen it somewhere before but can't place where. It was made out of rhinestones, with a gold letter *M* in the middle."

Ida dropped the last shirt and gave me her full attention, her blue eyes unblinking. "Those are the buttons I put on the doll they found Rita's body in, but there's no way you saw one of them in Abraham's room. I dug them up in an antique shop years ago. There were only four, and I triple-sewed every one of them on that doll's jacket, just like my mother taught me."

My pulse picked up, a slow, steady drumbeat growing louder, stronger. I closed my eyes and recalled the grisly image: the corpse, sprawled on the floor of the Turtle Stew, three bright buttons lining her front, each filigreed with a golden *M*. A detail lost in the chaos of death. "That means that somebody got their hands on one of the doll's buttons after you put her in the Stew, and that same someone visited Abraham's room after that. I'm guessing that same person crossed paths with Donald and Rita at least once."

Ida did everything in her power to avoid my eyes, looking everywhere in the room but at me. She could keep that up for only so long. When we finally locked gazes, hers was fear-soaked because we both knew there was only one person who fit the bill on all counts.

I was looking at her.

Chapter 47

Ida feigned tiredness and told me she didn't want to talk anymore.

I guessed both she and I felt a little queasy when I backed out of her room, unsure of what to say. She could be a killer. The sweet little old lady whose worst threat was that she wanted to destroy another woman's credit might have murdered two people. But why? And how did Little D trying to strangle Abraham—or not, if what he told his dad was to be believed—fit in with all this?

Abraham.

Somehow, that silent man held all the secrets. The person who couldn't answer questions seemed to be the only one who could clear all this up. I took the corner toward Abraham's wing just as Gary Wohnt, fully uniformed and looking as angry as a bull, disappeared inside his room.

I gargled my own tongue as I did an abrupt about-face, struggling to keep my breath steady. Had Gary spotted me? I didn't think so, but with him this close, it was only a matter of time until my goose was cooked. I speed-walked toward the Senior Sunset's rear exit, using every ounce of self-control not to run. Gary must have reached the same conclusion as I had: that Abraham was the one constant between all the hinky business in town.

Well, if Gary was in Abraham's room, that meant I was free to bolt to the library to research the guy more deeply. I had one more clue besides the button to track down, a hazy one that was emerging as the impossible answer connecting Rita's and Donald's deaths to Little D's desire to kill Abraham.

Evening had a solid black grip on the town when I stepped outside. The scent of the air dipped between snow and melt. I wore the night like a cloak, sticking to backstreets and alleyways, crisscrossing my way toward the library. My mind was copter-whirring.

Murder, money, coma. Foster care, cancer, dolls.

Heart medicine, infidelity, gambling.

An image of Johnny flashed into the mix. Man, I wished he were here. He could've held me while I talked through all the angles, helping me to find the solid truth under the shifting surface of stories, motives, and hunches. I was going to hug him so hard when he returned, beg him to take me back, drop to my knees, and pledge my eternal love.

The library was dark when I reached it thirty minutes later, after a walk that should have taken me fifteen. I was sure that I hadn't been followed, though. I let myself in through the back door, pausing a moment to absorb the utter ink-and-paper-scented quiet of an empty library. Once my eyes adjusted to the dim emergency lighting, I wove my way through the storage boxes crowding the back room floor toward the main library. It was eerie at this hour, the storage shelves rising like ancient obelisks.

The quiet made me imagine noises, and intruders, and capture.

I shook my head. No good would come of me scaring myself.

The public computers were all set up facing windows, which meant that the glow would spotlight my face if I used one of those. I elected to move the front desk computer screen and keyboard to the floor so I could crouch behind the counter.

The computer fired up quickly, its humming unnaturally loud in the library's graveyard quiet. I almost didn't want it to work, because here was the sticky, scary truth: my prefrontal lobe had worked out the killer on the walk through Battle Lake's backstreets, but my lizard brain wanted no part of it, was in fact wrestling like a sci-fi creature to push that genie back in the bottle. Because if the murderous quilt that

I'd finally pieced together was accurate, the creepiest *possible* explanation for Rita's death, and then Donald's, and then Little D's attack on Abraham, the most unbelievable answer, was actually the true story.

All three victims had discovered something they weren't meant to. If this computer in front of me verified what they'd uncovered, then I was in as much danger as they had been.

The database lit up my screen, bathing me in a sickly emerald glow. Four clicks, and there was Abraham's insurance policy.

My blood froze in my veins.

It was in the fine print, which I had previously only skimmed after discovering that Assurist had settled on $5 million plus a lifetime of ongoing medical care for as long as Abraham remained in a coma.

Pluck a duck.

My hunch had been correct.

Chapter 48

My route back to the Senior Sunset was much more direct than my trip from it had been, my speed fueled largely by the green gases of horror and disbelief. I hoped against hope that something would prove my theory wrong. If I was incorrect, the Sunset was the only place to find out. Gary's car was no longer parked in front. That meant I had at least one point in my favor.

It was after visiting hours, but I knew how to work the system, thanks to the orderly who'd let me check in this morning. I made my way to the back and slipped in through the employees' entrance, my mind galloping.

The button in Abraham's room. The shoes under his bed.

If my intuition was correct, they hadn't been offerings.

They'd been the tools of his trade.

I'd gone over it every which way but Wednesday, and Abraham as the killer was the only explanation that made sense. Yet it was so absurd, so horrifying to dip into the depths of his evil, that my brain slid sideways when I tried to address it head-on. So I had to slink at the truth.

I grabbed a set of scrubs in the employee room, yanking them on as a temporary disguise. I left my winter jacket and wig in an empty locker, using a loose rubber band from the floor to tie up my brown hair. Glancing in the full-length mirror, I barely recognized my own self. My face was still mildly distorted from the almonds, but it was more than that. I looked exhausted, drained, as if life had used me like an energy sack, sucking me dry for its own gain. In short, I was perfectly disguised to pass as a nursing home CNA. I made my way down the hall without so much as a second glance from the handful of staff I encountered.

Abraham's room was dim when I entered, only a night-light illuminating his sleeping form. But "sleeping" wasn't exactly the right word, was it? I glided across the room and yanked the blanket off.

I barely choked off the scream before it reached my lips. Kennie's doll lay on the bed, her garish mouth open.

"How did you figure it out?"

The voice was rusty, the vocal cords unused for 364 days. The sound froze my soul.

It took a lifetime of faking it to keep my voice neutral. I couldn't afford to show fear. "I looked up your life insurance policy."

I swiveled, slowly, my skin feeling thick. I should have told someone where I was going, brought a weapon. But I'd filed him into my brain as a benevolent figure, harmless. Even after realizing he was the killer, my brain couldn't make peace with it, couldn't move this man from the COMATOSE file to the DANGEROUS one. I wasn't the only one who'd made that mistake. "I read the rider. It says that if your coma lasts longer than a year, your settlement automatically doubles. That year is up tomorrow."

I faced Abraham, finally. He lurked in the dark shadows of his own closet, fully upright, watching me. His chest was heaving like that of an undernourished dog who'd been forced to run, his eyes overbright in his sunken skull. A smile flirted with his face, a knife slice where only a slack mouth had been for too long.

"When did you come out of the coma?" I asked.

Any hint of a grin vanished. "Three weeks after I went in. Maybe four."

I sucked air through my teeth. "Jesus."

His flesh hung off his upper body, papery, his muscle wasted on his bone. He'd lain still for months, allowing his strength to fade, his body to atrophy, to preserve the realistic appearance that he was in a coma. He truly was ruthless, and right now he was feeding off that like fuel.

"Jesus had nothing to do with it."

"Rita saw you move, and then Donald?"

He sneered. "Rita was an accident. She was giving me a sponge bath." He winked at me, lascivious, grotesque. "I might be in a coma, but I'm not dead. I had to take care of her right then and there. Surprised her for sure."

I swallowed. "Donald?"

"Unrelated, if you can believe it." He shifted in the closet, taking a step closer to me. "Told me he owed it to his wife to clear the path between her and a successful public offering, and so came by after Rita's funeral to smother me in my sleep. Apparently, he hasn't treated his wife well over the years and wanted to make things right." He leaned against the doorjamb. "You'd be surprised what people will say to you when they think you are in a coma."

I flushed. I'd been one of those people. "Little D?"

"The kid? He stopped by to swipe something. Saw me moving." Abraham put his own hands around his thin neck, looking for all the world like Gollum in the shadows. "It's easier to make it look like someone is strangling you than you'd think."

I swallowed a moan. Poor Little D. He'd tried to tell us that Abraham was a liar, but no one believed kids, most especially poor ones.

Abraham's slash of a smile twisted into something impossibly dark, his mouth a bottomless gate leading to the depths of malevolence. "You are the fourth, and the last, loose end. Sorry, my dear, but you made a ten-million-dollar mistake coming here."

I spotted a flash of silver before my head exploded in pain and my world went black.

Chapter 49

I groaned and blinked. My hands were pinned to my side, my worldview shrunk to the two peepholes of whatever box I was trapped in. Shifting my head even the tiniest bit brought earthquakes of agony. Abraham had beaned me good.

But he was no longer here. Was he?

My heartbeat tripped and rolled as I lurched nearer consciousness. *I must get my bearings.* I blinked again, my breath hot and sticky on my own face, as if I were wearing a small greenhouse, or a Halloween mask, or . . . *dear god no.*

I angled my head despite the searing pain and looked down.

Abraham had strapped pink stiletto cowboy boots to my feet, tugged tight leather pants onto my legs, and buttoned me inside a Western snap-front shirt.

I wasn't in a box.

I was inside the Kennie doll, wearing a Kennie mask, drowning beneath a Kennie wig.

Terror released my bladder.

I moaned as warm urine trickled down my leg. (There was one more reason not to wear leather, if you needed it.)

"You're awake." Abraham stepped into my sight line, looking terrifyingly calm. "Don't bother struggling. You're hog-tied, ankles and wrists."

"You're a dick," I said, only it came out as a squeak.

I recognized the desk to the rear of him. It was the same counter I'd hidden behind to look up his insurance policy. I was in the library, at floor level, trussed up twenty or so feet from the front door. I lurched upward, testing my binds. The sudden movement caused me to black out again, but not before I realized that I wasn't bound as tightly as I'd thought. It was pain more than rope that had me restrained.

When I came to yet again, Abraham was dousing the floor around me with gasoline. The pungent smell curled my nostril hairs. "Stop it." My voice was still too quiet. I pushed my consciousness toward the two bright holes in the mask. "I said stop it!"

"You bet." He squatted in my field of vision. "I'll stop tomorrow, when, after three hundred and sixty-five days in a coma, I'll miraculously awaken to not five, but ten million dollars. Or maybe I'll wait a day or two. No need to be greedy." He rubbed his hands together.

My brain fought against the bloody bunting that muffled it. This man I'd confessed to as if he were a tree, forever silent, had only been pretending. Murderously. "Five million dollars wasn't enough? You're no spring chicken, you know. You could have made that first settlement last." My feigned cockiness cost me. My vision began to narrow. I pushed back against the blackness.

"I've been poor my whole life, and I plan to live a long time after this," he said. "Ten million goes twice as far as five, right?"

Right. Right? My brain wasn't sure. How hard had he hit me? "You murdered two people."

He disappeared from view again. I heard more sloshing, and the realization of what was happening made it difficult to breathe. Abraham was pouring gasoline on the books. "Three, when I'm done here."

Three. He was going to burn me alive, scorch the books, torch the library. Rita's murder and Donald's would go unsolved. Little D would be forever branded an attempted murderer. It would disappear from his record when he became an adult, but the label would shape every decision he made from this moment forward.

Johnny would never know how much I loved him. He wouldn't hear my apology, or my proposal.

Tiger Pop would have to be separated from Luna and maybe given over to the humane society if none of my friends could adopt her.

"How did you carry me?"

His voice came from the back shelves. "I'm stronger than I look. It's a combination of lifting what I can find in my room while stretching out my skin so it hangs."

Good. He was out of sight. I rolled away from the strongest reek of gasoline, ignoring the horror of his words. If I could keep this up before Abraham saw what I was doing, I might make it to the door. I'd completed two revolutions before I rolled smack up against the front desk. I was now farther from escape than I had been.

But it wasn't all a loss. Something sharp poked me in the chest.

Kennie's Clothes for the Modern Cowgirl.

A flask and a nail file were sewn into the front placket of this shirt! Kennie had demonstrated them to Christie, Mrs. Berns, Bad Brad, and me when she'd first come to the library to explain why Christie was here. I'd hated it at the time. Now her ridiculous accessories might save my life.

"You can roll all you want," Abraham called to me. "At least all you want in the next sixty seconds, because that's how long until I start this carpet on fire and hightail it back to the nursing home for my last night as a vegetable."

I should have felt defeat, but instead, hatred blossomed inside me, powerful as a tsunami. Who was this horrible scrap of a man to snatch everything good from me? From Little D? I had no aspirations of rolling outside. I only needed to get at the nail file inside my shirt, and then I would entice Abraham near enough to drive the file deep into his neck.

But first, dangit, I needed to keep from blacking out.

"You wouldn't believe the tales people have told me over the past few weeks," he said over the sloshing of gasoline. "So greedy, humans, wouldn't you agree? They all want more money, or love, or luck.

Nobody's ever happy with what they have, which makes me feel better about what I'm doing here. I'm no worse than the rest."

He'd sounded like he was over by the shelves, but suddenly, his stale breath was near my ear. I'd rolled onto my stomach. My hands were under my chest, worming inside the shirt, feeling for the nail file.

"I'm just like *you*."

I drew a ragged breath. He continued.

"Well, maybe not just like you. It sounds like you really messed things up with that Johnny fellow. I'm sorry your dad was so *unavailable*," he said, his voice mocking. "You are an adult, however. It's time you stopped blaming your poor relationship decisions on your father and stood by your own choices, don't you think?"

My face burned as I remembered all I had revealed to him when I thought he couldn't hear me. I'd confessed truths to Abraham that I'd never told anyone, and here he was preparing to torch me. It really was dangerous to share secrets. I kept my voice level. "I'd like to hear about *your* dad. How proud of you would he be right now?"

My fingertips brushed cool metal. I didn't know if it was the flask or the file, and the way my hands were bound allowed little room for exploration. I strained against the rope, careful to keep my shoulder blades still.

Abraham rewarded my question with a splash of cold liquid on my back. I gasped. The greasy smell of gasoline assaulted my nostrils and amped up my adrenaline. He was turning me into human kindling. I didn't have much time.

"My dad was a farmer, my mother a farmer's wife. They rarely spoke to one another, worked me to the bone, and both died of cancer, leaving me the impossible job of turning a profit on a potato farm with poor soil." His voice grated. "How do you like that?"

I craned my neck to face him. I didn't black out. This was progress. Unfortunately, the movement shifted the mask, which left me only one eyehole. "I get why you killed Rita, but why in the world would you stuff her in a doll? And then me?"

His finger flew toward my eye, filled the peephole, and hooked the mask off my face. Cool, gasoline-scented air rushed at my naked skin. I sucked and coughed.

Abraham crouched in front of me. "When Rita saw me move, I had to knock her out. Once I did that, I had a body to deal with. Figured I'd make it look like a suicide, so I stole some medication from the storage room and shoved it down her throat just like we fed the calves medicine back in the day. I still had the problem of her body, though, and I didn't want it discovered too close to me or too soon. That's when I thought of Ida's dolls, placed all around town, going days without being touched or moved. The rest is history."

"And Donald, with the shears in my car?"

He leaned down so we were face-to-face. "Meet Battle Lake's Peeping Tom. I've kept my legs exercised with evening walks, borrowing cars when necessary. People are too trusting in a small town. I've visited the windows of Battle Lake's beauties over the past few months, getting to see them in their full, vulnerable glory. Speaking of, if you weren't about to die, I'd recommend investing in some new bras, now that you're on the market again."

I closed my eyes, fighting nausea from the gasoline fumes and Abraham's oversweet breath. "You spied on me?"

"Not just you, but yes. Enough to know that you were sniffing around, and that I needed you out of the picture. That made it easy to decide how to kill Donald and where to stuff the body."

My aching fingers finally closed around the cool metal Kennie had sewn inside the shirt. I fed it out the smallest bit at a time, my fingers cramping from the effort of keeping my spine and shoulders still, of presenting a compliant back to Abraham, who still crouched only inches away. "You're an active guy for a coma patient."

Abraham stood, bored with the conversation. "No thanks to Ida. That busybody made me more popular than the Taj Mahal. That's why it was especially satisfying to put her doll making out of business. At least until this last doll. You look good in this outfit, by the way."

"Thanks . . ."

I gripped the full heft of the nail file as the word trailed out of my mouth. He saw what was happening, but too late. I rolled onto my side, swollen with rage, and heaved my hands overhead, the cold metal glinting in the library's emergency lighting. The silver darted toward his neck. I plunged the thin blade in as deep as it could go, hot blood gushing from his wound. Progressing to my side, I was able to hoist myself to a standing position despite my hands and feet still being bound. I hopped to the front door and called for help. Abraham was rushed to the hospital, where he confessed to all the murders as his life was saved. Part of his settlement was used to pay the library's cleaning fees, and we lived happily ever after.

The end.

That was how the scene played out in my imagination. It was what *should* have happened. I actually got as far as rolling to my side and raising the nail file in the air with my bound hands. In the moments it took me to visualize the rest, he swiped the tool out of my hand, laughing as it fell onto the carpeted floor with a soft *whump*.

"This isn't a telenovela," he said. "There is no dramatic rescue for you, my friend. You're. Just. Going. To. Die."

He stood, talking as he walked toward the door, his voice laden with arrogance. "It should be quick, though I can't promise painless. You're about to be a very crispy lady, and I'm about to become an incredibly rich man. *Adios.*"

The click of a metal lighter was followed by a tremendous *whoosh* as all the oxygen was burned out of the library.

Chapter 50

The sonic boom of the gasoline eating the oxygen deafened me. Heat licked my eyelids. I kept them closed, rolling in what I hoped was the direction of the door. Sound returned in the form of crackling carpet fibers. The smell of burning plastic was overpowering.

I risked a peek.

The unbearable heat forced my eyes closed, but not before I saw that I had rolled the wrong direction yet again. I was nearer the computers than the front door, flames on all sides. I opened my mouth to scream, and heat rushed in. The tears burned off before they left my eyes. I couldn't breathe.

I wasn't going to make it out of this one.

Bye, Johnny.

Bye, Mom.

Bye, Luna and Tiger Pop. I'm sorry.

Bye, Mrs. Berns. Please take care of everyone for me.

The darkness beckoned, so much cooler than the library I found myself in. I rushed toward it.

I'm sorry, Little D. I hope you find your way out of this.

I tried one last breath. There was no air, only searing pain. I traded fire for rest. My last thought before plummeting downward was tinged with regret, a murky image of risks not taken and love not expressed. Still, it was a relief to leave behind the blistering skin and poisonous air and a lifelong accumulation of mistakes.

I hit the bottom of whatever I'd been falling toward. The force was so great that it jarred me back to the fire.

Except I wasn't falling down a tunnel. I was being picked up.

"Johnny?" My voice had been burned from my throat, rendering the beloved name unrecognizable. The fire grew impossibly hotter, and I smelled my own hair burning. The aroma turned my stomach.

Then, suddenly, it was cool, blessedly frigid, the frosty spring air kissing my blistered flesh like a thousand blessings, the respite so intense that I cried. I still hadn't opened my eyes. I was afraid that this was a hallucination, that I'd blink and see my skin bubbling from bone.

I felt someone untying the ropes around my ankles and wrists, gently rubbing snow on my hands and cheeks. The shock of it was ecstasy.

I could *feel*.

A mouth met mine, the lips firm, strong, a gentle breath guided inside my body. A radio crackled. The mouth left. I wanted it to stay forever and breathe that pure sweetness into my lungs. I reached, and a hand grabbed mine, and then a strong body bundled all of me into his arms, weeping softly into my hair.

"Johnny," I croaked.

I blinked. Firefly dots transformed into twinkling stars, their light dimmed by the blaze raging inside the library. As consciousness returned, so did pain, my singed nerves screaming in agony.

"Code Eight," he said as he held me. It took me a moment to realize he was speaking into a radio.

A police radio.

"We've got a fire at the Battle Lake Public Library, full blaze. Two victims, one the potential suspect. Both require an ambulance."

It wasn't Johnny holding me. Not at all.

Chapter 51

"Why didn't anyone tell me about yoga pants before?"

Mrs. Berns's question was a fair one. Yoga pants, if you didn't know, made every rear look firm, flattened any stomach, and etched muscle into the juiciest of thighs. Plus, they were comfortable. Neither she nor I had known how life-changing they were until we each purchased a required pair from Aquamarine, the instructor of the class we were attending.

"Amazing, right?" Aquamarine stood at the front of the room as we stretched and preened in our magic pants. "They're a bit expensive, but once you try them, you never go back."

"You've got that right." Mrs. Berns dropped onto a mat in the back of the room and patted the mat next to her to indicate I should sit. Kennie took the spot on the other side of me.

"I ogled some warm-up poses, in case you want to avoid looking like an idiot." Mrs. Berns dropped to all fours and raised her leg as if to urinate on a tree. "This one is called Up Dog."

I pushed her leg down. "I don't think you visited a real yoga site."

"What else do you think a website called 'Urolagnia' could be about?" She rolled her eyes and returned to her pose. "By the way, we're all traipsing over to Eustace's barn building after this, right?"

Kennie nodded. "You better believe it. Most of Battle Lake will be there."

I copied the pose Aquamarine was modeling, something called Child's Pose. It was right up my alley. As far as I could tell, it required dropping my knees and bowing facedown, which was essentially a fancy way to face-plant. I moved gingerly, careful not to stretch my gloves too quickly. I'd suffered second-degree burns on 20 percent of my body, or, if you preferred Mrs. Berns's vernacular, I'd been cooked to "medium rare."

My hands had taken the worst of it because I'd used them to protect my face. Since the fire I'd had to wear the gloves and keep my hands moist with a prescription lotion. The doctor said I had to keep up the regimen for fourteen days. I was currently on day four, and my throat still scratched like a two-pack-a-day smoker, but I was expected to make a full recovery, thanks to police chief Gary Wohnt.

I'd fallen in and out of consciousness the first few hours after he'd rescued me from the library. Him holding me and crying had taken on the submerged quality of a dream, and maybe it had been. I certainly wasn't going to ask him. The way he stayed in the hospital that first night and how he looked at me in the days since the fire vaguely unsettled me, though. Something had changed between us.

I was too much of a coward to ask what.

I'd since learned that, using evidence from the Turtle Stew crime scene, Gary had figured out what Abraham was up to about the same time I had. Unbeknownst to the public, a shoe print had been left near the newly emptied grease trap behind the Stew in roughly the same time frame that Rita's body had been dolled up. The shoe was a prescription orthotic traceable to a resident of the Senior Sunset, a man almost entirely wheelchair bound.

When the resident told Gary he'd offered his shoes to Abraham's altar in the hopes that it would land him a date with sweet Ida, Gary dug deeper into Abraham's backstory. He found a history of petty crimes and one felony charge for battery. With Abraham in a coma, he filed that information away for later, until such time as he heard there was a sighting of me at the Senior Sunset. Still keeping my jailbreak under wraps, he visited the home to investigate. Nobody at the Sunset would give me up (yeah!), so he stopped by Abraham's room on his way out.

That's when I had seen Gary. He hadn't made me as I'd slinked out of Ida's, nor had he spotted anything out of place in Abraham's room. Coming up short, like me, Gary had left the Sunset and located a computer to dig deeper into Abraham's past. When he'd found the fine print in Abraham's insurance policy, he'd returned to the Sunset to ask the staff some questions.

He'd also stopped by Abraham's room one last time.

No Abraham.

Pieces fell into place for him. He drove to my house, then Eustace's. The library was his third stop. He pulled up just as Abraham was leaving. Abraham didn't drop to the ground as Gary commanded, and so he shot him.

Gary had refused to answer me when I asked him if Abraham told him I was inside, and I was OK with that. I didn't want to know that Gary had risked his life on the slim possibility that he could save mine. That would shift my universe too far off the edge. I only knew that he had tried to run in through the library's front door after he'd shot Abraham.

The fire had been raging, an impenetrable wall that had melted the plastic on his belt when he tried to push through it. He'd run around the side and spotted me through the street-side windows, a tube of humanity in the raging flames. He'd fired shots into the windows, the backdraft of heat crisping his eyebrows, and dashed inside to pull me out.

Gary Wohnt was the reason I was breathing today.

Abraham was alive as well. He was also paralyzed from the waist down from Gary's bullet.

The irony was almost too much.

Once Abraham was released from the hospital, he would face trial and likely be imprisoned for the rest of his life for murdering

Rita and Donald, plus my attempted murder and a smattering of fraud charges.

Aquamarine's dreamy voice interrupted my thoughts. "Now that you're centered, let's move to Downward-Facing Dog."

"Ooh," Mrs. Berns said eagerly. "The website covered this one, too."

I averted my eyes. On my other side, Kennie was grunting in her effort to mirror Aquamarine. Kennie had really come through, first breaking me out of jail, and then, once she found out about Eustace and Little D being father and son, reuniting them and arranging for the entire town to come out to Eustace's house to build an addition to his cabin, one that would give Little D his own room. It was an orchestrated apology for judging Eustace and Little D, and I supported it wholeheartedly.

Christie had shown her true colors as well. When she heard the story of Eustace's cancer, and how he gave up his son so the boy would have a family, she founded the Assurist Medication Foundation right on the spot. Anyone with a medical need but without the money to pay for it could apply, and if they were accepted, Assurist would cover their entire financial costs. The timing was great, considering the company was going public soon, but I had no issue with them earning positive publicity for this.

It was too soon to be sure, but it looked like Eustace would be the first beneficiary of this program and like his cancer was a perfect fit for Assurist's latest medication. Dr. Gunderson had reviewed all Eustace's records and declared that he was about to feel much better than he had in a long time—if he took all the medication as prescribed and ate healthy, he might live to hold his grandkids.

For my part, I'd persuaded Christie to donate some extra money to the library. Our insurance would cover the cost of gutting and restructuring the existing space, but I wanted something better than we'd had before. I wanted a nap room so that kids of all ages could attend story hour at the same time, and a mom room so moms could have a break while I entertained their kids. My request was inspired half by Anita Ford, Little D's overburdened foster mom, and half by the invisibility cloak I'd had to don when I'd disguised myself as a mom. No one deserved to disappear for doing the most important job in the world. Christie had agreed wholeheartedly and donated the money for a fast-track rebuilding (money really did buy happiness!), plus started a trust fund large enough to keep the library going in perpetuity. She declared helping the library to be cheaper and more fun than having a husband.

That was the good news.

There was also bad.

Johnny didn't call when he returned to Battle Lake, not right away. It was OK. I understood that I might need to be patient. After what I'd put him through, it was crucial to demonstrate to Johnny that this time, I'd finally, permanently and forever, grown up. It was hard to wait, though, stewing in the juices of my own regrets.

It was a full twenty-four hours before he showed up on my front porch. Luna and Tiger Pop were thrilled to see him, of course. So was I, even though he looked ten years older than when he had left. His deep-blue eyes were sad, his mouth drawn.

"Want to come in?" I asked. I tried to hide my damaged hands behind me.

He shook his head, staring at his feet. My heart crashed to the ground. I knew what he was going to say, and I deserved every word of it.

"Mira," he began. He was still looking down.

My voice was small. "I know."

His eyes shot up, puffy but still beautiful. He reached toward me as if he were going to cradle my face in his hands, but he caught himself. "You *don't* know." A clear sound of pain tumbled out of his mouth. "You have no idea what the last seven days have been like for me. I wanted to call you. Hell, I wanted to drive here and take you in my arms and never let you go."

He leaned in toward me again, and I so desperately wanted to disappear into the strength of his arms. But he pulled away, and I had to mirror his gesture. He continued, his voice strained. "But I didn't drive here, or even call you, and it's not because I don't love you. I didn't know I could love anyone so much, actually." He ran his hands through his thick hair and stared off to the left. Tears glistened in his eyes.

I almost couldn't hold his gaze when he returned it to me. It was too raw, too stricken. "I didn't come back because I can't do this anymore." His voice was husky. "This relationship makes no sense, not like this." He gestured to encompass Battle Lake, Otter Tail County, the world. My heart fell. I knew exactly what he meant.

"It's my fault." Luna whined at my feet. It was agony to be this close to Johnny and not touch him. "I put us in this terrible position. I'm sorry."

He shook his head. "We're both responsible for this. And I think you were right to break it off. It wasn't working the way it was."

Because I hadn't let it. "I love you."

Something broke behind his eyes, and he held me gently, like I was made of glass. I knew it was only for the moment, but I drank it in, a flower thirsty for the only water she'd get for a while. "I love you too, Mira. I want the best for you. I hope you find it."

He pulled from the embrace and walked away without looking back.

Heartbreak was a quiet sound, shards of glass as bright and light as tinsel tinkling as they fall. Mrs. Berns's words in the doctor's office pierced the exquisite pain:

You need a man who can stand on his own, and who's firm with you. Until Johnny can be that man, you two can't make it work, and that's a guarantee.

I would fix this.

As god was my witness, I would win Johnny back, and I would never let him go. I had never wanted anything so much in my life. I would make this happen. What me and Johnny had was true love, magic and chocolate and fireworks, and that comes along once in a lifetime. You do not let love like that go once you find it, even if you have to do some growing up to earn it.

"Psst," Kennie said, startling me from my memory and back into the yoga session.

I glanced over to where she was poised on one bent knee, her other leg pointed behind her. "What?"

"I thought of a new business venture."

If there were ever words more guaranteed to make my butt clench, I had yet to hear them. "I thought the Minnesota phone sex was going well." I had been too busy healing to help out, but Mrs. Berns had said they were making money hand over fist. Hmm. Or maybe she'd only been practicing one of her phone sex lines on me?

"It's going gangbusters, thank you very much, but a businesswoman doesn't rest on her haunches."

It was a funny thing to say, as that's exactly what Kennie looked like she was doing. "What's the idea?"

"Potluck pants!" She pointed at her yoga pants. "These here beauties inspired me. Think of it. They look like regular jeans, beautifully tailored, except if you eat too much, you can let out the waist a bit. No one knows! What do you think?"

A slow grin curled the edge of my mouth until the grin dominated my whole sore face. *I'll be.* Kennie had finally done it. She'd come up with a good idea. "I don't hate it."

She smiled proudly before leaning forward into Warrior Pose 3D, which was similar to Warrior 3 except her arms sprouted in directions they were not meant to.

"Hey," Mrs. Berns said from my other side, farting like a sailor as she leaned forward into a position I could only describe as Drinking Thirstily from a Garden Hose. "Have I ever told you that I love you?"

I smiled, moving to copy her form. No reason she should have all the fun. "I love you, too."

My heart blossomed with an impossible, bubbly warmth. Everything was exactly right.

Or if it wasn't, it would be soon.

About the Author

Photo © 2023 Kelly Weaver Photography

Jess Lourey writes about secrets. She's the bestselling author of thrillers, rom-com mysteries, book club fiction, young adult fiction, and non-fiction. Winner of the Anthony, Thriller, and Minnesota Book Awards, Jess is also an Edgar, Agatha, and Lefty Award–nominated author; TEDx presenter; and recipient of The Loft's Excellence in Teaching fellowship. Check out her TEDx Talk for the true story behind her debut novel, *May Day*. She lives in Minneapolis with a rotating batch of foster kittens (and occasional foster puppies, but those goobers are a lot of work). For more information, visit www.jesslourey.com.